VILLA OF SUN AND SECRETS

JENNIFER BOHNET

Boldwood

First published in Great Britain in 2019 by Boldwood Books Ltd.

Copyright © Jennifer Bohnet, 2019

Cover Design by Lexie Sims

A CIP catalogue record for this book is available from the British Library.

Paperback ISBN 978-1-83889-220-3

Ebook ISBN 978-1-83889-221-0

Kindle ISBN 978-1-83889-222-7

Audio CD ISBN 978-1-83889-253-1

MP3 CD ISBN 978-1-83889-354-5

Digital audio download ISBN 978-1-83889-219-7

Boldwood Books Ltd
23 Bowerdean Street
London SW6 3TN
www.boldwoodbooks.com

For Richard with love.

PART I

1

Carla was not surprised when Tante Josette didn't come to the funeral. A nondescript wreath arrived – its white flowers already wilting. The words 'RIP Amelia. Your loving sister, Josette' scrawled on a black-edged sympathy card by some unknown hand at the florists.

A congregation of fewer than ten had gathered for the service. Carla knew her mother, Amelia, always a difficult person to get along with, would have been surprised at even that number. The owners of the care home, duty-bound to be there, two neighbours from Amelia's street, Carla, David and Maddy representing the family. Edward had left the week before for South Africa, impossible for him to return so soon. The wreath he sent his grandmother though, was lovely.

Standing in the crematorium watching her mother's coffin disappear behind the curtains, Carla felt the first stirrings of sadness, and anger. Sadness for a mother for whom she'd never felt good enough and anger for the fact that Amelia and Tante Josette had been estranged for over forty years. She'd written to Josette when Amelia had gone into the home, mainly to let her know about her twin sister, but a little bit of Carla had hoped Josette would visit and the two sisters would heal their decades' old rift. It wasn't to be.

Josette had written back saying she was sorry to hear of Amelia's decline but she wouldn't be coming to England to see her for one last time: It seems a pointless exercise, as you say, Amelia's mind has switched off so she won't know me. It would be equally pointless if she were still compos mentis because then she wouldn't want to see me.

An angry Carla had longed to reply, Come for my sake so I can believe that the two of you once cared about each other. That somewhere in the dim and distant past there was a loving, supportive family in the days before we became the prototype model for a modern dysfunctional one. But she'd recognised the truth behind Josette's words and had sighed before throwing the letter away.

Josette sat in the sunshine at her favourite pavement cafe on the quay in Monaco, the coffee on the table in front of her growing cold, her thoughts lost in the past. She and Amelia had often caught the train from Antibes and spent the day wandering around the principality hoping to see some famous people. Today, though, the memory of a long-ago visit that was to change everything in their lives was on her mind. Today, for the first time in years, she'd caught the train to Monaco to say a final goodbye to her sister in the principality where decades ago she'd been given the news that would start a chain of events that would ultimately change the course of her own life.

It had been Cannes Film Festival time and Amelia and

Josette had sat at another pavement cafe, the Cafe de Paris, hoping to spot some celebrities leaving the Hotel de Paris opposite. Or even sauntering up the steps into the casino for a game of roulette.

Josette had just exclaimed, 'Quick – look over there. I'm sure that's Sacha Distel,' and turned towards Amelia to make sure she was looking in the right direction when, to her dismay, she saw Amelia was sitting there with tears running down her cheeks. 'Que se passe-t-il?'

'I'm pregnant.'

Shocked, Josette stared at her twin. 'Is it Robert the sailor?' she had finally asked. Amelia had told her about meeting a crew member from one of the expensive yachts a few weeks ago. Twenty-three years old, he was spending the summer after his finals working on one of the prestigious boats before returning home and starting his banking career.

Amelia had nodded.

'Papa will kill you both,' Josette had said. She was silent for a moment. 'What does Robert say about it?'

'Je ne lui ai pas encore dit. You're the first to know,' Amelia whispered. 'I was hoping you'd help me decide what to do.'

'When d'you expect to see Robert next?'

'The yacht is due back in port tomorrow afternoon, so probably our usual place in the evening.'

'You have to tell him. Once you've done that and we know his reaction, we can decide what you do.' Josette had glanced at her sister. 'Do you love him? Do you want to keep the baby? Do you want him to marry you?'

'Yes. No. Yes. I don't know what I want other than I don't want to be pregnant.'

'But you are,' Josette had said, as a sudden thought struck her. 'You didn't go to Doctor Lefebvre, did you?' The old family doctor would have gone straight to their father, she was certain.

Amelia shook her head. 'Je ne suis pas si bête. I went to one in Cannes.'

Josette had caught hold of her sister's hand. 'If Robert is the kind of man I think he is, he'll marry you.'

'But his life will be in England. I don't want to leave here and live over there. I won't know anyone and his family will probably hate me and—'

'Stop it. Nobody could possibly hate you. And after you've married Robert and moved over there, I shall be a regular visitor. Tante Josette. Imagine!' Josette had looked at her sister and squeezed her hand. 'Try not to worry. Whatever happens, I'm on your side.'

The next evening, a shocked Robert had immediately said they'd marry when Amelia had told him she was pregnant. Had even braved the wrath of her father, holding her hand tightly, as they broke the news together.

Now, years later, Josette acknowledged Amelia's news that day had laid the foundation for the fracture that would tear their family apart in less than five years. If Amelia had never met Robert, so many lives would have been lived differently – she, Josette, wouldn't have been estranged from all the people she loved the most, would have had a stable life instead of always being on the move from one place to another, she'd have married and had a family with...

'Another coffee, madam?'

Josette dragged her thoughts back to the present. She shook her head. 'Non, Merci.' She paid for the undrunk cold coffee before standing up and beginning to make her way up to the old town and the cathedral.

Climbing the steps and strolling through the gardens to

the palace, Josette took her time, stopping once or twice to admire the view out over the town and the harbour. Eventually, she passed under the arch, skirted around the caped sculpture of the infamous monk and founder of the Monaco royal family, Francois Grimaldi, that she personally always found terrifying, and onto the palace precinct.

The large open forecourt in front of the palace was, as always, swarming with tourists and Josette crossed it diagonally, aiming for the small street that led down to the cathedral. Before she reached the flight of steps leading up to the entrance, she pulled a veil-type scarf out of her bag and placed it over her head, glancing at her watch as she did so. Perfect timing. The English funeral would be underway.

Inside, the ambience of the cathedral was hushed and reverent. Josette carefully lit a candle and placed it on the stand, whispering to herself, 'RIP Amelia. Je ne t'oublierai jamais, ma soeur chérie.' She stood for a moment, eyes closed, mentally saying a final goodbye to the sister who, for some still unknown reason, had cast her out of her life all those years ago. Now death had taken the final, irreversible, step of concealment of what had gone wrong between them all those years ago.

Ever since the news of Amelia's death had reached her, Josette had waited for the sorrow to engulf her. Now, standing in front of the flickering candles, the tears arrived with the realisation that any possibility of a reconciliation had died with Amelia. Oblivious to the looks of other cathedral visitors, even to the gentle touch of a sympathetic hand on her arm from a stranger, Josette stood waiting for the tears to subside, for her mind to return to its decade old default mode of 'it's in the past, let it go'.

It was ten minutes before she felt strong enough to

become a part of the shuffling crowd making its way around the cathedral, past the last resting places of Princess Grace and her Prince before making for the exit.

Blinking as her eyes adjusted to the bright sunlight, Josette thought about the future. She was free to do, to say, as she wanted. With Amelia's death the need to keep her own secret had died. Hadn't it? She was the last of the family who knew the truth. If she wanted, she could shout it out to the world. There was no one to gainsay her now. But was it worth upsetting another generation of people with the truth?

* * *

The Monday after the funeral, Carla collected the ashes from the crematorium before driving to her late mother's home to begin the task of sorting and clearing the house.

During the three months Amelia had spent in the care home, Carla had gone to the empty house once a week to keep an eye on the place and to water the house plants. David, her husband, had encouraged her to use the time to make a start on clearing and emptying the house.

'We all know Amelia won't ever go back there, so it makes sense to begin getting it ready for sale.'

Carla had shaken her head. 'It might make sense, but, sorry, I can't do it.' She'd tried to explain to David that, as illogical as it was, she felt she'd be invading her mother's privacy, even though she'd have no idea what Carla was doing. It would be easier when Amelia had passed. But, in truth, it was never going to be easy.

Inserting the key into the lock of No. 29 and letting herself in, she fancied that the house was even quieter than it had been over the last few weeks. As if the house knew Amelia was dead and had shut down on itself. Carla shook the thought away.

Placing the urn on the sitting room mantelpiece, Carla went into the kitchen to make herself a coffee. Waiting for the kettle to boil, she opened the back door and went out onto the small patio her father had created years ago. Looking out over the garden, she sighed. Never a keen gardener, Amelia had abandoned the garden the year Robert had died. Since then it had been left to Carla, or David when she could persuade him, to push the old-fashioned cylinder mower around the large patch of grass every couple of weeks in summer. The flower borders over the last ten years had simply merged into a weed-infested green border around the outside. Carla could see she'd need to get the mower out again soon.

A memory flitted through her mind of the garden when it was her dad's solace from work – and her mother. The Christmas he'd strung fairy lights around the bare branches of the gnarled apple tree in the far corner. Amelia had declared it an unnecessary extravagance and as soon as Christmas Day was over she'd demanded the lights were taken down. They were never seen again.

Back indoors, coffee made, Carla sat at the kitchen table and started to make a list of the things that she needed to organise. Emptying the house and getting it ready for sale would be her first priority. Clothes and books – charity shop; furniture eBay or local second-hand shop? Perhaps joining a local Facebook Buy and Sell group would be the easiest option. No, getting a house clearance firm to come and take the lot would be better.

She'd need to check with Maddy about the white goods – she might like the fridge for her new flat. Once the house was empty and clean, she'd contact some estate agents and get it on the market. The three or four boxes of papers and photos she knew were in a cupboard upstairs she'd put in the car and take home with her. Go through them, deciding what needed to be kept and what could be thrown away, in the comfort of her own home. Then there was the question of where to scatter Amelia's ashes.

Carla stopped and glanced through the door at the urn on the mantelpiece – looking for all the world as though it had been there forever but where it obviously couldn't stay. Another memory flashed into her mind. When her dad had died, Carla had asked Amelia if she could be with her when she scattered his ashes, to say a final goodbye.

Amelia had shrugged. 'Too late. Done the day I got them. I threw them in the river.'

Carla had never hated her mother so much as she did then. Not because of scattering her dad's remains in the river (the frustrated sailor in him had always loved being down by the river) but because she'd kept silent about what she was doing and denied Carla the chance of a last goodbye. Hadn't deemed it important enough to ask her to go with her.

But where to scatter Amelia? She wouldn't appreciate the river. Maybe Maddy would have an idea. There was no rush. It would be sometime yet before everything was finalised.

Her mobile rang. Mavis. The manager of the charity shop where Carla volunteered three mornings a week.

'Hi, everything all right?'

'Carla, I'm so sorry to have to ask, and I'll understand if you can't help, but I don't suppose there's a chance of you being available this afternoon?' Mavis asked. 'I'm one short and there's piles of stuff to sort through out the back of the shop.'

'Two o'clock okay? I need to talk to you about some of Mum's stuff too,' Carla said.

'Great. See you then. Thanks, lovely,' Mavis said.

Carla put the phone back in her bag. Looking out of the kitchen window at the grey day, she had a sudden longing to be somewhere else. Living a different life to the one she got up every day to exist through. David had never wanted her to work, insisting her job was the family, which when the twins, Ed and Maddy had been young was true. Her life had revolved around their needs, her social life around fundraisers for the PTA, brownies, scouts, ballet, football. You name the club, she had probably baked cakes for it. But these days that was all gone. With the twins away and David busier and busier with the business, she was spending a lot of time alone.

As she put her bag over her shoulder and picked up her keys ready to leave, Carla came to a decision. Once her mum's affairs were all settled she was going to change her life and start enjoying it again. Just how she would accomplish that she had yet to decide, but one thing was certain, she would insist she and David spent more time together.

The days were lengthening and the spring bulbs in the front garden were beginning to flower before No. 29 was finally clean and empty. Carla instructed the local estate agents who arrived to measure up and take photographs, ready for the house to go on the market once probate was finalised.

One evening in early March, Carla sat at her own kitchen table with the last box of her mother's papers and photos to sort. The previous five boxes had been uninspiring, but this one contained more photographs than paperwork and Carla had saved it for last deliberately. Secretly, she was hoping the photographs would give her a silent insight into the largely unknown history of her maternal French family.

Faded black and white photos of mysterious foreign relatives standing staunchly arm in arm on some mountainside; a Provençal mas; wide-eyed children fastened into cavernous whale-bellied prams. Two laughing little girls holding hands in a hayfield – 'Amelia et Josette. Juin l950' faintly pencilled on the back. Two older girls paddling on the beach holding their skirts high above their knees – 'Amelia et Josette, Juillet l962'. Proof that the twins had once been close.

A wedding photo dated September l964 taken on the steps of an imposing Hotel de Ville, showed her mother and father smiling in a stiff, grown-up wedding pose. Josette standing to one side looking happy. What row in later years could possibly have been serious enough to keep them apart for ever more?

Carla jumped as David appeared at her side with a glass of wine.

'Anything worth keeping amongst this lot? Or do we burn it all?' he asked, pushing some of the photos apart.

'I can't just burn things,' Carla protested. 'It's my family history. I need to go through it, maybe identify who I can, then the box can go in the cupboard in the spare room. Maddy's keen on genealogy, perhaps she'll want to do the family tree one day.'

David picked up a sealed envelope marked 'Josette. Private and Confidential'.

'Wonder what this is. Shall I open it?'

Carla took the envelope from him and examined it curiously. 'Tempting as it is, I don't think we should open it. I'll put it to one side and pop it in the post to Josette next time I go to the post office. I don't suppose it contains anything of earth-shattering importance to her though.'

'You could always go for a visit. Deliver it personally,' David said. 'You could do with a break after the last couple of months.'

Carla looked at him. 'True. But you'd be on your own now both the children are living away.'

'For god's sake, Carla, I'm quite capable of looking after myself, you know. You haven't been around looking after me recently anyway.'

'I didn't have the choice. Mum's house had to be sorted. I'm sorry you feel hard done by, but you were busy too. There weren't many evenings when you were even home to eat dinner.' She didn't add: *And you were clearly too busy to even offer to help me.*

'No point in coming home when you weren't here. Easier to work late and eat at the club before coming home.'

David's look challenged her to argue, but she couldn't summon the energy, so she ignored it.

'Don't worry about me. A break would do you good,' David said. 'At least think about it.'

'To be honest, I'm not sure about visiting Tante Josette. It's not as if she's ever issued an invitation.' Carla looked at David. 'Are you busy at work for the next few weeks? We could go together?'

'Not a chance,' David said. 'You don't have to stay with Josette. Just hand her the envelope and if she doesn't want to talk, you've done your bit. Find a hotel and have a few days' holiday.'

Carla shook her head. 'I don't want to go alone. It's better to post the envelope. I'll finish going through everything in here in case there's anything else marked for her.'

David shrugged. 'Whatever.'

* * *

A day later, the sorted box of photos was ready to go into the cupboard in the spare room. Pushing it onto the bottom shelf, Carla met with resistance and dropped to her knees to see what was blocking the way. An old shoe box had somehow wedged itself across the back, and as Carla tugged it free, the lid moved and she saw the black velvet jeweller's box.

Christmas was over months ago and it was too early for her birthday. Had David planned to give her a surprise? Something to help ease the pain of the last few months? Carefully, she took the diamond pendant necklace out of the box and held it against her neck. Beautiful. As she did so, a piece of paper fluttered out of the lid onto the floor.

Darling Lisa, all my love, David.

Carla felt a stab of real pain reading the words and tears spilled down her cheeks. After the stress of the last few months, she didn't know if she could cope with David having another affair. Her fingers trembled as she replaced the necklace in its box. He'd promised so often that each time was the last; that it was Carla he truly loved and begged her forgiveness. She knew that if she confronted him about Lisa he'd do the same this time. As she stood up clutching the velvet box, she mentally straightened her shoulders. This time she wasn't in a forgiving mood.

Twenty-four hours later, without a word to anyone, Carla fled to France and Tante Josette.

2

The Hotel de Ville clock struck the hour as the taxi driver took Carla's suitcase out of the boot and pointed, 'Vingt mètres à gauche.' He didn't bother to ask if she could manage, just took his fare and drove away.

Carla dragged her suitcase the twenty metres in the direction he'd indicated and looked around. The townhouse Josette lived in was hidden away in the old town of Antibes, down a narrow rue where few cars dared to venture. The sea was thirty metres away as the gulls flew, a three minute walk via the ramparts for everyone else.

An old collie, sleeping in the doorway of a decrepit building, opened an eye before deciding she was not interesting enough to disturb his slumber and closed it again.

Tall medieval houses faced each other across the cobbled street. Two, near the small square with the ancient wisteria and the even older fountain, were linked by an arch with a window overlooking the narrow rue, geraniums in pots hanging from its open shutters. Scaffolding was pinned to one of the houses, workmen on its planks whistling as they filled cracks and holes with grey mortar.

Josette's house, when Carla finally stood in front of it, was as shabby as its neighbours, but its front door had been painted a defiant scarlet. There was no bell or knocker so Carla banged on the door with her fist.

Above her head, a window opened.

'If that's you, Gordon, the door is open. Just give it a push. Anyone else, wait outside. I'll be down in a moment.' The window slammed shut.

Carla stayed where she was. Inside, a shadow flitted past the small window to the right. Seconds later, the door opened.

'Bonjour, Tante Josette,' Carla said. 'May I come in please? It's an emergency. Sort of,' she added.

Josette's blue eyes stared at her as if trying to gauge the depth of her emergency, before she shrugged and turned away. 'Don't see why not. I've a bottle of rosé in the fridge.'

Carla stepped over the threshold, closed the front door behind her and followed Josette into the open-plan room with its beams and unlit log-burning stove.

French doors opened from the kitchen area into a court-yard full of pots of lavender and gaudy geraniums, where jasmine and honeysuckle entwined together, covering the walls. A pair of pigeons canoodled in a recess in the corner, taking off with ruffled feathers as Josette shouted at them. A green wrought-iron table with matching chairs, made comfortable with cushions covered in the inevitable Provençal blue and yellow fabric, was placed in a corner. A large square white parasol provided shelter from the over-head sun.

Josette poured two generous glasses of wine and handed one to Carla. 'Santé.'

They clicked glasses before Josette asked, 'Why are you here?'

'I told you. I had an emergency.' Carla hesitated before saying, 'You didn't come for the funeral. I thought maybe you would.'

'I sent a wreath. You came to berate me?'

'No. I've several reasons for coming. One of them is to learn about the French side of the family. Mum never told me much – you're the last one who can tell me. I also wanted to spend some time with you – a spot of aunt–niece bonding if you like. The last reason is,' Carla stopped and drained her glass. 'The last reason can wait. Any more wine in that bottle?'

* * *

Josette phoned Gordon once she was certain Carla was busy making up the bed in the spare room.

'We'll have to forget our island excursion for a while,' she said. 'My niece has come for a visit.'

'She might like to come with us,' Gordon suggested.

'Peut-être, but not this week. She has things on her mind.'

'Do I get to meet this niece of yours?'

'Maybe I'll invite you to supper later in the week. If she stays that long.'

Putting the phone down, Josette placed another bottle of wine in the fridge before returning to the courtyard and sitting at the table, closing her eyes and thinking about Carla's words.

Merde. She wasn't mentally prepared for this encounter.

Aunt-niece bonding. Learn about the French family. Both ridiculous notions. It was far too late for more than a superficial telling of family history. Josette prayed Carla wouldn't push her quest for information about the family too far. The truth could serve no real purpose now. Thirty, twenty, even ten years ago when... Josette shook her head. She'd decided in the cathedral the morning of the funeral, the truth was best left to be buried with her when she died. She wouldn't be leaving one of those 'tell all when I'm gone' letters either.

'I've brought some photos,' Carla said, joining her at the table, holding two large envelopes.

Josette opened her eyes and came back to the present with a start. Carla had changed into a floral maxi dress, her feet were bare and her hair was pinned up haphazardly. Her niece had grown into an attractive woman in the thirty years since she'd last seen her.

'I can't believe you're fifty this year. You've certainly got the right kind of genes,' Josette said.

'You're not the only one who can't believe it,' Carla said. 'I find the prospect terrifying, particularly now.'

Josette looked at her and waited, but Carla shook her head.

'Later,' and she opened one of the envelopes and began to hand things to Josette.

'Pictures of Maddy and Edward,' she said, holding photographs out to Josette.

Josette took the photos. Twins, like her and Amelia. A great-nephew and niece she'd never met. Knew only the basics facts about them and their lives. 'What are they up to these days?'

'Edward is doing locum veterinary work in South Africa.

Maddy is just starting her own PR business. Here's a photograph of them taken at Christmas last year.'

Josette looked at the pictures of her great-nephew and niece, inwardly regretting the years of enforced separation.

'This is one of the last photos of Mum,' Carla said quietly, handing over another picture.

Josette stared at the picture of Amelia, her late sister. The family likeness to their mother had strengthened down the years. Both had the thin lips that had shrivelled into hard lines as they'd aged and the bitterness in them had shown.

'It's hard to believe you were twins,' Carla said. 'Mum changed so much as she aged. Whereas you,' she shrugged, 'you've always looked the same to me on the rare occasions I've seen you.'

'Was she very difficult at the end?' Josette asked, ignoring the last comment.

'No more than usual,' Carla said simply. 'Once her mind had gone, she did become more aggressive though, especially to me. Nothing I did was right.'

Josette nodded thoughtfully and was silent for several seconds before asking, ''What's in the other packet?'

'Photos of babies and people I assume are French relatives. I'm hoping you'll be able to tell me who they are and fill me in on some family history,' Carla said, picking it up and pulling another envelope out. 'And I found this amongst Mum's things. It's marked private and confidential with your name on it. I was going to post it but...' she shrugged. 'Things happened and it seemed a good idea to deliver it personally.'

'Thanks.' Josette turned the bulky sealed envelope over in her hands before glancing at Carla. 'Did you open it?'

'No. David wanted to but I wouldn't have been happy

opening something so clearly marked for someone else. Are you going to open it?'

Josette shook her head. 'No. Not tonight.' She stood up and went into the house and pushed the envelope into the bottom drawer of the kitchen dresser – the one where she threw miscellaneous things that might come in useful one day.

She didn't need to open the envelope – she knew without looking inside what it would contain. It could stay in the drawer until the next time she lit the wood burner. Then she would burn it. Destroy the evidence forever.

* * *

Carla watched through the open doorway as Josette closed the dresser drawer with an impatient push. At seventy-three, Josette was still slim. Her white hair was folded into a tidy French pleat, her fingernails neat and rounded, painted a soft coral. Unlike her toes, with their flashes of scarlet peeping out from her strappy sandals.

As a teenager, Carla had been fascinated by this enigmatic aunt of hers and longed to get to know her better. Decades ago, she'd asked her mother why they didn't see more of Josette – more of any of their French relatives in fact – and received the brusque answer 'Family rift.' No details were ever volunteered.

Amelia had relented once when Carla was about nine. The three of them – Carla and her parents – had travelled to Antibes for her grandmother's funeral. Young as she was, Carla had sensed the tension between her mother, Josette and her grandfather both in the church and back at the villa for the wake. It had been the only time during her childhood

Carla had seen her aunt. When her grandfather had died a year later, Amelia had gone to France alone, leaving Carla at home with her father for five days.

'She mixes with the wrong sort and moves around a lot,' had been her mother's excuse when a teenage Carla had asked why they didn't see Josette. But the year Carla was due to go to Paris with the college, a Christmas card arrived with a Parisian address, a telephone number and a scrawled message: Living in the City of Light for a while. Secretly, Carla copied the contact details. And daringly rang her aunt.

For two hours, they'd sat and chatted in a small cafe on the Left Bank. Josette interested in Carla's life, deflecting questions about her own. When Carla had asked if they could keep in regular touch, Josette replied it was best to leave things as they were – but any emergency and she'd be there to help if she could. She'd told Carla not to forget that she travelled a lot in her freelance photography job so couldn't promise to always be available.

Down the years, Carla had contacted her at different times hoping to chat, but Josette had always been strictly impassive. 'Not an emergency is it?' she'd ask and the conversation would stall.

Well, now she had a crisis and, thankfully, Josette had taken her in, although admittedly Carla had given her little choice.

'We'll eat supper out tonight,' Josette said, returning to the courtyard and shrugging herself into an ancient linen jacket. 'Nothing fancy,' she added. 'Place in the market does good pasta.'

When they got to the market, restaurants lining the pedestrian side of the market had placed tables and chairs where, earlier, trestles piled with fruit and vegetables had stood.

Josette ignored the restaurant tables without cloths and offering cheap plastic chairs, making straight for a restaurant where the tables were covered with pink and white checked cloths and the chairs had comfortable woven cane seats.

'Bonsoir, Josette,' the patron said, kissing her cheek before shaking Carla's hand in welcome as Josette introduced her. 'Ça va?'

A carafe of house red appeared on the table, as Josette looked at the menu before ordering carbonara. Carla ordered a salad Niçoise.

'You don't like pasta?' Josette asked.

'I just don't fancy it tonight,' Carla said. 'A salad will be fine. I'm not very hungry.' She picked up her glass, already filled by an attentive waiter, and looked at Josette. 'David's got a mistress,' she said. 'Again.'

'So, find yourself a lover,' Josette replied.

Stunned, Carla laughed. 'If only it was that easy.'

'It is.'

Carla shook her head. 'Haven't got the energy to fight tit for tat. Waste of time too, I think.'

'Having good sex is never a waste of time,' Josette said. 'Mind you, it has to be good sex. Merci,' she addressed the young waiter placing their cutlery and the bread basket on the table. 'Wham bam and thank you mam does not constitute good sex however desperate you are. I learnt that a long time ago.' She picked a piece of baguette out of the basket before saying, 'Maybe we can find you a French lover while you're here.'

'I can't believe we're having this conversation,' Carla said. 'I didn't come for advice about my sex life.'

'What did you come for?'

Carla swirled the wine in her glass round and round for several minutes before looking up at Josette.

'I told you, to learn about the French family and I needed to get away. Coming here seemed as good an option as any. But if it's a problem, I'll find a hotel tomorrow.'

Josette shrugged. 'Up to you. Just don't expect me to behave like your average aunt dispensing good advice. Never been my thing and I'm too old to change now. Plus de vin?' she asked, picking up the carafe.

Carla lay on the bed in the small guest room at the back of the house, staring up at the ceiling, her body tired but incapable of overruling her active mind and sleeping. What was she doing here? Her problem might now be a thousand miles away, but it still existed.

She glanced at her watch. Ten o'clock in the UK. Had David read the cryptic note she'd left propped against the coffee machine telling him she was going away for a few days, to think things through? Or was he out with his lover?

Maybe she should have stayed, patiently ridden out the storm and taken him back when the affair ended, as it would, she had no doubt, in about six months. Heavens, it was their silver wedding next year. How could they not celebrate that together?

Instead, she'd run away within twenty-four hours of learning about the affair, telling no one where she was going. As the plane had flown southwards high above France, the unexpected sense of delicious freedom that had engulfed her as she'd obtained the last available seat on the flight had evaporated, leaving a drowning sense of despair in its place.

She closed her eyes. What had she hoped to gain by coming here? By conveniently running away, she'd inadvertently given David the freedom to engineer more adulterous meetings with this Lisa, whoever she was. More time to see a lawyer. Get things organised in his favour.

Dammit, she wasn't some deluded little woman, clinging to her man, no matter what he subjected her to. But of all the things she'd been expecting to happen in the rest of her life, leaving David wasn't one of them. That wasn't what she'd anticipated at all. She didn't know if she was strong enough to survive on her own, even as the magazines kept telling her it was technically her time.

She'd coped with his affairs before, making a scene over only one of them in the early days when he'd complained of feeling neglected when the twins were newborn. Hurt and humiliated, she'd decided to stay to give the children a secure childhood. Later, his redundancy and the setting up of his own advertising business had made finances tight and divorce too expensive an option – there would have been nothing to divide between them. The house, mortgaged to the hilt and signed over as security for the business, certainly wouldn't have raised enough money to provide her and the children with a home.

She suspected he didn't even realise she knew about any of the others. Elaine the dentist, Fiona his bank manager were just two she remembered from down the years. And now this unknown Lisa. Did she work with David? A new secretary he'd employed? Maybe she was one of the new assistants he'd talked about employing and taken on to ease the workload.

Carla shifted restlessly as she remembered toying with the idea of leaving when Maddy and Edward left home for university, but by then her life with David had morphed into a habit. It had been easier to stay than go.

Water gurgled its way along a pipe above her head as Josette brushed her teeth in the small bathroom across the landing. Carla sighed, picturing her aunt getting ready for bed. She hadn't exactly welcomed her with open arms, but at least she'd let her stay. Hopefully she'd mellow as they got to know each other, although she was certainly living up to her family reputation of being a loner. Self-contained and undemonstrative were the words used by Amelia once to describe her twin sister to Carla. She clearly hadn't changed as she'd aged.

The bathroom door opened and closed. A tap on the bedroom door before Josette pushed it open. Carla turned her head and regarded her aunt.

'I don't sleep too well these days,' Josette said. 'Five thirty usually finds me downstairs. Don't feel obliged to get up early – although I doubt that you'll sleep beyond seven o'clock anyway. Bonne nuit.' The door closed before Carla could answer.

3

There was no sign of Josette when Carla made her way downstairs the next morning. Josette had been right about Carla not sleeping after seven. When the nearby town hall clock had boomed the hour, she'd woken with a jolt.

There was a note on the kitchen table: Croissants in the tin, help yourself. Coffee ready to go. See you later. J. Was Josette deliberately avoiding her?

Taking her breakfast out into the courtyard, Carla thought about the day ahead. Ringing Maddy was the first priority. She needed to speak to her before she turned up at the house and discovered her absence. Edward was away for at least another three months so she didn't need to bother him right now. He'd promised to try and get back for her big birthday later in the year. Things should have sorted themselves out by then. One way or another.

Carla looked at her mobile. 8 a.m. here, 7 a.m. in the UK – Maddy would be busy getting ready for work. How do you tell your grown-up daughter that her parents' marriage had suffered an earthquake fracture off the Richter scale? Risk the blunt truth – 'Dad is having another affair and I had to get away' – or try to soften the news – 'We're having a few problems so we've decided to have some time apart to sort things out.' Make it sound like a joint decision – not hers alone. Was there a chance that this separation was not permanent – that David would break it off with his latest mistress, grovel and apologise and promise to behave in the future? Was that what she wanted to happen?

The booming chimes of the Hotel de Ville clock striking once again died away as Carla selected Maddy's number and listened to the ringing tone. When the message service clicked in, she switched off. Leaving Maddy a message about the current situation wasn't an option. She had to break the news to her in voice, if not face to face.

A break in the sound of footsteps in the street was followed by a bang on the front door. Carla hesitated. Should she open the door? Her limited French was rusty and she dreaded struggling to make herself understood with a stranger. As she stood there undecided, she heard the footsteps walking away. Relieved not to have to take any action, Carla realised she'd been holding her breath.

Josette was still not back when Carla left to explore the town. She knew little about the place where her mother and aunt had been born other than it had long been an ancient trading port, with its fortifications built by the French engineer Sebastien Vauban. The town's modern marina, Port Vauban, was named in his honour.

A brisk onshore breeze was whistling around the narrow rues of the old town as Carla walked away from the market area. A narrow ally led her to the ramparts and she walked along the coastal road until she reached the bottom of Boulevard Albert Premier, near an open park area.

Without stopping to think, Carla stepped off the pavement, looking to her right rather than her left, and found herself jerked from under the wheels of a car by a man who pulled her back onto the pavement. A furious fist wave and an angry honking of the horn from the driver emphasised how close the car had been to knocking her down.

Shocked, Carla tried to stop shaking. In a daze, she realised the man had his arm around her shoulders and was leading her to a nearby cafe.

'Deux cafe, s'il vous plait,' he called out to the waiter, while he gently eased Carla onto a seat. 'Prendre des respirations profondes,' he instructed, sitting down opposite her and watching her.

Carla closed her eyes and tried to stop the thumping of her heart. How could she have been so stupid?

'Vous Anglais?' the man said.

Carla nodded. 'Yes.'

'In that case – I translate. You need to take deep breaths.' He watched her for several seconds, making sure she did as he said. 'Your habit is to look right. Here you 'ave to look left. It is a mistake the English make all the time.'

Two coffees were placed on the table in front of them, a sachet of sugar and a small biscuit in each saucer. Whilst the man opened his sugar packet and poured it into his coffee, Carla automatically placed hers to one side. She'd stopped taking sugar in coffee a long time ago.

'May I suggest you take the coffee with sugar this time, good for shock I think?'

Carla sighed but obediently emptied the sugar into her

coffee, stirred it and took a couple of mouthfuls. She pulled a face. Gross. She looked at the man. 'Thank you for what you did. I was lucky you were there, otherwise...' she shuddered.

'I think you will remember better to look both ways now,' he said. 'Good – you 'ave stopped shaking and the colour it returns to your face.'

Carla picked up the biscuit, tore the plastic open and took a small bite.

'You are at the beginning of a vacance?' the man asked, picking up his demitasse coffee cup.

Carla nodded. 'Yes. I am visiting my aunt for a few days.' Easier to agree than to admit to a stranger she'd run away.

'I hope you enjoy your stay,' he answered. 'Now I must go. I am late for a meeting.' He stood up and placed a few euros on the bill in the saucer that had arrived with the coffees.

'Please let me pay for the coffees,' Carla said. 'I owe you that at least.'

The man brushed aside her protest. 'Non. It is my pleasure, but please, remember to look left in future.'

'Definitely,' Carla promised.

'Ciao,' and he left.

Carla finished her biscuit and, when the waiter came to clear the table, ordered a fresh cup of coffee, which she drank without sugar. Feeling better, she was about to make a move when her mobile rang. Maddy.

'Mum? Your phone sounds funny. Are you okay? What's going on? I've had Dad on the phone saying you've left him.'

Carla caught her breath. Damn. David had got to Maddy before her. She took a deep breath. 'I'm fine. I was hoping to talk to you before Dad did. I just need some time away to think about the future.'

'Why? What's happened?'

Carla took a deep breath. David clearly hadn't explained his part in her decision to leave. Time for Maddy to learn the truth. 'Dad's having an affair.'

Maddy's shocked 'What?' was barely audible. The question that followed 'How d'you know?' was a little louder.

Conscious of the interested looks from a couple at a nearby table who clearly understood English, Carla kept her own voice low.

'Maddy, I'll call you later. I'm in a cafe at the moment. It's not very private.'

'That's another thing – where are you? Dad thought you might be with me. I think that's why he rang me.'

'I'll ring you this evening and explain everything,' Carla said. 'Seven o'clock a good time for you?'

'Yes. Mum?'

'I love you.' Carla pressed the off button on her own phone. What a morning.

Josette had told Carla the truth when she said she didn't sleep well and was up early most mornings, but getting out of the house and walking along the coast road was not a part of her normal routine. Generally, she made for one of the cafes in the market for a coffee. Today though, she'd needed to get out and walk by the sea in an effort to try to organise her thoughts before Carla started to ask her inevitable questions about the family.

As Josette strode along, she thought about Carla. The last person she'd expected to see when she'd opened the door yesterday. How big was the crisis in her marriage? How long was she planning on staying? How little she knew her. How much family history could she divulge without devastating her world? Did she need to know the truth? How would she react? Would she accept a sanitised version of the family history? Or would she want to dig deeper, ask more questions?

Sitting on a bench by the Plages de la Salis and staring out over the Mediterranean hoping for inspiration, the questions continued to go round and round in Josette's mind. Answers though were elusive. Watching a pair of seagulls fighting over the remains of a discarded takeaway burger, a troubled Josette came to a decision. A promise was a promise, even if it had been made under pressure decades ago. She'd carry on keeping it. Any question of Carla's she could answer honestly – and for Josette that was the key word – she would. Any others, she'd shrug her shoulders and say nothing; keep her fingers crossed that Carla would learn enough to satisfy her and not press for more information.

In the meantime, she'd try and enjoy having Carla as a house guest and introduce her to some of the Cote d'Azur sights. Life could be lonely at times, having company for a little while would be good. Maybe some bonding would be possible even at this late stage, if she dodged the problem questions and skirted around others carefully.

Walking home, she stopped off at the market and picked up salad and some sardines, a baguette and two individual tartes citron from the artisan boulangerie stand and that was lunch sorted. She'd cook Carla lunch on her tiny barbecue in the courtyard.

Josette had been home for ten minutes when Carla banged the door. Letting her in, Josette took a key off a hook near it.

'You'd better have this while you're here,' she said,

handing the key to Carla. 'Don't lose it. It's my last spare one. Lunch will be ready in about ten minutes. Wine's in the fridge.'

Carla set the table and made the salad before pouring two glasses of wine and taking them out to the courtyard while Josette barbecued the sardines.

'Santé,' Josette said, taking her glass. 'Did you have a good morning exploring?'

Carla laughed. 'Yes, thanks – apart from when I nearly walked under a car.'

'Ah, the old right versus the left mistake?'

Carla nodded. 'Thankfully, this man grabbed me and literally pulled me to safety. Took me ages to stop shaking. I had fun exploring afterwards though. A couple of places I vaguely remembered from when we came to Nanna's funeral. The market for one, oh, and the Picasso museum.'

'Did you see the old family home?'

'No. To be honest, I wouldn't recognise it if I saw it.'

'We'll take a walk sometime and I'll show you. It's rented out at the moment, but the current tenants leave soon,' Josette said. 'Which means I have weeks of hassle trying to find new ones. So many fraudsters about these days.'

'I would have thought the villa would have been sold years ago?' Carla said. 'When Grandpapa died.'

'Under French law, Amelia and I inherited it together. Whilst I was keen to sell, Amelia refused to agree. She didn't want anything to do with the place but was determined to stop me benefiting. Insisting any monies went into a special fund that neither of us could touch. Said the next generation could fight over it when the time came. The notaire, he try every year to get her to sign a release mais... she always refuses.' Josette's voice faded away as she stared at Carla, a look of consternation on her face. How could she have forgotten about Villa Mimosa? 'Have you heard from the French lawyers about Amelia's will?'

'No. Her will was an English one basically leaving everything to me, with small bequests to Maddy and Edward. A few thousand each. After the house sells.'

'And there was no mention of Villa Mimosa?'

Carla shook her head.

Josette picked up the bottle of wine and, despite Carla's protest, topped both their glasses up. 'In that case we need to make an appointment with the notaire to organise things legally.'

'What things?' Carla asked, puzzled.

'Principally the fact that you, as Amelia's legitimate heir, now own half of Villa Mimosa with me. Santé.'

4

That evening, a few minutes before eight o'clock, Carla switched on her laptop ready for a video chat with Maddy. Josette had surprised her earlier by giving her the password and telling her to use the house broadband internet connection. Carla hadn't been expecting her aunt to be a silver surfer. Besides, there was no sign of a laptop, not even an iPad, in the house. Josette had shrugged her shoulders nonchalantly at Carla's surprise.

'C'est difficile not to be online these days. The French government close offices, create websites and expect everyone to become computer literate overnight. I keep my tablet in the bedroom so I can play online poker at night when I can't sleep.' The fact that Josette played poker surprised Carla less than the fact she did it online.

Carla scribbled a couple of things she wanted to say to Maddy on a piece of paper so she didn't forget them, before bringing up Skype and pressing Maddy's name and struggling to marshal her thoughts into a logical and sensible order while waiting for Maddy to answer. She didn't want

Maddy knowing, or even suspecting, how terrified she was of what the future held. If she could hold it together and make her daughter believe that she was coping and wasn't about to dissolve into a teary blob, then there was a chance she might convince herself too, that things would come right. The smile she greeted Maddy with was genuine, even if the first words her daughter uttered were almost guaranteed to make the mask slip.

'I phoned Dad after I spoke to you and we've had a major bust-up over his affair. He told me to grow up and stop being such a child. These things happen. You and I apparently have to learn to live with it.' The name she then called her father made Carla wince.

'Maddy, don't. That's a horrible name to call him. He's right though – I do have to accept the fact that it's happened and I'm afraid you do too.'

'No way. He's even suggested I meet this Lisa. Thinks I'll like her and we'll get on. He's delusional as well as being a...' Maddy bit back on saying the word again. 'Have you spoke to Ed? I tried to ring him but couldn't get through.'

'I was waiting until he came back later in the year,' Carla said, swallowing hard. David wanting to introduce Maddy to this woman was something she hadn't anticipated. He was obviously serious about her. 'Ed is so far away, I didn't want to worry him. Besides, there's nothing he, or anyone, can do.'

'Are you in a hotel, Mum?' Maddy asked. 'Dad thought you might have gone to Gran's house but said there was no sign of you when he went round there.'

'No, I'm not in a hotel. I'm... I'm staying with a friend.'

'Which friend? Mavis?'

'No one you know.'

'Why aren't you telling me where you are?'

'Because, in all probability, Dad will demand you tell him and I don't want him knowing yet.'

'But it's not fair not to tell me – I'm on your side. Tell me.'

Carla sighed, looking at her daughter's red-rimmed eyes. 'Sorry, I can't. Not yet. I promise I'll tell you soon. I just want some time away from everything, to think, calm down and make plans.'

'If he gives up this tart will you go home? It's got to be just a midlife crisis. It's not as if he's ever done it before, is it?' Maddy said, rubbing her nose, a nervous habit she'd had as a young child. When she realised Carla hadn't answered, shock registered on her face. 'He has, hasn't he?'

Carla nodded. 'Several times. I don't think he knows I know about most of them though.'

'So surely this won't be any different, he'll be back with his tail between his legs in a couple of months – maybe even weeks.'

Carla was silent, working out in her own mind what was so different this time. Was it just that she was so much older? That she didn't have to stay for the 'sake of the children'? Or was it because she was tired of being married to David and condoning his affairs? She'd spent enough years in a loveless marriage, surely she deserved a life of her own? Besides, did she even have the option this time of forgiving and forgetting?

'Dad talking to you about this Lisa tells me this affair could be different. It's not clandestine like the others were. It seems he's happy for this one to come out into the world for everyone to see. Saying he'd like you to meet her is a clear indication that he wants to be free of me. To move on,' Carla took a deep breath, trying to force a note of optimism into her voice. 'I wouldn't have chosen to end my marriage this way, but joining the ranks of divorced women at my age doesn't signal the end of my life. I'll treat it as an opportunity to try new things, go to different places, enjoy a new direction.' The thought *And try to rediscover the woman I used to be* she kept to herself. Was that even possible?

'But where are you going to live? What are you going to do? You can't just let him walk all over you. You have certain rights that Dad will have to adhere to legally.'

'Don't worry, I'm sure we're both old enough to be civilised with each other. I just have to work out the best way to deal with things for me,' Carla said. 'I'll be back soon. I'll have a clearer idea of what I'm going to do by then.'

By the time Carla ended the call, she was exhausted with the effort of keeping up the pretence of a cheerful front for Maddy when inside she felt desolate, bereft and close to tears. She hadn't begun to think about finding the answers to the questions Maddy had asked.

Downstairs, Josette was sitting in the courtyard, a bottle of rosé on the table in front of her. She held out a glass to Carla.

'Thanks,' Carla said, swallowing a large mouthful of the chilled wine before sinking onto the spare seat.

'Maddy well?' Josette asked.

Carla nodded. 'Except for being upset for me and angry with her father.'

Josette regarded her steadily. 'She'll get over it. Probably quicker than you.'

'I think she'll struggle to accept things, she's always been a daddy's girl. And the fact we'll no longer be playing happy families in the eyes of the world will upset her. Instead we'll be busy trying to live our segregated lives with the family torn apart.'

'Nothing new in that. Families have been dysfunctional

throughout history. People survive and get on with their lives as best they can. There is no other choice,' Josette said. 'It's called living. Bien sûr. I know that from experience.'

Carla looked at her, waiting for her to expand on the remark. Instead, Josette picked up the bottle and topped up her own glass when Carla shook her head and placed her hand over the top of her own still half-full one, wondering about the life this enigmatic aunt of hers had lived. Would she ever tell her about it?

5

Carla was sitting in the courtyard eating her breakfast croissant the next morning when Josette returned from her usual
start-of-the-day coffee in the market.

'We have a rendezvous with the notaire at the end of the
week about Villa Mimosa,' Josette said, helping herself to a
coffee from the cafetière. 'We'll go for a walk later along the
bord de mer so you can look at the outside at least.'

'Thanks,' Carla said. 'I was so young when Nanna died, to
be honest, I can't remember visits to the villa at all. I do
vaguely remember being told to stop asking so many questions when we came for the funeral. No idea what I was
curious about.'

An hour later, after dodging the tourists as they made
their way along the coastal road, they were standing at the
top of the short drive leading to the Villa Mimosa. The tall
metal gates were pushed open, giving a clear view of the
typical Provençal maison with its olive-green shutters and
terracotta roof tiles. A single tall mimosa tree stood on

sentinel duty to one side of the drive, seed pods hanging from it now that the blossoms had finished.

'Originally there was a bank of mimosa trees along here, hence the villa's name,' Josette said. 'The smell in spring was wonderful. Sadly, this is the last one.'

A small van was parked to the side of the front door, but there was no sign of anyone.

'Can we walk up the drive?' Carla asked. 'Look around the garden?'

'I don't see why not,' Josette replied. 'We do own the place. The van belongs to the gardener whom I pay to keep the place looking presentable. I can always say I needed to speak to him if the tenant appears. Obviously, we can't go in the house without prior arrangement, but the garden...' she shrugged. 'They've given notice anyway.'

Gravel crunched under their feet as they walked up the drive with its low rosemary hedges on either side. A short flight of four curved shallow steps with a mixture of colourful pots, some with trailing white and pink geraniums, others with sweet smelling lavender, stood in front of the door like a welcoming committee. Turning left, Carla followed Josette down the path at the side of the house to the back garden, where the water of a large swimming pool glistened in the sunlight.

'Oh, I wasn't expecting there to be a pool,' Carla said. 'That definitely wasn't here when I came last time. I would have remembered that. I would have been in it at every opportunity.'

'Down here it's de rigueur for a villa of this size to have a pool. We had it put in about thirty years ago. Amelia was dead against it but...' Josette tailed off. 'People looking to rent for a year or two always demand a pool. Joel here is the pool boy as well as the gardener. Bonjour, Joel,' she called out to a man busy scooping leaves and other debris out of the pool. 'Je montre juste ma niece Carla la villa,' she added.

Joel, a tanned, fit, fiftyish man with close-cropped grey hair and stubble, acknowledged their presence with a short look in their direction and a brief 'Bonjour' but carried on concentrating on what he was doing. Carla watched as he carefully manoeuvred himself and the cleaning hose around one of the painted stone elephants that stood either side of the far end of the pool.

While Josette walked around the pool to speak to Joel, Carla stayed where she was, drinking in the garden's details. The small cane couch with its colourful cushions under the shelter of a large cherry tree in the far corner, an ideal place for relaxing and curling up with a book after a swim. Neat flower beds down the left-hand side of the garden in front of the oleander hedge dividing Villa Mimosa from its neighbour, lemon trees in pots, roses climbing an old metal arch, a tall pagoda, a bird feeder. Four pairs of French doors along the width of the house opened onto the terrace, where a long teak table and chairs were positioned under the loggia, perfect for lunches al fresco and romantic starlit suppers.

Carla stood there trying to match this garden to the one that should be somewhere deep in her memory from her childhood visit. Her head began to hurt with the effort of trying to force her brain to give up its memories of the garden from that visit. She had only been young after all, how could she expect her mind to throw up any pictures of the past. It had been a short visit. Two days at the most. Nothing here was familiar. What had been where the pool was? Overgrown shrubs? A lawn? A large tree? A tumbledown shed? A swing?

Something she couldn't grasp began to niggle in her brain. She jumped as Josette returned to her side.

'What was where the pool is now?' Carla asked.

'An apology of a lawn and a large oak tree. And didn't that give us a problem, getting the roots out. Took days. I was désolé to see it go if I'm honest. Amelia and I loved that tree. We used to climb it and hide from Papa,' Josette said. 'Amelia fell out of it once, broke her wrist. We didn't climb it much after that.' She sighed and took a quick look at Carla. 'I remember you getting into trouble because of the tyre swing that was fixed to one of its lower branches when you came.'

A picture of a chunky rope and a large tyre with herself swinging to and fro floated into Carla's mind. She smiled. A memory at last. 'I remember that tyre. I got black from it. Mum was furious with me. Wouldn't let me near it again for the rest of the time we were here.'

'I remember your tears,' Josette said. 'You were inconsolable. Seen enough for now?'

Turning to walk back up the drive, Carla glanced at Josette. 'Do you have good memories of growing up here?'

They had almost reached the gates at the end of the drive before Josette sighed and answered. 'Growing up, yes, but in the end I couldn't wait to get away. Everything had become so tainted, I couldn't bear to stay.'

'I remember the occasional postcard arriving from different places down the years. I learnt to tread gently around Mum when a new one arrived. They always upset her.'

'I didn't realise that,' Josette said.

Carla nodded. 'As I grew older, I realised it was probably because she was jealous of your life. D'you remember that year I met you in Paris? We talked and talked. I'd hoped you and I would keep in touch more afterwards but...' Carla shrugged. 'Mum was furious with me when she found out I'd met up with you.'

When Josette didn't say anything, Carla continued.

'When you left here the first time where did you go?'

Josette smiled. 'Paris – a place I returned to again and again. Initially, I thought about going to Italy, but Paris was the obvious choice for losing myself in and finding work.'

'You never married. Did you ever want to? Maybe have a family of your own?' Carla asked, knowing she was probably pushing her luck with the question.

There was a brief silence before Josette laughed. 'I enjoyed the era of the late sixties far too much to tie myself down. I was a bit of a hippy in those days.'

'Mum always said you were a rebel. That you mixed with the wrong sort. Was that true?'

'A rebel? I've never thought of myself like that. We just reacted to circumstances differently. As for the wrong sort – who's to be the judge of that?'

* * *

Back in town, Josette declined to join Carla on a visit to the Picasso museum, instead she wandered along to the square by the post office and ordered a coffee at a pavement cafe. Watching the children play in the little park alongside the square, Josette smothered a sigh. Yesterday, after she'd refused to elaborate on her remark about life giving you no choice but to get on with it, she'd found herself trying to ignore the guilty feelings that swamped her. Had she been undiplomatic, harsh even, when she'd dismissed Carla's worries about Maddy? Today, as she and Carla walked back along the bord de mer, their conversation had stirred up more guilty feelings. Making her think about things she'd hidden deep in the recess of her mind for years.

Having given her word all those years ago that she would never talk about the rift in the family, she'd made a life for herself that had turned out happier in the end than she'd ever hoped after the devastation of being cut adrift and having to find a different path to the one she'd expected.

Carla's physical presence in her life for only a matter of days had shown her it would be all too easy for ripples to begin to disturb her hidden past. A past that could fragment into a thousand pieces if the ripples ever grew in size, pushing sorrow, resentment and recriminations into the present. A present that she had allowed herself to be content with, not permitting even the tiniest suspicion to grow in her mind that the life she'd been denied would have been the one to have made her truly happy. The bad family stuff had lain dormant for so long, she'd made the mistake of thinking it would stay that way for ever. She should have realised it would resurface one day and taken steps to... what? Minimise its effect? Deny it happened?

One thing was becoming clearer. It was time to take a step back. Reinstate that 'only in an emergency contact me' rule she'd put in place with Carla years ago. Aunt–niece intimacy or bonding was too dangerous a path to follow. She had to curtail the relationship before it destroyed the pretence her life had been based on.

6

After her tour of the Picasso museum, Carla wandered down to the quay and stood watching the boats for a while. When her phone rang and she saw the caller ID, David, she hesitated before answering. She knew she couldn't put off talking to him for ever but hadn't planned on being in a public place for their conversation. She moved to one side of the pavement, trying to stay out of the way of other people heading towards the International Quay where the superyachts were moored.

'Thought you were going to ignore me,' David said. 'I was about to hang up.'

'What d'you want?'

'Answers to a few things, like: where the hell are you? When d'you plan on coming home? The estate agent wants to know if probate has been completed yet as he has a couple of people who could be interested in Amelia's house. And I'd like that diamond pendant you stole back.'

Carla took a deep breath. No conciliatory words then. No heartfelt apology for cheating on her. She took a deep breath.

'I do not have to tell you where I am. I'll be back when it suits me. I'll ring the solicitor and check on the probate and let the estate agent know. As for the pendant, I think I'll hang on to it – at least for a while.' She ended the call with a shaking finger and switched the phone off. No way was she going to listen to a furious David ranting and raving at her.

And had she really 'stolen' the pendant? She was pretty certain the money to buy it would have come out of their joint account, which technically meant, maybe, the jewellery could be construed as being half hers? Not that she wanted the damn thing anyway, but it was the principle behind it.

As for his question, when was she going home, she didn't have an answer. Inevitable as seeing him was, she didn't feel strong enough yet to stand up to him and face down his bullying tactics. She'd planned on staying with Josette for maybe three days but the unexpected meeting with the notaire about Villa Mimosa had delayed things, so it would be a couple more days at the earliest before she was free to go back to the UK. And then where did she plan to go? Back to the marital home? Maddy's? Her mother's now empty house? Could she live there rather than sell? No, if she was going to start a new single life it couldn't be in that house where Amelia's presence would hang over her forever. It could never be more than a stopgap whilst she decided what, where and the kind of life her future would hold. She could even use the money to buy a simple bolthole and spend the rest on travelling if she wanted to.

Time to start formulating some plans. Make a list of things to do to move her life on. Before she could change her mind, she turned her phone back on and opened the note page and, standing there on the quay, she began to organise her immediate future.

Desperate to get away, she'd not given a thought to buying a return ticket so she'd need to book a flight for after the notaire's appointment. Once back in the UK, she would need to:

(a) see the solicitor about probate progress

(b) pass the information onto the estate agent

(c) make sure the agent contacted her in future and not David, and

(d) enquire about the cost and initiate divorce proceedings whilst at the solicitors

That last note to herself scared her rigid if she were honest and she quickly closed the phone down rather than think about the consequences of setting that particular item into motion. She couldn't believe she was finally thinking along those lines after all these years.

Walking back through town, a scarlet leather tote in the window of one of the designer dress shops caught her eye. Carla wanted it the moment she saw it on the arm of the mannequin. It was a statement bag that screamed: the owner of this bag means business, don't mess with me. David would say it was over the top and ostentatious. She hesitated for a nanosecond before going into the shop and buying it.

Back at the house, Carla hummed to herself as she sat at the table in the courtyard, emptying the contents of her nondescript functional bag into the new one that in no way could be described as ordinary. The scarlet leather was lovely to look at and so soft and supple to the touch.

'Glass of rosé?' Josette said from the kitchen. 'C'est un beau sac,' she added, joining Carla in the courtyard.

'Thanks. I'm not usually an impulsive shopper,' Carla admitted. 'But I had to buy this. I'm hoping that it will be my lucky talisman for the future,' she added quietly.

Josette handed her a glass of wine, held her own aloft and said, 'Santé – and here's to the powers of the red bag.'

Carla tapped her own glass against Josette's. 'To the red bag,' she said, wondering whether her aunt was poking gentle fun at her. 'I do know it's not going to make an iota of difference in reality to what happens to me in the next few months, but it does make me feel that by simply deciding to buy it for no reason other than I love it, I'm the one in charge of things. Plus, the fact I know David will hate it is a bonus.' She smiled at Josette. 'Shall we eat out tonight? My treat? A thank you for having me to stay.'

'If you like,' Josette shrugged indifferently. 'Couldn't turn you away, could I?' She went back into the house, leaving an unsettled Carla staring after her.

Carla deliberated between two restaurants for treating Josette that evening. Both had good reputations. Both had a table for two free. In the end she went for the one with a sea view, reasoning that if Josette was still grumpy with her at least she'd be able to watch the yachts out at sea rather than sit staring aimlessly around at other diners.

But Josette was in surprisingly good spirits, happily agreeing to a Kir Royale aperitif while they chose their meal.

'Santé – and thank you for letting me stay,' Carla said, raising her glass at Josette. 'I've booked a late-afternoon flight home the day of our appointment with the notaire. I can't run away forever. I have to make a start on sorting things out. I expect you'll be glad to have your cottage to yourself again.'

Josette shrugged. 'An emergency is an emergency.'

'May I come back and stay later in the summer – by then I hope to have everything at home under control? I'd ring you first this time.' Even as she spoke, Carla sensed a certain tension in Josette and was cross with herself for asking to return. Tonight was meant to be a happy occasion. She didn't want to upset her aunt.

'I'd appreciate a call first,' Josette said. 'In case it's inconvenient.'

'Sure.' Carla took a sip of her drink, forcing herself to stay calm and not make a sarcastic retort. Despite trying to be a good house guest, she'd clearly been in the way more than she'd realised.

To her relief, the waiter arrived at their table, pencil poised to take their order, and by the time he'd written it down, Josette seemed to have relaxed again and the two of them sat there discreetly people-watching as the restaurant began to fill up.

Carla sipped her drink and sighed as she listened to the buzz of conversation around her, understanding little of it.

'I wanted Mum to speak to me in French so often,' she said quietly. 'When I went to secondary school, learning French was one of my options and I was thrilled at the thought of Mum and I chatting away to each other. She wouldn't even let me join the class. She seemed to eschew anything French.' Carla looked at Josette, a rueful smile on her face. 'At home she refused to cook anything French and Dad did love his magret de canard.'

Josette was about to say something when a man stopped by their table and bent his head to kiss her in greeting.

'Carla, this is my friend, Gordon,' Josette said. 'Gordon, my niece, Carla.'

'Enchanté,' Gordon said, shaking Carla's hand. 'Would you two ladies like to join my table? Sylvie and André will be here in a moment,' he said to Josette. 'We could have a party.'

'Thank you, but not tonight, Gordon. We've already ordered.' Josette glanced across at the waiter, making his way towards them. 'I think our starters are about to arrive.'

Gordon looked disappointed but didn't argue. 'Another evening then. Bon appétit,' and he moved away just as the waiter placed their first course on the table.

'Gordon seems nice – I love his Scottish accent. Is he a special friend of yours?' Carla said, looking at Josette with a smile.

'When you get to my age, all friends are special – there aren't that many of them left,' Josette said, picking up her fork to tackle the prawn and salmon terrine she'd ordered. 'Your salade de chévre chaud looks good – best eat it while it's still warm.'

Carla sighed. Josette's friendship with Gordon was clearly another subject that was not up for discussion.

* * *

A couple of hours later as the two of them made their way home along the ramparts, Carla sighed happily. 'I really enjoyed this evening. I hope you did to,' she said, glancing sideways at Josette.

'I did, thank you. Food is always good there,' was Josette's uncompromising reply before she surprised Carla by saying, 'Peut-être we have a nightcap to finish the evening off? I've got a bottle of St Honorat liqueur which is rather good.'

Sitting in the moonlit courtyard ten minutes later, sipping their nightcaps, Carla said, 'You never did go through the family photos I brought over – shall I leave them here and maybe next time we can?'

'We could have a quick look now,' Josette said. 'I can't

promise to know and name everyone, but hopefully I'll recognise a few people.'

Startled by the unexpected offer, Carla jumped up and fetched the packet from her room. Minutes later, Josette was thumbing through the black and white pictures.

Josette smiled and joked her way through family groups, babies in huge perambulators, pictures of women strolling arm in arm along the Promenade des Anglais in Nice, she even named a couple of cousins – 'all dead now of course' – before sighing. 'Il y a si longtemps – I feel so old looking at these. They're a bit of a... Oh, what's the English word? Time warp?'

Carla had to agree. 'Is this one of you and Mum? You're both looking very glam in your long dresses. How old were you then?'

'Let me see. That was taken at a dance in Cannes the year Amelia met and married Robert, your father, so we would have been eighteen.' Josette sighed. 'We were such good friends then. As close as it was possible to be. We could always tell what the other one was thinking.'

'You look very alike in this photo,' Carla said. 'Hard to tell who's who. Did you ever pretend to be each other?'

'Oh yes, c'était très amusant. But it was something we outgrew. By the time this photo was taken we didn't tease people so much, but at school we were always pretending to be each other.'

'So what happened to stop the two of you caring about each other for all those years since? And for you to become known as the black sheep of the family,' Carla said quietly, amazed that Josette was talking about Amelia and not daring to look at her face as she risked such a personal question.

There was silence for a second or two before Josette

shrugged her shoulders. 'There was a family row, the details of which are best left buried in the past.' She began to gather up the photos and put them back in the envelope.

Realising the subject was closed, Carla started to hand Josette some of the loose photos for the envelope. 'This one of Mum and Dad looks as if it was taken in the garden of Villa Mimosa,' Carla said. 'They look so young – and so happy together. Grand-mère's standing by a pram in the background, so I guess that was taken the year I was born.'

Josette held her hand out for the photo, looked at it for a couple of seconds and gave a brief nod.

'In all the photos I have at home it's hard to find a smile amongst them. After I left to marry David, they seemed to have grown even further apart.' Carla glanced at Josette. 'Do you think they were happy?'

Josette gave a gallic shrug. 'No idea. Other people's marriages have always been complete mysteries to me.'

Carla sighed as she picked up the remaining photos, knowing she was unlikely to get any more information out of Josette. 'Okay, last one – oh, not sure which of you it is, with a man, taken in Cannes. I recognise the Le Suquet tower up on the hill. Lovely photo.'

Josette held out her hand for the photo and the colour drained from her face. 'I didn't know Amelia had this.' She sat looking at the photo silently. 'It's me, a lifetime ago.' She slipped the photo on top of the others. 'Right, I think we've done enough reminiscing. I'm off to bed. I'll put these in the bureau for now, shall I?'

Carla watched as Josette, not waiting for an answer, picked up the packet and went indoors, calling out 'Bonne nuit' as she went. The last photo had definitely spooked her.

But why? And just who was the man in the photo with his arm around Josette's shoulders?

7

The notaire's office, situated on the third floor of a modern building on the bord de mer, positively hummed with quiet but serious efficiency. Monsieur Damarcus and Josette were clearly old friends as he greeted her with a kiss on the cheek as well as a handshake before turning and shaking Carla's hand.

'So, now we do the official paperwork for you to inherit your half of the Villa Mimosa. And then you sell, n'est pas? Like Josette has wanted to do for years.'

'Josette and I haven't discussed it, but would it be possible to keep it and carry on renting it out?' Carla asked. She glanced across at her aunt who was shaking her head.

'No discussion necessary. I want to be rid of the place,' Josette said. 'Amelia made life difficult, refusing to sell and leaving it to me to deal with while she stayed in England doing nothing. You're not likely to be a hands-on landlord either, are you?'

'I would come across on a regular basis,' Carla promised.

Josette stared at her. 'Non. Selling is the better option.'

'Ladies,' the notaire interrupted. 'The formalities will take a few weeks, once Carla's name is on the deeds you can decide then. I have to say, if you do decide to sell, I don't doubt there would be a lot of interest locally. It would probably sell for four or five million euros.'

Carla felt her mouth fall open at his words, but before she could say anything, Josette ended the discussion.

'Good. In that case we'll go to auction.'

The rest of their appointment time was filled with various forms Carla had to fill in and sign, but eventually it was done and Carla and Josette said their goodbyes to Monsieur Damarcus, who promised to be in touch very soon.

Walking back to Josette's cottage, Carla again broached the subject of not selling Villa Mimosa. It had been in the family so long, it felt wrong to sell it without at least exploring the possibility of keeping it.

'I promise I wouldn't leave you with all the hassle of managing the place and finding tenants. I'd come over whenever you needed me.'

'I need the money,' Josette said. 'I wasn't going to say that to Monsieur Damarcus, but it's the truth.' She glanced at Carla. 'I'm at the age when you start thinking about what happens when you need help. Residential care doesn't come cheap.'

'I understand,' Carla nodded. 'But if and when you need that help, couldn't you sell your cottage?'

'It's rented, And my money would disappear with residential home fees très rapidement.'

'I didn't realise that,' Carla said. 'But how about when the tenants leave, you move into the villa? At least it would be rent-free.'

'Rent-free maybe, but the maintenance wouldn't be. Besides, it's too big. What would I do with five bedrooms?'

'Monsieur Damarcus mentioned a separate fund to pay for essential maintenance. You could even rent out a couple of the rooms and have an income.'

'Non,' Josette said. 'It is best to sell. Close the past down.' The look she gave Carla dared her to argue further.

Regretfully, Carla let the subject go. She didn't want to leave her aunt with bad feeling between them, but secretly she promised herself the next time she was over to sign the inheritance papers, she would talk again to Josette about the possibility of keeping Villa Mimosa. Surely if she was in need of money, giving up the cottage, moving to the villa and living rent-free made economic sense?

Josette walked to the end of the rue with Carla, where the taxi ordered for the journey to the airport was waiting. The tight hug Carla gave her was unexpected.

'Thank you so much, Tante Josette. I promise I'll give you a ring before I descend on you next time. You take care.'

The taxi was moving down the narrow street almost before Carla had slammed the door shut. Watching the car disappear, Josette sighed. She knew was going to miss Carla. Despite herself she'd enjoyed getting to know her better over the last few days and was already looking forward to her return once the notaire had the final papers ready for signature.

Back indoors, Josette cleared the lunch things away and tidied the kitchen before taking her secateurs out of the gardening drawer in the cupboard and going into the courtyard. Trimming back the rampant honeysuckle, she inhaled its perfume, taking care to avoid the bees busy feeding on the flowers.

Deadheading the geraniums in their pots and generally tidying up the jasmine and the passion flower she was encouraging to climb the trellis Gordon had fixed to the back wall for her recently, Josette hummed happily to herself. She loved pottering about out here, the nearest she got to a proper garden these days. Remembering how beautiful the garden at Villa Mimosa had been looking the other day, the old longing for a decent-sized garden sprang uninvited into her mind. Together with the thought, *If I lived in the villa I'd be able to garden whenever I wanted to.*

'Not. Going. To. Happen,' Josette said, startling herself by uttering the words out loud as she over-trimmed an unlucky plant. 'Merde.'

Whatever Carla said, the villa was going to be sold. Josette hadn't been lying when she'd said she needed the money, but it wasn't just that. It was the memories the place contained. Memories she'd be forced to confront on a daily basis if she lived there. Besides, it was too big for just one person. As for renting rooms out, she was too old for the hassle. Even if Carla was serious about visiting regularly, her own life for the next few months was likely to be difficult with the David situation.

Placing her hand on the small of her aching back and rubbing it, Josette looked around the courtyard. Enough for today. Back in the kitchen, she loaded her favourite Ella Fitzgerald disc into the player while she waited for the coffee machine to do its stuff. Sitting out in the courtyard sipping her coffee and listening to Ella singing 'The Man I Love', her thoughts drifted back to the days when listening to Ella had literally gone hand in hand with loving Mario. They'd both adored Ella's singing.

The photograph of them that Amelia had kept for some strange reason evoked so many happy memories. Josette half started up to fetch it from the bureau to look again on Mario's handsome face, before sinking back down onto her seat. Later. She didn't need to look at the photograph itself to relive the day and her unrestrained happiness of that summer. The summer she'd believed she was destined to marry Mario and spend the rest of her life with him.

She'd met Mario at a mutual friend's party a year or two before. The attraction had been instant on both sides and their new friendship had quickly developed into something special. The day the photo was taken Mario had asked her to be at Antibes station ready to catch the morning train travelling in the Marseille direction. He wanted them to spend a day together in Cannes.

Waiting on the platform clutching her ticket, she'd scanned the growing crowd, hoping to see him. When he still hadn't shown up when the train arrived, she hung back, letting people board and cursing the fact he hadn't turned up and she'd wasted money on a ticket. She turned her head at a sudden whistle from the third carriage and smiled. She should have realised he'd be on the train already.

'Josie, over here,' Mario had shouted from the open door of the carriage. She ran across the now empty platform and jumped in next to him. The doors had closed as Mario moved away from them. Josette realised later he'd illegally kept his foot against it to prevent its closure. Seconds later, the train had begun to move.

'I thought you weren't coming,' she'd said.

'I had to work at the pizzeria last night, Mama, she's not

well,' Mario had replied, his face clouding. The family lived just over the border in Italy at Ventimiglia and his parents had run a lively pizza bar for decades after taking over from Mario's grandparents. Mario's brother, Alexandro, had gone into the family business as soon as he left school.

'I'm sorry,' Josette had said. 'What's wrong?' She'd met Mario's mother several times and liked the Italian woman who welcomed everyone as part of her extended family. She loved it when Mario invited her to eat with his family. Mealtimes at Mario's home were so different to those at her own home, especially since Amelia had married and gone to live in England, leaving Josette alone with their parents.

'A bad cold. She'll be better tomorrow and back at work. But my father, at times like these, he take the opportunity to try to bully me into working full time at the pizzeria along with Alexandro. He knows I will do anything for Mama, but I will not work for him,' and his face had clouded over at the thought.

Seconds later, he'd shrugged before smiling at Josette. 'Enough. Today belongs to us and we enjoy! You can take some more of your photographs,' he'd said, looking at the camera Josette carried with her everywhere.

She'd always loved taking photos from the moment her grandfather had placed an old box camera in her hand when she was about twelve. By the time she met Mario she'd graduated to a five year old Canon and was saving hard to buy one of their new models.

Moving through the carriage, they'd found a couple of seats together and sat holding hands as the train rattled along the coast towards Cannes. Watching the waves of the Mediterranean lapping the various beaches they passed, some sandy, some full of pebbles, Josette couldn't imagine living anywhere else – although if moving to Italy to be with Mario was necessary, she wouldn't hesitate.

'Your sister, she arrive for a visit soon, yes? I'm looking forward to meeting another you.'

Josette had laughed. 'I'm looking forward to her coming too, but I'm still worried. Robert says she is still far from well. I think he's placing too much hope on their visit helping Amelia recover.'

When Amelia had married and moved to England, Josette had felt a shift in their unique twin relationship. No longer in daily contact, it was only natural their total oneness would diminish somewhat now that Amelia was married and had a new family. But even before Robert had told them of Amelia's recent illness, Josette had suffered some terrible nightmares that she knew were telepathically linked to Amelia and her fears. Robert had simply told the family that Amelia was suffering from depression and it would take time before she was completely well.

'I'm sure being back in France and seeing you will be good for her,' Mario had said. He stood up. 'Come on, Cannes station is next.'

Jumping off the train in Cannes, they'd run down through the narrow streets towards the front and the old quay where the fishing boats unloaded their catches. They'd stopped by the imposing Hotel de Ville building to watch a wedding party posing for photographs in front of the entrance.

'One day, my Josie, it will be our turn,' Mario had breathed in Josette's ear. 'But first I make my business work. Make some proper money. Come, we buy ice cream and look at the boats.'

The words 'our turn' had stayed in Josette's mind long after Mario had whispered them. She was still hugging them to herself as, hours later, they'd climbed up to Le Suquet tower and stood looking out over the town and its curved bay with the Îles de Lérins in the distance. She knew she was in love with Mario and surely with those words he'd confirmed he loved her too. Even if he'd not actually said so.

She'd taken a step back from the wall and Mario, lifted the camera to her eye and taken a snapshot of him gazing out to sea, the expression on his face unfathomable. As the shutter clicked, she'd asked, 'What are you thinking?'

'That one day I will have a boat or three taking the tourists out to the islands every day. Tourism is on the up down here. A few years and it will be the biggest employer in town. And it's going to be good for you and me, Josie. You wait and see.'

A passing tourist had offered to take a photo of the two of them and Josette had handed over her precious camera. She remembered the excitement she'd felt collecting the developed film from the pharmacy days later and seeing her and Mario standing so close.

A blackbird up high on the honeysuckle in the courtyard burst into song as Ella's voice faded away. Josette stayed where she was for several moments, lost in the past, before pulling herself together with a sharp mental shake. Daydreaming about what might have been was not something she'd ever indulged in. She'd always believed that life was what it was and one got on with whatever hand it dealt you. Even if it did turn out to be a lonelier and less satisfying life than you'd expected or wanted.

Josette sighed as she picked up her cup and went indoors. The house felt different, empty now that Carla had left. 'Get a grip, you knew she wasn't a permanent fixture,' Josette muttered.

A sudden urgent need rose in her to have the company of a real man tonight – not a ghost from the past. She'd phone Gordon and see if he was free for supper. If not, she'd go to one of the cafes in Place National, have a bottle of wine to banish the demons and forget how much she'd loved being Mario's 'Josie'. Nobody else since had ever called her that.

* * *

An hour after she'd said goodbye to Josette and checked her luggage in at Nice airport for her flight home, Carla still had time to kill. With at least another hour to wait before her flight, she bought an English magazine in the newsagents and then, rather than spend the time in the departure lounge, made her way upstairs to the restaurant with a view out over the runways, in search of coffee and a comfortable seat.

Sitting at a window table in the restaurant overlooking the Mediterranean and the runways, Carla left the magazine unopened, watching the planes landing and taking off – wondering who was going where was way more entertaining.

A smiling waitress placed coffee and the pain au chocolat she'd ordered on the table. 'Merci,' Carla said automatically.

Sipping her coffee and slowly allowing the chocolate and buttery pastry to melt in her mouth, Carla felt herself getting uptight as she thought about the reception she could expect from David when they met.

She hadn't told him, or Maddy, that she would be back today. She'd booked herself into a local hotel for a couple of nights to give her time to sort things with the solicitor and the estate agent and, crucially, find herself somewhere to live. She was determined not to go back to the house she and

David had lived in for over twenty years. She'd ring Maddy and tell her she was back but make her promise not to tell David until she was ready to face him.

'Bonjour. I'm happy to see you managed to survive your holiday in one piece,' a male voice interrupted her thoughts, making her jump. The man who'd saved her from certain injury that first day in Antibes.

'Bonjour. Yes, thanks to you,' she said. 'May I buy you a coffee?'

He shook his head. 'I've already ordered and paid, but I'll join you if I may? I'm Bruno, by the way,' he added as he pulled a chair out.

'Carla. Nice to meet you officially!'

'Your holiday was good, I hope?'

'Just the break I needed,' Carla said. 'Back to the real world now.' She glanced at him. 'Have you been on holiday down here too?'

Bruno shook his head. 'Non. I live in Cannes. Today I meet my uncle who comes for a short stay.'

'I didn't get to Cannes this week, but maybe next time when I visit my aunt.'

'Of course, I'd forgotten you said you have family down here.'

'My mother was born in Antibes, although she rarely returned after she married my father. She died a few months ago and this visit was to... to deal with family stuff.' Not a complete lie, but not the total truth either. Bringing the package down to Josette had been a convenient excuse for her to run away from her own family, but she wasn't about to tell Bruno, a stranger, that.

'My condolences for the loss of your mother. It is always a difficult time, the months after someone loved passes. Sorrow does not go well with the things that officialdom sometimes requires us to deal with.'

'That is so true,' Carla said, smiling at him. 'I've some more officialdom to deal with next week.'

'Bon chance. Ah,' he said, glancing out of the window. 'The Italian plane lands. My uncle will be in Arrivals soon.' Bruno stood up and held out his hand. 'Au revoir, Carla. Perhaps you visit Cannes one day and we'll meet again.'

'Perhaps,' Carla smiled. 'And thank you once again for saving my life.'

She watched Bruno stride away and disappear into the crowd before finishing her coffee and picking up her bag and magazine.

Time to make her way through security and on to the departure lounge before boarding the Bristol flight and flying back home to face her problems. Tomorrow she'd begin the process of pulling the pieces of her fractured life back together, even though she knew, with absolute certainty, a major piece was fractured beyond repair.

8

'So, how long will the sale of the house take to go through?' Carla asked.

The estate agent moved some papers on his desk. 'The couple whose offer you've accepted are selling their house, so...' he shrugged. 'Between eight and ten weeks is the usual. As you're not looking to buy something else, it all depends if the buyer is in a chain, really.'

'The thing is, I'm thinking of moving into the house until it sells,' Carla said, taking a deep breath. 'I'm divorcing my husband, so I need somewhere temporary to live. Eight to ten weeks should be long enough for me to sort something out. And I will have to buy somewhere too, eventually.'

'I'm sorry for your situation, but maybe I can help?' the estate agent offered. 'Tell me your price range and the area and I'll look for some suitable properties.'

'Thanks. I'm not sure yet which area I'm looking at,' Carla said. 'I've got to get my head around certain things. Make a few decisions.'

Five minutes later, leaving the estate agents and clutching

a handful of leaflets, she found a cafe, where she ordered a lunchtime sandwich and coffee. Sitting there staring unseeingly out of the window at the passing traffic and thinking about the morning's meetings, Carla felt strangely detached from reality. As if she was watching someone else altogether make decisions about her life without any regard for the consequences.

'Yes, I want you to issue my husband with divorce papers,' she'd told the solicitor without hesitation – citing unreasonable behaviour. At the estate agents, she'd agreed to the offer price for No. 29 without demurring. Two decisions, both of which would spawn innumerable changes and problems in her life, taken so easily.

Selling Amelia's house was an inevitable outcome after her mother's death, and one that she was mentally prepared for. But divorcing David? That was something she'd not thought about in years. Once, after his second affair, she'd made all sorts of secret plans for a life without David, only to pathetically accept that the devil she knew was the best option. Now, an impulsive reaction less than a fortnight ago had sent her careering towards an unknown future. A future it would be down to her alone to plan and make work.

During her time in France it hadn't seemed so daunting. Carla had drawn comfort from the fact that Josette had always lived on her own and seemingly enjoyed being single. At least now she'd have the freedom, for the first time in her life, to do what she wanted without asking anyone's permission. No parents or husband to question her actions. No children to be responsible for. But the question, what did she intend to do with the rest of her life, had to be faced and an answer found. Something that Maddy had no hesitation in pointing out later that day as she prepared them both supper in her flat.

'I know Dad's in the wrong, but running away was an overreaction, wasn't it? Might have been better if you'd stayed and made him confess to your face. Where the hell did you go anyway?'

'France. I went to see Tante Josette.'

'Granny's sister? Why?'

'Seemed like a good idea at the time. And it was. I needed to get away and think about what to do.'

Maddy looked at her expectantly. 'Reach any decisions?'

'A couple, but right now I think I'm just going to, "wing it". I think that's the best expression,' Carla said.

Maddy pulled the cork out of a bottle of Merlot before looking at Carla. 'Wing it?'

'Yes, you know – see where these decisions lead me.'

'So, these couple of decisions are?'

'Today I accepted an offer on Granny's house. And,' Carla took a deep breath and looked Maddy directly in the eye, 'I've filed for divorce from your father.' She picked up the glass of wine Maddy had pushed towards her. 'Those two decisions should be enough to kick start things, don't you think? Cheers.'

'Oh, Mum, have you really thought things through, though?' Maddy said. 'Selling Granny's house is one thing, although if you and Dad do divorce, you could keep it and live there?'

Carla, catching the emphasis Maddy placed on 'if', shook her head. 'There is no "if" about the divorce. It's going ahead. As for No. 29, I am thinking about going to live there for a few weeks until completion, but after that I want a fresh start somewhere.'

'Have you told Dad you're back? Has he been in touch?'

Something in the tone of Maddy's voice made Carla glance at her.

'Yes. He's asked me to meet him for lunch tomorrow,' Carla said. 'Can't say I'm looking forward to it. He said there are things we need to talk through.'

'I think he wants you to forgive him,' Maddy said quietly. 'He probably also wants to tell you he and this Lisa have broken up.'

Carla stared at her. 'Oh. I wasn't expecting that. When did that happen?'

'Three days ago.' Maddy turned away to take their lasagne supper out of the oven and place it on the table. 'Lisa told him she'd made a mistake and dumped him.' Maddy topped up their wine glasses before sitting down and joining her silent mother. 'Will it make a difference? Will you forgive him?'

'Not a difference in the way your father maybe hopes it will,' Carla said. 'And no, I can't and won't forgive him this time. Whatever he says, or promises, it's too late. Years too late.'

'Are you not scared about divorcing Dad?' Maddy said. 'I can't bear the thought of you being alone.'

Carla reached across the table and touched her daughter's arm. 'Hey, I'm fifty this year, not ninety. I'm actually looking forward to having a new life. Doing things I want to. Pleasing myself for once.' She took a helping of lasagne before saying, 'Right, can we please change the subject. Tell me about the business. Any interesting new clients?'

Changing the subject worked. Maddy had soon launched into an enthusiastic conversation about her business and nothing more was said about her parents' marriage problems.

It was gone nine o'clock when Carla reluctantly picked up her tote and said she had to get back to the hotel.

'Hey, nice bag, Mum. I could do with one like that,' Maddy said, stroking the leather.

'Hands off, it's mine,' Carla said. 'Using it gives me confidence. Reminds me while I mightn't want to paint the town red, I'm going to enjoy my new life on my terms.'

'I just want you to be happy, Mum,' Maddy said, hugging her.

'Thanks, darling – it's what I wish for us both.'

Walking back to her hotel, Carla thought about how she'd assured Maddy she was looking forward to enjoying her new life, and she truly was. But there was no point in kidding herself the next few weeks – months – were going to be easy, because they weren't. Tomorrow's meeting with David was going to be more difficult than she'd anticipated if he did indeed want her to forgive him.

Knowing the way David thought, the fact that this Lisa had dumped him would mean he'd assume that Carla would feel sorry for him, and a forgiving reconciliation would be possible. He wasn't a man who could live alone. This time though she would not give in and forgive him. No way.

9

Carla stood in the kitchen of No. 29 the next day trying to view the house objectively and not let her emotions override her head. She needed somewhere to live until the current mess her life was in was sorted out. The house had been left to her and was the sensible, money-saving answer. She'd remember the happy times here, times that mostly involved her dad, and push other unhappy memories to the back of her mind. Doing that, surely she could bear to live here for a few weeks?

But what about furniture? If she'd known she was going to leave David all those weeks ago when she'd stripped the place ready for sale, she'd have left the basics – bed, table, settee, cooker – in place. A ready-made bolthole.

She only needed a room really. If she lived downstairs, she could make do with a bed settee, some sort of table with a chair and a small combi oven... A kettle, crockery, cutlery, bed linen, suddenly the 'need to have' list in her head was growing longer by the second. So annoying when she knew that everything she needed was in duplicate, triplicate even, in her old home. Could that be her answer? If she moved in here, she'd ask David if she could take whatever she needed. Even as the thought occurred to her, she banished it. When they divorced, half of the old marital home would be hers by right, so she would tell, not ask, David that she was only taking what was rightfully hers. And then, when she moved into her new home, she'd at least have a head start in furnishing it and having familiar things around her.

Moving into the sitting room, Carla saw with a jolt that the mantelpiece was empty. The urn with Amelia's ashes had gone. She'd not decided where to scatter Amelia before running away to France and had deemed leaving them where they were was the best thing. So who had taken them? What had they done with them? Not scattering them was one thing, but losing the ashes would be another something else entirely. Maybe the estate agent had hidden them? Tactfully banishing them from the view of potential buyers. But where?

The obvious place was one of the old-fashioned cupboards built into the alcoves on either side of the fire-place. Cupboards which her mother had always refused to have removed, saying they were too useful to take out. Holding her breath, Carla opened the door on the right-hand side. Empty.

She moved across to the left-hand side of the fireplace and peered into the cupboard. And breathed. The urn was there, pushed to one side, out of sight. Lifting it out, Carla put it back on the mantelpiece as a reminder to dispose of them urgently.

Right now, though, she needed to get across town to meet David for the 'we need to talk' lunch he'd insisted they had. She'd wanted to meet somewhere neutral for both of them but in the end David had over-ruled her, saying the pub restaurant near his office was the most convenient for him, and as she was a free agent, it made sense for her to go there.

Carla deliberately arrived early and chose a table in a quiet corner where she could sit and wait out of sight of prying eyes. She ordered a bottle of sparkling water, asked for the menu and ordered a ploughman's lunch.

Of course David was late. Carla had finished her lunch and pushed the plate to one side before he arrived in a flurry of laughter and bonhomie with a couple of people from the office – Helen his P.A. and his senior manager, Simon. Carla saw him make a quick assessment of tables around the restaurant before he spotted her. She gave him a small nod of acknowledgement and waited as the three of them made their way over to her. Surely he wasn't going to invite Helen and Simon to join them?

'I'd ask you to join us,' she heard David say apologetically, 'but we've got some catching up to do now Carla's back from holiday.'

Ah, that's the way he was playing things, was it? He wanted people to think they were still a united couple.

After the usual 'nice to see you again' and 'enjoy your lunch', Helen and Simon moved on to their own table. Carla knew she didn't imagine the sympathy she saw in Helen's smile as she said 'Bye'.

'Sorry I'm late. You know what it's like.' David pulled out a chair and sat down, noticing her empty plate as he did. 'You've eaten already?'

Carla shrugged. 'I can't stay long. You were late and I was hungry.'

'So where did you disappear to in a huff?'

'I took your advice and went to Antibes,' Carla said,

deciding to ignore his use of the word huff. It was anything but a huff. Besides, even if it had been, as far as she was concerned he was the last one to condemn her actions.

'You could have told me where you were. Did Josette welcome you with open arms?'

'It was good getting to know Josette a bit better after all the years she and Mum were estranged,' Carla answered calmly, pouring herself a glass of water as the waiter appeared to take David's order. She waited until he'd left before saying, 'So what do you want to talk about?'

'Us, of course,' David said. 'Why the hell haven't you come home? Where are you staying?'

Carla shook her head. 'David, you know full well why I haven't come back home. Her name is Lisa.' She paused before adding, 'I've got a hotel room for the moment.'

'You can't live in a hotel indefinitely,' David said. 'You need to come home.'

'I don't want to live in the same house as you right now,' Carla said. 'Certainly not while you're seeing another woman.'

She waited to see if David would tell her what she already knew about Lisa dumping him. He didn't.

'I've instructed a solicitor and you should receive the divorce papers this week from him,' she continued.

'I don't want us to divorce. I apologise for the hurt I've caused you by this affair, which, by the way, I've ended, and I promise I will try my damnedest to make it up to you.'

'I'd heard she dumped you.' Carla stared at him. 'David, I've had enough of your broken promises and lies. Lisa is the latest in a long line of women you've had affairs with down the years. I've had enough of being taken for granted, of being the little woman behind her man. I want a life of my own, and with the children independent and Mum gone,' she shrugged, 'well, I want a shot at being truly happy. I refuse to let you hold me back any more. I want to go places.'

David reached his hand out and grasped hers before she could move it out of the way. 'Once No. 29 is sold we could do that together. I've always wanted to go to the Maldives. It could be a second honeymoon.'

Trust David to put his wants first. 'I was actually thinking of an eco-camp in the Amazon forest, not a luxury resort anywhere.' Not true. Going travelling had been a vague idea, with no definite destination in her mind. One thing she did realise, though, she didn't want to go anywhere with David. She jerked her hand out of his.

'Okay, we could do that too.'

Carla shook her head at him. The message that she'd had enough was clearly not getting through. As she opened her mouth to tell him how she felt again, David was already speaking.

'Look, I've got a week's conference to go to up in Cumbria – I leave this weekend. Why don't you at least move back in while I'm away. When I get back you might have changed your mind and decided to stay.'

About to tell him no, Carla stopped and looked at him thoughtfully. 'I do need to sort out my stuff and pack it up ready for...' she shrugged, 'ready for when I decide where I'm going. It would be easier if I did it while you're away.' Carla looked at him. 'I won't change my mind though about staying on afterwards.'

David sighed. 'I can't say the thought that I've made it easier for you to pack up your things while I'm away fills me with joy but...' he shrugged. 'just live in the house and we'll see what happens when I get back.'

'When you get back I'll still be divorcing you, David. What part of that sentence do you not understand?' Carla stood up and slipped her red tote over her shoulder. 'I'll leave you to settle my lunch bill. Have a good conference.' She turned on her heel and walked away, leaving David staring after her.

10

When Gordon phoned and suggested they made their long overdue visit to have lunch on St Honorat now that Carla had left, Josette readily agreed.

Gordon was waiting for her, tickets in hand, by the landing stage when she arrived, a queue of passengers already boarding the boat. The two of them found a couple of seats out on deck. Minutes later, the boat was making its way across the Mediterranean on its fifteen minute voyage to the Îles de Lérins.

Josette took a couple of deep breaths, filling her lungs with the tangy salt air and feeling the breeze on her face. 'I do like being out on the water,' she said.

'Did you sail when you were young?' Gordon asked.

Josette shook her head. 'No. Friends of my parents had a small day cruiser and often took us out fishing or brought us here for a picnic.' Josette gestured towards the islands. 'So many boats these days,' she said, looking at the multitude of yachts anchored in the broad reach between the two islands as the passenger ferry slowed to approach St Honorat's landing quay.

Ten minutes later, they'd disembarked. 'I've booked a table for lunch at the restaurant, shall we go straight there?' Gordon said.

'Would you mind going ahead on your own?' Josette asked. 'I'd really like to have a few moments in the Abbey first.' She knew Gordon wouldn't want to visit the Abbey. He'd told her soon after they'd met he didn't have time for any religion and had no real interest in even looking at the buildings that encompassed their ideology.

'Of course,' Gordon said. 'Take your time.'

'I won't be long.' Josette smiled at him gratefully before making her way alone along the rustic path towards the entrance to the Abbey.

The monks were just leaving after morning mass and she stood to one side as they passed, their long white robes swishing across the ground. Once inside the ancient Abbey, Josette slipped into a pew at the back and closed her eyes. Sitting there, inhaling the special atmosphere that had surely been created by centuries of silent worship trapped forever amongst its high rafters, she felt her spirits lift. Not a religious person by nature, sometimes she just needed the utter calm that only an ancient church like this one seemed able to give out.

Having Carla visit had unsettled Josette more than she'd expected. Could returning to live in Antibes on something of a whim and an overwhelming yearning for her roots a year ago have been a mistake after all the years she'd spent travelling around? Was it time to move on again? Her love of photography, once all-consuming, had dwindled away. She hadn't picked up her camera since she'd returned to Antibes. Was it because she was getting old and everything was so much more of an effort that it was easier to do nothing? Or was it something else? Regret of the choices she'd made throughout her life?

She'd never been one for living by routine, preferring a more free and unfettered lifestyle. Her previous nomadic life, flitting from one place to another as a freelance photographer, had had its drawbacks, but on the whole it had suited her. However unsettled she felt now, she didn't want to get sucked into a life of routine at her age. Or start reminiscing about the past, every day. It was the future that mattered. However short that might prove to be. After all she'd had her three score years and ten.

Several moments passed before she came to with a start when a shooting pain in her right leg made her jump and she realised she'd been sitting awkwardly. Carefully flexing her leg, she stood up and hobbled to the exit, hoping the pins and needles would go away once she was moving.

By the time she'd walked down through the flower filled cloisters and out of the Abbey grounds, the pain had dispersed and she felt better. Spending quiet time in the Abbey had worked its magic and she felt soothed and comforted.

Gordon got to his feet as he saw her approach and she threaded her way through the crowded tables to reach him.

'Sorry, I lost track of time,' Josette said, accepting the aperitif he handed her.

'No problem, we've got all the afternoon. Have a look at the menu and then we can order.'

'Thanks. I don't need the menu. I saw the special of the day board as I came in. I'll have the set meal please.'

While Gordon placed their order with the waitress,

Josette sipped her drink, thinking about their friendship. It had been one of those fortuitous encounters when complete strangers know they've met a kindred spirit.

Back in early January, after a disturbed night listening to a ferocious blizzard battering the coast, Josette had got up early and discovered the Riviera slumbering under a heavy and unexpected snowy duvet. Within minutes, she was dressed and stepping out into an eerily silent town, making her way through the empty streets to the nearest park, just one thing on her mind. Once in the park, she began to make a snowball, rolling it through the pristine snow and patting it together. When it was too big to move, she began to make a smaller one.

She barely registered the first snowball that hit her in the back, she was concentrating so hard, but the next one, arriving seconds later, got her full attention. Oooh – somebody wanted a snowball fight, did they? Carefully, she placed the smaller snowball on top of the first one before swiftly bending down, gathering a handful of snow and turning, throwing it expertly at the child who'd thrown the snowball. Except it wasn't a child. It was a man. A man who smiled and threw another snowball at her, calling out, 'Game on,' as he did.

For five minutes, they had laughed as they flung snowball after snowball at each other before a breathless Josette had said, 'This is fun, but I need to finish my snowman.'

The man had closed the gap between them. 'May I help you?'

Josette had nodded and together they had set about creating the biggest snowman they could.

'I'm Gordon,' he'd said, scooping up another large handful of snow.

'Josette. Nice to meet you.'

'You too. Think Jack's head is big enough now,' Gordon said. 'What?' he'd asked as Josette had stared at him crossly.

'You're calling my snowman, Jack. Why?'

'After Jack Frost of course. I'm going to find him some eyes.' Gordon had wandered off and started to kick around in the snow at the edge of the park. A minute later, he'd returned with two smallish stones and placed them carefully on the snowman's face. 'Bit tiny, but they'll do. Really need something for his nose,' he'd said, looking around for inspiration.

'I came prepared for that,' Josette had answered, pulling a carrot out of her coat pocket and positioning it below the stone eyes.

'Looks good, although I think he could do with this,' and Gordon had unwound his tartan scarf and tied it around the snowman's neck. 'Now he's a proper snowman. Fancy a hot chocolate?' he'd asked, looking across the park. 'Looks like the cafe is opening up.'

'Sounds good.'

Standing near the café's outdoor gas heaters, drinking the hot chocolate, Josette had glanced at Gordon. 'Thank you for this and the snowball fight. I haven't had so much fun in years.'

'Doesn't do to be serious all the time,' Gordon had said. 'Life is always better with friends and fun in it.'

'Are we going to be friends?'

'I think we're going to be really special friends,' he'd said.

'Special friends?' Josette had looked at him. 'What does that mean?'

'Special friends have lots of fun together. Having fun is king in my book.'

'D'you have a wife who might object to us having fun together?'

Gordon shook his head. 'No. D'you have a husband at home?'

'No.'

'There you go then. Nothing to stop us having fun together.'

Josette had laughed and since that day in the snow their friendship had flourished and they did indeed have fun together. Discovering that they'd both lived unconventional lives formed a surprising but happy bond between them. Josette had been on the fringe of a celebrity crowd, while Gordon's life of writing songs for famous singers had meant he'd actually met and mixed with lots of them – something which he said he'd hated, preferring a quieter life really, out of the limelight.

Josette came back to the present with a jolt, realising Gordon was asking her a question.

'Want to talk about whatever it is that's bothering you?'

Josette looked at him. His pragmatic Scottish attitude towards solving problems always made Josette smile. There were no grey areas as far as Gordon was concerned. Things were either black or white, nothing in between. She was far too analytical to ever see anything in such a cut-and-dried manner. Maybe it would help sort things out in her head to talk them through with Gordon, without going into too much detail. He knew something of her past life but not everything.

'Having Carla here has reminded me of stuff that has been buried a long time,' Josette began. 'Things I feel that are best left buried but will, I'm afraid, force their way out in the foreseeable future. The catalyst is likely to be the fact that Carla has inherited her mother's half of Villa Mimosa.'

'Will she agree to selling the place like you've wanted to do for so long?'

'She's already mentioned keeping it and promising to make regular visits to help with the renting et cetera.' Josette placed her empty glass on the table.

'At least you'd have support and practical help. Wouldn't that be a good thing? You said your sister was always difficult and uncooperative as far as the villa was concerned.'

Josette shrugged. 'The trouble is I've lived for so long without any proper family contact, I'm... I'm not sure how I'd cope with being Tante Josette on a regular face-to-face basis. Part of me thinks family contact would be good as I get older, but a larger part is telling me keeping the status quo would be better.'

She didn't add she was also beginning to get the feeling that she was no longer in total control of her own destiny. Carla's appearance in her life was like a ticking time bomb waiting to go off.

11

Carla waited until lunchtime the day David had said he was leaving for Cumbria before going home. She heaved a sigh of relief that there was no sign of his car when she turned onto the drive and parked.

Taking her case upstairs, she ignored the open door of the master bedroom with its queen-sized bed she'd shared with David, opening the door of the guest bedroom instead. She'd sleep in here for the week.

Leaving her unpacking until later, Carla went down to the kitchen and switched on the coffee machine. Waiting for it to heat up, she opened the fridge door. No need to go food shopping. The shelves were full; there was more than she could possibly eat in a week. Was David trying to lure her back? Well, if he thought a few packets of her favourite foods, not to mention the bottles of wine in the rack, would make her change her mind, he could think again.

She pressed the button on the radio and Classic FM filled the kitchen with a Chopin piano piece she recognised but couldn't name. Pouring a mug of coffee, she went through to the sitting room. David had clearly made an effort to keep it tidy. A note was propped against a large vase of red roses in the sitting room: *Welcome home. See you in a week. Love David. xxx.* Carla screwed up the note before she went back into the kitchen to throw it in the bin.

Somewhere deep in her tote, her mobile rang. Carefully, she lifted out the urn, placing it on the kitchen table, before scrabbling around for the phone. Maddy.

'How are you, Mum?'

'I'm fine. Just having a coffee before I make a start on sorting my things out. Dad's left me a fridge full of food – fancy Sunday lunch here?'

'Can we make it an early supper? Say about six-ish? And can I bring a friend?'

'Sure'

'I've got to go, Mum. See you Sunday.' And the phone cut off, giving Carla no chance to ask the question 'which friend?'

She put the phone back in her bag before taking the urn and placing it on the kitchen windowsill. She hadn't liked to leave it in No. 29 on her last visit there in case she forgot about it again. Maybe Maddy would have an idea as to where the ashes could be scattered. She'd mention it on Sunday, depending, of course, on who Maddy brought with her.

Right, time to get on. She only had a week to sort her possessions. Resolute, she made her way back upstairs. She'd start with emptying her wardrobe, chest of drawers and cupboards.

Two hours later, in the small spare bedroom, there were three piles: keep, give to the charity shop and throw away. Tomorrow she'd find a couple of suitcases to pack the stuff she was keeping and the rest could go in black bags.

What she needed now was a long soak in a hot bath.

Walking into the en suite of the master bedroom, she turned on the taps before pouring some of her favourite bubble bath into the water and lighting a couple of the candles she always kept on the edge of the bath. Just time to go downstairs while the bath filled, pour a glass of white wine and grab the magazine she'd bought at the airport but hadn't yet finished reading.

Undressing and slipping into the hot water felt so good. Carefully placing her glass of wine on the side tiled shelf of the bath after taking a large sip, Carla lay back and opened the magazine. An article with the headline title 'The Law of Attraction. Dream it. Visualise it. Live it' caught her eye. Not that she had any faith in what most motivation gurus urged one to do to improve one's life, but sometimes there could be a germ of a good idea hidden amongst the hype.

This particular feature was all about writing things down and visualising exactly what you wanted, which would apparently help it materialise in real life. Making a vision board and imagining how your life could be in five years with the things you dreamed about accomplished was the key to success. If only it was that easy.

Carla dropped the magazine onto the floor. She reached for her glass before topping up the cooling water with some more hot and sliding back under the bubbles. Trying to work out where she'd be in five years' time was a joke. Five weeks ago, she hadn't had any idea her life was about to implode the way it had, so how the hell could she plan five years in advance?

As for visualising the house and lifestyle she wanted, she already had it. This house that she was planning to leave had been the only house she'd wanted for the last twenty-odd years. Right this minute she couldn't imagine not living here.

The moment she'd unlocked the front door and walked in, she'd felt safe and happy to be back. Walking away from it with no real plan for the rest of her life was going to be so hard. Maybe she should move back in, insist that David left – he was the one at fault after all.

Getting out of the bath and towelling herself dry, she muttered, 'Get a grip.' Lots of women her age had to make unexpected new starts. Besides, she did have a plan, albeit a sketchy short-term one. Once Amelia's house had sold and the divorce was underway, she'd be able to make proper long-term plans. It was a question of one step at a time. But where the hell was she going to live in the meantime?

Sorting out her clothes, she'd realised even living in one room at No. 29 she'd need more than just the basic stuff she'd put on her list. The more she thought about it, the clearer it became how fraught arranging a temporary move there would be. Maybe renting a small furnished flat would be better. She'd buy a local paper in the week and see what was available.

Grabbing her towelling dressing gown from the hook on the door, she went downstairs. The house phone rang while she was preparing a brie and avocado sandwich for her supper. Guessing who the caller would be, she let it ring until the answerphone clicked in and, as expected, she heard David's voice.

'Carla, darling, if you're there please pick up. I just wanted you to know that I've arrived in Penrith.' A short pause before he continued. 'Maybe I'll catch you later. Love you,' and the call ended.

The routine calls telling her of his safe arrival whenever he'd been away travelling had ceased about a year ago. David had shrugged when she'd mentioned it. 'No news is good news. You'd hear soon enough if there'd been an accident.' Now, when she didn't have the slightest interest in his where-abouts, he'd decided to tell her. Swatting the guilty 'I should have picked up' thought away, Carla sat at the kitchen table to eat. Knowing David of old it would be part of a ploy to smother her with kindness, wear her down and come round to his way of thinking. Idly Carla wondered how long it would take for him to realise that there was no way that was going to happen ever again.

It was an hour later when he rang again. This time on her mobile. Deciding it would be childish to ignore him she picked up the phone. 'Hello David.'

'Carla, darling. Everything all right? Settled back in okay?'

'Thank you, yes. I've made a good start on sorting out my things. Planning a charity shop run first thing Monday morning.'

Silence at the other end.

'David, are you still there?'

'Yes, I'm still here, wishing you didn't feel the need to move out.'

'Well, you're the guilty party in this so why don't you move out and I'll stay until the house is sold.' Carla heard David's sharp intake of breath.

'I'm not moving anywhere. I think we can work through this. Did you like the roses?'

'The roses are beautiful, thank you,' Carla said. 'But I wish you'd accept the fact that I need to move on with my life.' When David didn't respond, Carla added, 'Filling the fridge with so much food was very generous of you. Maddy's coming for supper tomorrow to help eat some of it.' No need to mention she was bringing a friend. David would only demand details and she didn't have any to give him.

'That's good,' David said. 'Wish I could join you both. Long time since we had a family supper in the kitchen.'

'You've been busy in the evenings for a long time, David,' Carla said, trying to keep her voice neutral but determined to make him realise whose fault that was.

'I'm sorry about that,' David said before lapsing into silence again.

'Was there anything else? I'm planning an early night.'

'I'll say goodnight then. Talk to you in the week. Sleep well.'

* * *

Sunday morning and Carla was up early to fetch a couple of suitcases from the rack in the garage ready to start filling with her things. It was mid-afternoon before everything was tidied away, the car full of bags ready for delivery to the charity shop and rubbish in the boot to throw away and she could begin to prepare supper. Roast chicken with all the trimmings. Followed by upside-down apple cake with cream for dessert. She hummed happily to herself as she worked. The house was full of delicious cooking smells when she jumped in the shower to freshen up before Maddy and her friend arrived.

Sam was a surprise. Maddy's recent boyfriends had all tended to be sophisticated men about town with high-powered jobs in banking or IT. Sam, at six feet, with a physique that could only be described as burly, ginger stubble and a smile that went all the way up to his eyes, was the complete antithesis to them. Carla liked him immediately. She couldn't help but wonder what David would make of him though. The fact that Maddy seemed nervous as she introduced Sam made Carla wonder if she was serious about him.

Chatting over aperitifs in the sitting room, she learnt that Sam, a qualified architect, had recently started his own ecological building business.

'I like getting hands on,' he explained. 'Being in an office for too long frustrates me. Now I design, get my hands dirty with the building and help the environment. Win-win,' and he smiled disarmingly at Carla.

'I'm looking at a couple of houses this week,' Carla said. 'But I doubt that any of them will tick many boxes on the ecological front, none of them are new-build.'

Sam looked as if he was about to say something, but Maddy got in first.

'I can't imagine you and Dad not being together in this house any more. I'm so cross with him. I still can't get my head around the two of you divorcing.'

'To be honest, neither can I, but it will happen,' Carla said. 'I'll go and check on things in the kitchen. I'm sure Sam would appreciate a change in the conversation, so take a look at the house brochures on the coffee table. Sam, you can tell me if any of them would be considered environmentally friendly. I've got an appointment to view the top one next week.'

The phone rang at eight o'clock, just as Sam was spearing the last roast potato.

Carla sighed. 'That'll be David. I'm not answering it. If you want to, Maddy, you can.'

'Hi, Dad.'

Carla took a sip of her wine as she tried not to listen to

the one-sided conversation. Sam leant across the table and whispered, 'I survived my parents' divorce three years ago and Maddy will do the same. Don't worry.'

Carla smiled at him gratefully.

'Mum's fine considering what you're putting her through,' Maddy said, an edge to her voice. There was silence for about a minute as Maddy listened to David, before taking a deep sigh. 'Whatever, Dad, but you're going to have your work cut out to persuade her, she's looking at houses next week. No, she doesn't want to talk to you, that's why I answered the phone. Bye,' and Maddy ended the call.

Carla got up from the table. 'I'll fetch dessert and then I need to pick your brains about Granny's ashes. I have no idea where to scatter them. I'm hoping you'll come up with a place and come with me when I do the deed.'

12

Over the next week, Carla slipped into a routine that, apart from the fact that she had a couple of house viewings with the estate agent, was depressingly similar to the one she'd followed before going to France. But she did manage to fit in a couple of hours to help Mavis out in the charity shop one afternoon, something she enjoyed.

The estate agent had reacted with a relieved sigh when she'd told him her plans for using No. 29 as a temporary bolt-hole looked unlikely to happen. He'd been worried about things delaying completion.

The solicitor, too, had reacted with caution when she'd mentioned her plans. 'Moving out of the marital home before a settlement is reached is never a good idea.'

Scouring the local paper and letting agencies proved futile, unless she fancied renting a top-floor flat in the prestigious block overlooking the park, which, to be honest, she did quite fancy, until she saw the price per month, £1800. The obvious solution was to find a house she liked enough to buy and push for a same-day completion date as No. 29. But so far none of the houses she'd seen had appealed. Despite having told David she had no intention of staying in the house with him, she was realising that, sensibly, she had no real alternative. But if she stayed, she was determined it would be on her terms. She'd spell it out so that David would be left in no doubt the divorce was going ahead. Having insisted she wouldn't be staying when he returned, he was sure to take her continued presence as a hopeful sign of her forgiveness.

Driving home after yet another disappointing house viewing, she thought about the next day when David was due back. Even with a six hour drive ahead of him, he was unlikely to set off before ten o'clock, so hopefully it would be late afternoon before he arrived home and she had to face him.

Swinging quickly onto the drive, she almost drove straight into the back of the car parked in front of the garage doors before slamming the brakes on and stopping a mere millimetre away from its bumper. David was home.

She was sitting there shaken and trying to resist the urge to reverse and drive off when David appeared and opened the driver's door. Carla turned off the engine, pulled on the hand-brake and got out of the car.

'Thought I'd surprise you and come home early,' David said.

'You certainly did that and you very nearly had a surprise dent in your car,' Carla said. 'How long have you been back?'

'About a minute. I thought you'd be here and we could spend some time together. Haven't even got my things out of the car yet.' David opened the rear door of his car and took out his case. 'Where have you been?'

'Viewing a house.'

'Any good?' David asked, clearly trying and failing to sound interested.

Carla shook her head. 'House could be fine, but I got the feeling the neighbours could be a problem. Lots of dogs.' She locked her car and followed David into the house. 'I'm going to make a cup of tea. Want one?'

'Thanks. I'll just pop my stuff upstairs.'

When he came down, he looked at Carla. 'You didn't sleep in our room.'

Carla, pouring the boiling water into the teapot, didn't answer. She wasn't yet ready for where that conversation would lead. Instead, she said, 'How come you left the conference early?'

David shrugged. 'I'd done my bit and the last day of these things is always a bit of an anti-climax. I'd rather be at home. With you,' he added. 'I thought I could take you out for dinner this evening.'

Carla took a deep breath. There was still lots of the food that David had filled the fridge with left. Going out to dinner with him was not on her agenda. 'I'd rather eat in. I need to talk to you and it would be easier to talk here.' It would be churlish not to make a meal for the two of them. She moved across and opened the fridge. 'How about I make us steak and sauté potatoes with a salad?'

'Food sounds great, not sure about the talk though,' David said. 'I was hoping you...' his voice trailed away as Carla looked at him. 'Okay. I'll open a bottle of red to breathe. Then I'm going to jump in the shower.'

Before starting to make supper, Carla opened her iPad and started to make a note of the things she needed to remember to say to David. It was important that he understood exactly where she was coming from. When she was sure she'd remembered everything, she clicked save and switched it off.

By the time David came back downstairs, the salad was made, the potatoes were cooking ready to be sautéed in the steak juices, fried mushrooms and onions were keeping warm in the oven set on low and the steaks were seasoned and ready to hit the hot pan.

David poured two glasses of red wine and handed one to Carla. 'Cheers. It's good to be home.'

Carla clinked his glass with hers silently and returned her attention to the stove.

Ten minutes later, when they were both sitting at the kitchen table with their meal in front of them, Carla spoke. 'David, I'm sorry, but I'm not moving out as I said I would.'

'I'm not sorry. I'm glad you're staying. We'll work things out, you'll see,' David said, reaching across the table to hold her hand and sighing as she moved it out of his grasp.

'No, David, I'm not staying to "work things out" with you. I'm staying for two reasons. The first is my solicitor has advised me to stay until we've reached a financial settlement. The second reason is moving into No. 29 isn't practical and I don't have anywhere else to go yet.' She took a deep breath. 'Lots of people are having to stay living in the same house for financial reasons these days when their marriage fails, so we're not alone. At least we're lucky in that we know it won't be for ever – probably no longer than three months, six, maximum. Once Mum's house has sold, I'll be out of your way.'

'That's lucky, is it?'

Carla ignored his remark. 'But we do need to talk about a few ground rules for living separate lives in the same house. I've taken over the guest room, as you know, and I'll use the family bathroom. I'll do the cleaning necessary for both. Master bedroom and en suite is down to you.' She held her hand up as David went to speak. 'Let me finish. I won't be doing any washing, cooking or shopping for you, so you'll need to organise yourself there. I'll clear a shelf in the fridge for my food. Lastly, I will endeavour to stay out of your way as much as possible. Anything you want to add to the list?'

David sighed. 'You seem hell-bent on ending our marriage without giving me a chance to prove how sorry I am. Other couples survive infidelity.'

'Foolishly I've ignored your infidelity for years. If this was the first time you'd cheated on me and you were promising it would never happen again, I might have considered staying,' Carla said. 'But we both know it's not the first time and we know that six months, a year, down the line the chances are you'll meet someone else you fancy and it will all start again. Sorry, but I don't want to hang around waiting for that to happen – I deserve better.'

In the silence that followed, Carla continued to eat her meal, although her appetite had diminished somewhat and she had difficulty swallowing. David seemed to prefer drinking the red wine to eating and pushed his food around his plate. When Carla stood up to put her things in the dishwasher, David pushed his plate away and stood up.

'I'm going to watch the sports channel,' he said and he poured the last of the wine into his glass.

'This came for you while you were away,' Carla said, taking the large white envelope with the name of her solicitors postmarked across the top from the dresser and handing it to David. From the look on his face, David realised what it was and he took it from her without a word and left the kitchen.

Carla sank back down onto her chair, exhausted. That had been harder than she'd expected and, as unresponsive as David had been, she knew there was every chance he'd make life as difficult as he could for her rather than let her walk away.

Her mobile rang. Wearily, she picked it up and glanced at the caller ID. And was instantly alert.

'Tante Josette. Ça va?'

'Oui merci. The notaire has the papers ready for signature. Can you come soon? The tenants moved out of the villa yesterday, so you will be able to see inside when you come.'

'I'll book a flight for early next week. May I stay with you again or shall I book a room somewhere?'

'Of course you can stay here,' Josette said. 'We have a lot to discuss. Let me know the flight details and I'll book a rendezvous with the notaire. A bientôt.'

Carla smiled as she put the phone down on the table. A short reprieve from living in the house with David. Her smiled faded as she realised she had yet to tell him about inheriting a half share in Villa Mimosa.

13

Carla dragged her suitcase down the ancient street towards Josette's cottage past the same collie dog asleep in a doorway. Overhead, the sun shone from a cloudless blue sky and Carla could feel the perspiration trickling down her back.

Josette answered her knock on the door immediately with an 'Entre, it's open' and enveloped her in a hug as soon as she was inside.

'Gordon and I have just finished lunch. You remember my friend, Gordon? Can I get you something to eat?' Josette asked.

'I had a sandwich on the plane, but a glass of ice-cold rosé would be welcome,' Carla said. 'But, first, can I change into something cooler? I can't believe how hot it is here.'

Five minutes later, she'd slipped into her favourite sundress and was sitting under the shade of the parasol in the courtyard sipping a glass of wine.

'Oh, it's good to be back.'

Gordon stood up. 'Sorry, ladies, I have to leave. Got a date with a horse in Cagnes-sur-mer. Wish me luck. I'll see both of you tomorrow evening. I'll let myself out,' he said to Josette as he took his empty wine glass into the kitchen.

'We've both been invited to a May Day party on board a boat moored in the marina. A friend of Gordon's,' Josette said when Carla looked at her questioningly. 'Should be fun. How's things at home?'

Carla pulled a face. 'Not good. Glad to get away. David is not happy with the current arrangement of us living separate lives in the same house.'

'Can't be easy for you either,' Josette said. 'Fancy a walk round to Villa Mimosa this afternoon?'

'Please – I can't wait to see inside. Wonder if I'll recognise it after all these years. When's our rendezvous with the notaire?'

'Ah, I hope you're not planning on rushing back home? He couldn't fit us in until Wednesday afternoon of next week in the end.' Josette didn't add that she'd refused the offer of a meeting first thing in the morning, suspecting that Carla would feel she ought to go home soon afterwards, which Josette thought would be a waste of the air fare.

'No, not rushing anywhere. Right now I don't care if the meeting had been postponed until next month,' Carla said. 'I'm just happy to be here. Away from the atmosphere at home. And having to make important decisions when I'm not sure about anything.'

'That bad, hmm?'

'David doesn't believe we should be divorcing. He seems to think if he pays me more attention and is extra nice to me I'll forgive him and our marriage can be saved. When I told him about Villa Mimosa, the first thing he did was to start speculating about what we could do with the money.' Carla shook her head. 'My solicitor has already told me that any assets I own separately will have to be divided between the two of us unless we agree to settle otherwise. Apparently, that includes the money from Mum's house as well as the villa.'

'So it would be better for you if we do continue to rent the place out?' Josette asked.

'Yes, I think so. I know Mum left you to deal with everything via the agency, but I wouldn't do that. I'd come over regularly and if you rang to say you needed me here, I'd jump on a plane.' Carla glanced across at Josette. 'There's something else I need your advice and, possibly, your help with. But I will understand if you don't want anything to do with what I'm about to ask.'

'Sounds ominous.'

'It's Mum's ashes. I don't know what to do with them. Maddy couldn't think of anywhere to scatter them either. I thought you might have a suggestion. Somewhere over here that Mum loved.'

Josette was silent for so long, Carla thought she'd upset her with the request.

'Don't worry, Tante Josette. It was just a thought. I know Mum wasn't always happy living in England – I heard her berating Dad often enough for making her leave France, but I'm sure I'll find the perfect place eventually.'

'Did you bring them with you? The ashes,' Josette asked, a distinct tremble in her voice.

Carla nodded. 'They're upstairs in my case.' Was Josette about to cry at the thought of her dead sister's ashes being upstairs?

'Oh dear – Amelia swore it would be over her dead body before she and I were ever in the same house again. Semble avoir raison,' and Josette made a choking noise.

'I'm sorry. I didn't mean to upset you,' Carla said before

realising Josette wasn't crying, she was trying to hold back a laugh.

'I'm not upset. I just can't get over the irony of it after all these years.' Josette finished the wine in her glass before standing up. 'Come on, let's go and show you the villa. I'll think about the ashes problem later.'

Twenty minutes later, Josette unlocked the villa's front door and Carla followed her into the spacious hallway with its terracotta tiled floor and pale yellow walls.

'We had the whole of the ground floor retiled about fifteen years ago,' Josette said. 'The kitchen and the salle de bains were upgraded about five years ago. Tenants were allowed to decorate according to their personal tastes but no structural alterations. The family who have just moved out were here for three years.' *And this is the first time I've set foot in the place for forty years,* Josette said in her head, saying out loud instead, 'It will be interesting to see the changes.'

Carla looked at her, surprised. 'You didn't see them when they were done?'

'The letting agency has always handled everything. Amelia was in England and I was never here. It was easier.' Josette shrugged. 'Since I've been back I've been in the garden a couple of times to talk to Joel but never in the house.'

The kitchen, to the left of the front door, was huge, with a large oak plank table that could easily seat twelve placed in the centre, granite work surfaces sat on top of pale distressed units and the open shelves matched the units below. A large green La Cornue stove stood against one wall and a huge American-style fridge was by the window.

'The kitchen, I sort of remember, was a mismatch of

dressers and cupboards and was smaller. And darker,' Carla said.

Josette nodded. 'It was. And the meals that came out of it were a bit unmatched too. It's lovely now.'

The sitting room that led to the terrace at the rear of the house had two comfortable looking red leather settees and an insert log fire.

'I didn't realise the villa was let furnished,' Carla said.

'The agency suggested we put enough furniture in to qualify it as a furnished rental,' Josette said. 'Apparently, it's easier to get people out of furnished accommodation if it all goes sour than unfurnished. Only two of the bedrooms have beds and we didn't provide terrace or conservatory furniture, so it all looks rather bare now.'

Carla opened a door in the left-hand corner of the sitting room and walked into a narrow corridor that led to two empty rooms with a bathroom between them. 'I can't get over how big it is,' she said. 'How many rooms upstairs?'

'Now, there are three bedrooms, all en suite, and a smaller room used as a study.'

'The house has a lovely feel to it,' Carla said, as they climbed the uncarpeted wooden staircase. 'I wish I could find something half as nice to buy back home. Which was your bedroom? Did you share with Mum?' she asked as they walked into the first room they came to.

The unexpected question took Josette by surprise. 'We shared this front bedroom until we were, oh, about nineteen, I suppose. Then Amelia moved into the back bedroom until she got married,' Josette answered, opening the French doors and stepping out onto the small balcony.

'I love how you can see the sea and right along the bord de mer from up here,' Carla said, joining her outside. 'The grandparents must have rattled around in here after you both left.'

Josette shrugged. 'They basically closed off the rooms they didn't use and lived downstairs for years.'

'So how much does the place rent for these days?' Carla asked.

'Around €2,300 a month for a yearly lease. If we rented it out as a holiday let, we'd get that per week in the season. More in August,' Josette said. She shrugged. 'Too much hard work.' She turned to go back inside. Despite the bedroom being altered to accommodate the en suite, the view from the balcony was the same and memories were flooding into her head. Unwanted painful memories she didn't need.

Back downstairs, Josette opened one of the French doors that overlooked the garden and stood on the terrace looking at the pool and garden and taking a few deep breaths, trying to banish the upsetting emotions flooding through her.

'Keeping a garden looking this good in the constant heat must be difficult. Your Joel does a great job,' Carla said thoughtfully, wandering out to look around. 'How long has the house been in the family?'

'A hundred years or so. Your great-great-grandfather had it built between the wars.'

'So it's always belonged to the family. Shame selling it will mean I'm the last generation,' Carla said, bending to sniff one of the white rambling roses over the pool house. The ground to the rear of the pool house had been left wild and as well as the roses there were daisies and sunflowers all growing haphazardly and providing nectar for the large number of bees who were buzzing around.

'If you've seen enough I'll lock up,' Josette turned away,

ignoring the clear message behind Carla's words. 'I'll see you by the front door in five minutes.'

Leaving Carla in the garden, Josette closed the French door and locked it securely before walking slowly back through the house to the kitchen. Carla was right. The villa these days did have a good feeling to it, downstairs at least, almost a welcoming one, even to her. The bad feelings, though subdued, were still lurking in the air upstairs.

Locking the door behind her, Josette went slowly down the front entrance curved steps. Waiting for Carla to join her, she absently picked a few dead leaves off the geraniums. If Carla was serious about being involved and helping her, maybe she shouldn't insist on selling. Unlike Amelia, Carla would surely agree to the rent money being available, not left in the bank, so she would finally have an income from the place, which would make her life a lot easier. But could she bear to be more closely involved with the villa again?

Hearing Carla's footsteps coming round the side of the house, Josette straightened up and smiled.

'All locked up,' she said.

'I've just had a thought,' Carla said. 'Two actually. The first is – how do you feel about scattering Mum amongst the wild bit with the roses and daisies around the pool house? I know she wasn't much of a gardener, but it's really pretty around there. D'you think she'd be happy to be back in the garden of the house she grew up in?'

Josette looked at her, lost for words. Never mind whether Amelia would be happy or not, she, Josette, would have to give some serious thought to having her twin sister scattered in the garden of the villa where both their lives had been irreparably shattered. Would Amelia really want to be scattered here? She thought not. But how would she explain that to Carla without a sound reason? There was no way she could tell her the truth.

'I think we need to close the main gates while the villa is empty,' Josette said instead, opening the door of a boxed-in panel on the inside of the pillar at the entrance and pressing a button.

Standing on the pavement watching the electric gates swing together and clang shut, Josette knew Carla was waiting for her to say what she thought about the idea of scattering Amelia behind the pool house. But it wasn't until they were walking along the ramparts and nearly back at the cottage that Josette spoke. And then she didn't mention the ashes.

'If you still want to keep the villa and rent it out, we will,' Josette said. 'But you can't do an Amelia and leave it all to me. You will have to come over regularly. The rent money will have to be divided equally between us both and the maintenance account. No more ridiculous banning access to it.' When Carla didn't answer, Josette glanced at her. 'Continuing to rent the villa out was what you wanted. Or have you changed your mind and want to sell it now?'

Carla shook her head. 'No, I don't want to sell, but I do want to talk to you before we decide what to do. You go on back to the cottage. I'm going to buy one of the roasted chickens from the shop in the market, a baguette and a bottle of wine. Tonight we're going to have a family discussion about my second thought.' Carla turned and walked rapidly away in the direction of the market.

While Josette waited back at the cottage, putting some plates to warm, and knives, forks and wine glasses on the table in the courtyard, the phrase 'family discussion' played on her mind. It was many years since she'd taken part in any family discussion.

And just how could she discourage Carla from scattering Amelia's ashes around the pool house or in any part of Villa Mimosa's garden? She was still trying to think of a reason for saying no to that particular suggestion when Carla arrived back with the food. Within minutes, they were both tucking into the delicious meal.

Carla picked up her glass of wine with a sigh and drank. 'Food tastes so different over here, no idea why though.' Putting the glass back down she said, 'So, family discussion time.'

'Not had one of those for a long time,' Josette admitted. 'Besides, now I've agreed not to sell Villa Mimosa surely the only things we need to discuss are the new arrangements – and finding new tenants, of course.'

'I'm really pleased you've come round to the idea of us keeping the villa in the family, Tante Josette, but,' Carla glanced at her, 'do you know the English expression "light-bulb moment"?'

When Josette nodded, Carla said, 'You know my life is currently in a bit of a state and I've already had to make some life-changing decisions. I've looked at so many houses recently and haven't seen even one that I could consider living in. The moment I walked into the villa I loved it and knew I could live in it happily. That's when my light-bulb moment happened. I'm going to move to France – and I'd like to live in the Villa Mimosa.'

Josette stared at her. 'But it's too big for one person.'

'Eventually I'd like to run the villa as chambre d'hôte. Or a British-style B&B. I love cooking and that kitchen is calling out to me. So, what d'you think?' Carla fingered her glass nervously. 'I can either rent your half from you or buy you out. There should be enough money from Mum's house to do that. Either way, you'd be assured of an income. And the villa would remain in the family. Which feels important to me,' Carla added quietly.

Josette held out her empty glass. 'I need to think – and for that I need another drink please.'

14

The discussion between Carla and Josette was lively and went on all evening. Once she'd got her breath back after Carla had talked about her plans, Josette started to pull them apart. 'You've been to France for three brief visits and now you want to move here. You're looking at things through a daydreaming haze. The sun might shine every day down here, but life still throws the bad stuff around. One of your biggest problems will be your French – it's rubbish.'

'I'll take lessons. Using it every day, it will improve.'

'As for running a chambre d'hôte. You don't have any catering experience, do you? I thought not,' Josette said when Carla shook her head.

'No, but I have run a family home for years and I love cooking. If I start small, just offer bed and continental breakfasts for a couple of people at a time, I know I'll manage.'

Josette sighed and shook her head. 'I'm not convinced it's the right thing for you to do. You must talk things through with someone at home.'

'I hope you're not suggesting I talk to David. He's the last person I want advice from.'

'No, of course I'm not suggesting David,' Josette said. 'But how is Maddy going to feel about you moving to a different country? And Ed when he returns?'

'Of course I'll talk to the children, but they're living their own lives now and I'm determined to grab the chance to live the rest of mine the way I want to.'

It was late when Josette finally took a deep breath. 'I hope I don't come to regret this, but okay. We'll talk to the notaire about it, but I'm not selling you my half share, in case it all goes wrong for you. You can pay a small rent, like a normal tenant, for the first year and if your B&B is successful then we can talk about it.'

'Thank you,' Carla said. 'I do know it won't be easy, but I haven't felt this excited about anything in years.' She stood up and started to carry the empty plates into the kitchen. 'If I can have the keys I'll go back tomorrow and start making some plans. It's all right if I spruce the place up a bit, isn't it?'

'Mais oui,' Josette said.

As she got ready for bed in Josette's guest room, Carla hummed happily to herself. Back in France for less than twelve hours and she was buzzing with excitement at the thought of the future. David, when she told him her plans was sure to play the superior male and tell her she was out of her mind – both moving to France and running a guest house. Ed and Maddy would hopefully be supportive of her. Ed, she knew, would tell her to do whatever made her happy and she knew that living in the villa would.

It was only as she switched off the bedside light that she realised in all the excitement Josette hadn't answered her question about scattering Amelia's ashes in the garden. She'd have to ask her again tomorrow.

* * *

The next morning, Carla was up early and found Josette in the kitchen making coffee. 'Shall I go for the croissants while it brews?' she offered.

'Thanks. Don't be surprised to find the town quiet this morning,' Josette said as Carla opened the front door. 'May the first is La Fête du Travail, when the workers have a day off.'

Carla stopped. 'Will the boulangerie be open then?'

'Bien sŭr, for an hour or two this morning.'

Walking through the streets to Josette's favourite boulangerie and back again, Carla passed several pop-up stalls on street corners selling sprays and small pots of lily of the valley flowers. The smell was wonderful. Impulsively, she stopped and bought a pot for Josette.

To her surprise, when she handed the pot to her, Josette brushed a tear away. 'Merci Carla,' and leant and kissed her on the cheek. 'It's a long time since anyone gave me May Day muguets.'

'I'm guessing it's a tradition associated with today's fête?'

Josette nodded. 'Everyone buys a spray of muguets for family and loved ones.'

Carla smiled at her aunt. 'What a lovely tradition.'

After breakfast, Carla set off for the villa. The drive gates were open when she arrived and Joel's van was parked near the house. The man himself was busy sorting the large terracotta urns on the terrace.

'Bonjour, Joel,' Carla said. 'I'm sorry, je ne parle pas le

Français,' she said slowly and smiled, hoping he would recognise her from their brief introduction the other day. She hoped too he wouldn't answer her in rapid French. Briefly, she wondered if she should try to tell him about her plans for the villa – no, that was best left until Josette was with her and could explain in French far better than she could.

'Bonjour,' Joel said, glancing at her. 'You are alone? No Josette? I was hoping to speak to her.'

'No Josette today. I didn't expect to find you here on a fête day,' Carla said. 'You speak good English.'

'A day off from my main job means more time for my own business. I speak English with a couple of clients. Do you speak any French?'

'A little. Taking lessons is top of my list when I move here.'

'You move to France?'

'Yes, I'm going to live here,' Carla said.

'What, in the villa?' Joel said, sighing.

Carla nodded and looked at him questioningly.

'I was hoping Josette would rent me a room for a few weeks before she took on new tenants.'

'Oh,' Carla said. 'I'm sorry. You're looking to move?'

'I 'ave to find another apartment,' Joel said. 'My landlord wants to do summer rentals. It's not always that easy to find something suitable I can afford. Never mind, c'est la vie. Something will turn up – it always does.' He smiled at her before turning away and carrying on with his work.

Carla walked round to the front door and let herself in. First, she went into the two rooms downstairs, which she thought, to begin with, she'd keep for her private quarters. Plain white walls, terracotta tiles covered the floor and French doors instead of windows opened on to the path that ran down the side of the house. She'd get away with not decorating down here. The bathroom too was all right apart from needing a new shower curtain.

The bedrooms upstairs, though, were a different story. Definitely needed painting, new rugs on the wooden floors and new curtains. The two double beds with pine head-boards were fine, but she'd buy new mattresses. A complete new bed for the third bedroom. And lots of bed linen. Dressing tables, wardrobes, bedside tables, lights, lamp-shades, a comfy chair for each room, trays with crockery and tea-making facilities. The en-suite bathrooms were all good, but towels and bath mats went on the list.

The kitchen was next. Carla bit her lip, thinking of her well equipped kitchen back home, as she surveyed the empty work surfaces and cupboards. At least there was a good cooker and a fridge in situ. She'd just have to get the basics she needed and buy the rest slowly. Setting the villa up was going to take time and would clearly be expensive. It was also unlikely to be ready for any guests before the end of the summer season this year.

Carla took a deep breath. She'd focus on moving to France and having a new life, part of which would entail preparing the villa for guests, but the most important thing would be living life on her own terms.

'Joel was at the villa today,' Carla said to Josette as they sat out in the courtyard under the shade of the parasol eating lunch. 'He seems to be a nice man.'

'He is,' Josette replied.

'When I told him I was moving into the villa soon, he told me he'd been planning to ask you if he could rent a room temporarily. He's having to move and can't find anything suitable at the moment.'

'It is difficult down here, especially during the summer,' Josette said.

'I didn't want to say anything until I'd spoken to you, but I was wondering whether it would be possible to let him stay in the villa until he finds somewhere? I'm going to be back and forwards for a couple of weeks at least, so having someone living in the house might be a good idea?'

'I don't think Joel would take advantage, so why not? If it helps him. He's not had the best of luck in the last few years,' Josette said. 'I have to admit I didn't like the thought of the villa being empty for too long. I'll ring him tomorrow and tell him he can have a room if he still wants it.'

15

Carla was busy sandpapering doors upstairs a couple of days later when she heard the driveway gates opening and saw Joel parking his van at the front of the villa. She ran quickly down stairs.

'Joel, can we talk? Did Josette ring you?'

Joel shook his head. 'She might have done, but my phone is currently out of charge. Something cropped up she wants me to do?'

'It was about you looking for somewhere to live. We've both agreed you're welcome to a room here until you find something.'

'But what about you moving in?'

'I'm going to be toing and froing from England for a couple of weeks and when I am here I can stay at Josette's. I'm ordering three beds this week. I'd appreciate a hand with assembling them, but once they're here you're welcome to move into one of the downstairs rooms. I've started decorating the other bedrooms.'

Joel looked at her. 'Vraiment?

Carla nodded. 'Yes, truly. We'll have to sort something out about a little rent, but we can talk about that later.'

'Brilliant news, thank you.'

'I have to warn you, the villa is going to be pretty basic for a bit. Not much more than the furniture that's here already.'

'No worries. I'm just happy to have a roof over my head. Pas problème helping with the beds – or anything else. Just give me a shout.' Joel said.

Carla returned the happy smile Joel beamed at her with one of her own. Returning upstairs, she couldn't help wondering about him. If she'd met Joel somewhere else, she'd never have guessed he was a gardener, although he did exude a certain attractive sexy earthliness. Maddy would certainly describe him as fit, in more ways than one. Sandpapering the door of the second bedroom, she wondered what had happened in his past. Maybe Josette would tell her more if she asked. But then again maybe she wouldn't. Carla was learning that Josette kept her own secrets and thoughts tightly guarded. Gossiping about her gardener with Carla, with anyone, was something she was unlikely to do.

The days leading up to the notaire's appointment were busy ones. The beds and mattresses, ordered online, arrived and Joel assembled the two for the downstairs rooms and promised to do the third one upstairs as soon as Carla had finished decorating. She painted the walls white with just a hint of sunshine yellow and all the woodwork plain white. In less than a week, the upstairs was transformed and Carla began to think that she might be ready to open her doors to guests during the long school holidays later in the year.

David rang one evening, asking how she was and when would she be back.

'I'm fine. I'll book a flight after I've been to the notaire's.' No point in telling him about her decision to move to France until she was back.

The appointment with Monsieur Damarcus the notaire went well. Once the formalities were over and all the paperwork signed in triplicate, Carla told him her plans for the villa and he offered to help her with registering both herself and the business with the French authorities. An offer Carla knew she'd gratefully accept when the time came.

Afterwards, Josette went with her to the large hypermarket on the edge of town, where they literally spent hours choosing bed linen, crockery and the hundred other small things on Carla's list. She'd decided things like dressing tables, wardrobes and other furniture would have to be bought when she returned after her trip back to the UK. In thirty-six hours, she would be at the place she used to call home, explaining to her husband and her daughter that her future home was going to be in Antibes. Not something she was looking forward with any enthusiasm to doing. Particularly as far as David was concerned. Still, once she'd done it, she could return to Antibes and get on with her new life.

Joel was at the villa moving in when Carla and Josette got back from the hypermarket and he gave them a hand carrying the shopping into the villa from the taxi before finishing unloading his van.

'I'll see you back at the cottage,' Josette said. 'Pizza for supper okay with you?'

'Sounds great,' Carla answered. 'See you later.'

Pulling two packages out from the pile of shopping waiting to be sorted in the kitchen, Carla went through the sitting room and into the small corridor that led to the down-stairs bedrooms. The door was open to Joel's room and he smiled when he saw her.

'Are you sure you're going to be okay in here? Sorry about the lack of furniture other than the bed. I bought a clothes rail and a hanging organiser today,' and she held them out to Joel.

'Thanks. I was planning on living out of my suitcases, but these will definitely make life easier.'

Carla noticed an upended wooden box at the side of the bed with a bedside light and a framed photograph of a laughing young woman. 'I'll find you a cloth or something to go over that. That's one beautiful young lady,' she said, looking up at Joel, wondering who she was but not liking to ask.

'Tamara, my sister.'

'Does she live in France?'

Joel shook his head. 'No, she lived in the States before she died.'

'I'm so sorry,' Carla said. 'I didn't mean to pry.' Maybe this was what Josette had been referring to when she'd mentioned Joel having a hard time recently?

'I know you didn't. I'd better start assembling the rail,' Joel answered.

'I'd better get back to sorting my shopping,' Carla said, hoping she hadn't upset him. He'd clearly been very fond of his sister.

* * *

The next evening, her last before she flew back to the UK, Carla invited Josette, Gordon and Joel too, of course, for drinks and nibbles at the villa. She got the feeling that Josette had accepted reluctantly. Champagne in the fridge, salmon bites, a selection of tomatoes stuffed with various fillings, nuts and crisps were lined up on the kitchen work surface. She'd taken Josette's advice to go to the artisan stall in the market for the nibbles. Normally, Carla would have prepared the food herself, but the kitchen was not a working kitchen yet in any sense of the word. A kettle and a microwave, glasses, cups, crockery and cutlery were all there now, but baking utensils and ingredients had yet to be purchased. Still so much to do when she returned.

The sitting room French doors were open and while waiting for Josette and Gordon to arrive Carla wandered out onto the terrace. The low sound of music drifted on the air from Joel's room, adding to the lovely balmy south of France evening, which was perfect for sitting and relaxing in the garden. Only they couldn't, she realised. There wasn't any furniture to sit on. Carla made a mental note to add garden furniture to the list that didn't appear to be getting any shorter. Tonight they'd have to stand around outside or sit indoors.

She turned as Joel appeared at her side. 'The garden is a real credit to your hard work. It's beautiful. I love the colour of that bougainvillea along the back – it's almost purple. And what's the name of that tallish shrub with the blue flower by the rockery?'

'Plumbago.'

'I was thinking some solar lights dotted around would look good. And candles in containers out here on the terrace.'

'But peut être not too many solar lights as they can confuse the insects.'

'I didn't realise that. I'll stick to candles then,' Carla said, looking around. 'I can barely believe I'm going to be living in a house with lemons and oranges growing in the garden. It's like a dream come true. Ah, I can hear Josette and Gordon. Time to pour the drinks.'

Joel opened the champagne for her and she handed the flutes around. Carla raised her glass in Josette's direction. 'Thank you, Tante Josette, for agreeing to let me start my new life in Villa Mimosa so, can I just say, here's to family and new beginnings.'

'Family and new beginnings,' everyone echoed.

Only Gordon noticed that Josette omitted the word family and simply toasted 'new beginnings'.

16

It was raining when Carla landed back on English soil, which put an additional damper on her already low spirits. As the plane had taken off from Nice airport, she'd sighed. Knowing what lay ahead of her for the next couple of days, she'd have given anything not to have been heading back to the UK. She'd emailed David yesterday to tell him she was returning and would see him this evening. She'd refrained from telling him they needed to talk again because she knew he'd only misunderstand and think she'd changed her mind about the divorce. Easier to wait until they were together.

She also emailed Maddy, inviting her for supper. That way, she could tell the two of them at the same time about her exciting new plans as they ate.

To her relief, David wasn't home when she arrived at the house. She took her case up to the guest bedroom before going downstairs to make a cup of tea. A note on the kitchen table told her he'd be home about seven and he'd bring Chinese for them all to share. A few more hours' reprieve then. Time enough to make a few phone calls to the estate agent and the solicitor.

The phone call to the estate agent went well. Contracts on No. 29 had been exchanged and completion would be in about three weeks. After speaking to the solicitor, though, about the divorce, Carla was cross. David was apparently dragging his heels over everything, but mainly their financial settlement. Maybe when he heard her news tonight he'd finally realise trying to hold things up in the hope she'd change her mind was a waste of everyone's time.

Maddy and David arrived within minutes of each other. Carla returned Maddy's hug and accepted David's kiss on the cheek. When David went upstairs to change, leaving the two of them to sort the takeaway food, Maddy whispered to her mum.

'Don't mention Sam tonight.'

'Why? You haven't broken up, have you?'

'No, of course not. I just haven't told Dad about him yet.' Maddy looked at Carla. 'You do realise Dad is still hoping you'll change your mind about the divorce?'

'Well, he's going to have to accept it when he hears my news.'

Maddy looked at her questioningly.

'Later.'

Carla poured the red wine she'd opened earlier and handed a glass to Maddy.

'I hope you've poured me a glass,' David said, coming into the kitchen at that moment. 'Could do with a drink after the day I've had.'

Carla handed him a glass. 'Let's eat.'

'So, how was France?' David said, helping himself to some sweet and sour balls and savoury rice. 'Are you now officially half owner of an Antibes villa? I'm looking forward to you showing me around soon. I was thinking we'd go for a long weekend later this month.'

'David, what part of the word divorce do you not understand?' Carla said quietly, before taking a deep breath. 'Yes, I now officially own half of the family villa with Tante Josette. And my big news is – I have decided to move to France, so I've come to an agreement with Josette that I will live in the villa and – eventually –- run it as a chambre d'hôte.'

Complete silence greeted her words. Maddy was the first to speak.

'You mean you're moving to Antibes? You can't just up sticks and go like that. What about us?'

'Us?'

'Me and Ed.'

'You're grown-ups living life the way you want to,' Carla said. 'Both of you are unlikely to live at home again. Besides, you both know wherever my home is will be your home too.'

'But it won't be here where we grew up,' Maddy wailed.

'True, but you'll always have the memories. Villa Mimosa is a lovely old house with plenty of rooms, not to mention a pool. I know you're going to love my new home as much as I do already,' Carla said, injecting an upbeat tone into her voice.

Maddy turned to her father who, having drained his glass of wine and poured himself another, was now pushing his savoury rice around the plate. 'How come you're so quiet, Dad. This is all your fault. If you hadn't had an affair with that tart, Lisa, none of this would be happening.'

'Actually, I don't think that's totally true. The chances are it would have happened anyway,' Carla said. 'I think Dad would agree that our marriage has been in trouble for some time. His latest affair was just the catalyst.' She threw a pleading look in David's direction. 'I'm sure we're all old enough to be civilised about everything. Even when the divorce is finalised, Dad and I will always be there for you and Ed.'

'In different countries!' Maddy said, pushing her chair back and standing up. 'I'm going. I half promised to meet S— someone. I'll give you a call tomorrow, Mum, when I've got my head around things. Bye, Dad.'

David winced as the front door slammed behind her. The two of them sat in silence for a minute before Carla spoke.

'So, we are going to be civilised about things, aren't we, David?'

'I've been a bloody idiot I know, but I do wish you'd think about trying again. No? Okay then,' wearily David nodded. 'Civilised it is.'

'Good. I was talking to my solicitor earlier and he said you're holding things up, particularly my financial settlement.'

'Yeah, well I was hoping... I'll ring my solicitor in the morning and speed things up.'

'You do that. He'll want to tell you about a few things I've instructed my solicitor to offer. There's a couple of conditions attached to what I've asked him to propose, but he agreed they were fair.' Carla stood up. 'I'm off to bed, it's been a long day. See you tomorrow. Oh, I nearly forgot. I've put the necklace back in its box in your room. Night.'

'Night,' David said, not looking at her as he poured the last of the wine into his glass.

* * *

The next morning, Carla stayed in her room until she heard David leave for work before she got up. She had a busy few days ahead of her. There was so much to organise with a move to another country. She also needed to phone Maddy to check she wasn't still upset after last night. After breakfast, she picked up the phone to call Josette.

Standing, looking out of the window at the drizzle, waiting for Josette to answer, Carla thought longingly of the sunshine that Josette would no doubt complain about, saying it was too hot, too early in the day. Carla, though, was looking forward to enjoying a proper summer with lots and lots of sunshine. In truth, she couldn't wait to get back.

17

Josette straightened several of the framed photos she'd hung in the privacy of her bedroom. Photos that were representative of her life for the past fifty years and ones that she was proud to have taken. Hanging them elsewhere in the cottage would have felt like showing off and Josette had never been one for bragging. Placing them in full view of visitors would also encourage questions about her past. Questions that Josette preferred not to answer.

Most of the photographs were black and white ones she'd taken all over Europe during the course of the last fifty years. Subjects ranged from young children to old women, from deluxe buildings to bombed-out streets in war zones, from crowds to solitary figures in a landscape. Some had won awards.

Getting ready to meet Gordon for a day out, her eyes were drawn as ever to a certain photograph. A young child, no more than two years old, reaching out to be picked up by the father. Her camera had captured the father's look of pure unadulterated love as he bent down towards the child. It had always been one of her favourite photos. Josette closed her eyes as the familiar wave of sadness that had swept through her the day she'd realised how a man's life had been destroyed by the loss of that simple unconditional love, swept through her again.

Picking up her bag, a pashmina and putting on her straw sun hat, her hand hovered over her camera on the dresser, where the sun streaming in highlighted the dust particles forming over its case. Once the Nikon would have been an automatic accessory every day, but in recent months the desire to take photographs had died. Today, though, the camera's neglected presence stirred memories as well as a feeling of sadness at what she had given up.

Maybe it was time she dusted off the camera, but not today. Gordon had promised her a fun day out and they were off to Monaco. If she wasn't careful, she'd be late meeting him down by the station. Josette ran downstairs and out of the cottage, slamming the door behind her.

* * *

'Sorry, am I late?' she said as he greeted her with the usual cheek kisses. 'We'll have to hurry getting our tickets.'

'Today we don't need tickets. Come with me,' and Gordon took her by the hand and led her in the direction of a white convertible MG vintage sports car parked nearby. 'I thought we'd travel in style today,' he said, moving round and opening the passenger door for her. 'If madam would take a seat.'

Josette did as she was told and fastened her seat belt and waited while Gordon did the same. 'I didn't think you had a car?'

'I've hired this little beauty just for today,' Gordon said.

'We can pretend we're young again and can afford a fun car. The coast road, I think,' he said, pressing the start button. 'Monaco, here we come.'

Josette put on her sunglasses and took off her sun hat before the wind could whip it off her head as Gordon drove fast and expertly along the bas corniche. The small waves of the blue Mediterranean on their right gambolled in the sunlight, rolling up the pebbled beach and back again. In the sky, planes making their descent for Nice airport travelled a faster parallel line to the coast road before disappearing from view to touch down gently on the runway.

It was only yesterday that Carla had taken off in one of the planes flying in the opposite direction. She missed her already. The telephone call early this morning had been an unexpected surprise. She sighed and sensed Gordon giving her a fleeting glance.

'Carla rang me this morning to check I was all right. Wasn't that kind of her? Things are falling into place for her to move over and live in the Villa Mimosa.'

'That's good,' Gordon said.

'I'm not so sure,' Josette sighed, 'I'm not used to being involved with family. All I've ever wanted from the day Amelia and I inherited the place was to sell it and close that part of my life. Now, when it seems the opportunity has finally arisen, I cave in and agree to Carla not just moving into Villa Mimosa but running a chambre d'hôte in the future.'

'Why were you so desperate to close that chapter of your life?' Gordon asked.

'I have some unhappy memories of the place.'

'No happy ones at all?'

'Probably my own fault, but the unhappy ones have, over the years, pushed the good ones out of my mind,' Josette said.

'It seemed a happy place to me when we were there the other evening. The garden was lovely too. I think Carla will make a success of her business and in a few months you'll realise how much you like having family around you.'

'Maybe. Having close family nearby is something I'd accepted would never happen because of the feud with Amelia. Anyway,' she added determinedly, 'today I'm not going to think about what the future may hold. I'm going to enjoy the fun day you promised me.'

Josette sat up straighter and pushed herself back against the car seat. A phrase her mother would have used 'blowing the cobwebs away' came into Josette's mind minutes later as the car flew along, eating up the kilometres and the invigorating wind blew around her head.

'I love this car. Wish I'd had one like it when I was young,' Josette said. 'It's years since I've been along this road. We always came to Monaco by train. It was easier.'

'We? And why?'

'Amelia and I. And the why was because our father agreed with Somerset Maugham's words, "it's a shady place for shady people", and didn't approve of us visiting. We used to come in secret.' She glanced at Gordon. 'D'you know Monaco well?'

'In a previous life I used to be a regular visitor. Almost bought an apartment here.' He shrugged. 'It's changed a lot since those days. But it still has a certain *je ne sais quois*.'

Gordon rarely mentioned his past life and Josette waited, hoping he'd enlarge on his comments. When he didn't, she said. 'Life's a funny thing, isn't it? Changes of which we are aware happen, we even instigate and accept some of them.

Then, ten, twenty, years pass and you realise certain of those changes had an unseen domino effect on other things, and almost without noticing you've lived a whole different life. One where you forgot your dreams.'

'That's a sad reflection,' Gordon said quietly. 'It's never too late to have dreams, you know.'

'Maybe not, but turning them into reality could be a step too far, too late. *C'est la vie*.'

Gordon, concentrating on overtaking a lorry, didn't answer.

'Tell me what you have planned for today?' Josette asked once they were safely past.

'After parking the car, I thought we'd walk up through the town and start with coffee in the Café de Paris, followed by a visit to the casino, where we'll play the slot machines. After which I'm hoping we'll come back down and my plan for lunch in the Automobile Club happens. There is a fair amount of walking involved in these plans as you probably realise.'

'That's fine. J'adore me promener around the principality. There's always something or someone to see.'

Leaving the car in the underground car park on the quay, the two of them wandered along the wide harbour front, strolled up the hill past the Princess Grace Theatre, along Avenue de Monte Carlo with its designer shops and into Place du Casino. By the time they sank onto chairs on the terrace of the Café de Paris, they were both ready for a reviving coffee.

Waiting for the coffee to arrive, Josette smiled at the scene in front of her. Numerous tourists, under the watchful eye of the uniformed security man, were busy posing as close as possible to the luxury cars parked in front of the casino for photographs. All around them was a babble of international languages: Japanese, Dutch, English, Russian, Italian and, of course, French.

The waiter placed her coffee on the table. 'Merci.'

'Amelia and I used to love coming here when we were teenagers,' Josette said. 'We'd pretend we were famous, talk in loud voices, giggle together over something that had happened "on set" and haughtily ignore everyone. The reality, of course, was that nobody was the slightest bit interested in us anyway. C'était amusant quand même.' She drank some coffee, conscious of Gordon watching her. 'I took one of my more infamous photos here too.'

'Infamous as in of famous people behaving badly?' Gordon said.

Josette nodded. 'It was of the Burtons having a major tiff on the casino steps,' Josette said. 'I was lucky in that the paparazzi that usually hung around had all gone off to chase Rainier and Grace. That photo has earnt me a few euros over the years.'

'I've never seen you with a camera in your hand. Do you not miss taking photographs these days? Just for your own pleasure.'

Before Josette could answer, Gordon's mobile pinged with an incoming text and the moment was lost.

Reading the message, Gordon pulled a face.

'Sorry, lunch at the Automobile Club is a no-go. Never mind. I know a good restaurant in rue Princess Caroline. Come on, time to gamble with the fruit machines first.'

Josette and Gordon decided twenty-five euros worth of tokens each would be enough for them to have fun with and they joined the crowds in the slot machine room. Josette wandered around for a while watching other people and trying to work out how to play the modern electronic devices. 'Wish they still had the old-fashioned models,' she said, stopping to watch Gordon. 'I knew how to play them. All these flashing lights confuse me.'

'Just choose one and dive in,' he replied. 'You'll soon get the hang of it. If not, it's only a small amount of money you've gambled.'

So she dived in as instructed and doubled her money on her first play, after which she was hooked. When Gordon tapped her on the shoulder half an hour later saying it was time to make their way back down and find a restaurant, she smiled at him.

'That was so much fun,' Josette said. 'And while I didn't exactly break the bank at Monte Carlo, I've still got my original twenty-five euros.'

'In that case, you can buy a cream gateau later to take home with us for tea.'

'It's a deal,' Josette said, laughing.

18

Sunday afternoon and Maddy drove Carla to the airport. A strangely subdued Maddy.

'Stay and have a coffee with me?' Carla said. 'I'll check the cases in first. Then I've got at least half an hour before I need to go through security.'

'Okay. I'll go and order. There's always a queue,' Maddy said and walked off.

When Carla joined her ten minutes later, Maddy was wiping the tears away.

'I wish you weren't doing this, Mum.'

Carla sighed. 'Maddy, you know why I'm doing it. Can't you just wish me well in my new life? A new life for me that still includes you in it. The world has Skype now. We can speak and see each other every day if you want. Besides, I'm going to be less than a two-hour plane ride away.' When Maddy didn't answer, Carla sighed. 'Darling, don't you think you're being rather selfish? You are an independent young career woman with your life in front of you. You also have Sam.'

'He says I'm being selfish too.' Maddy looked at her. 'It's all happened so quickly. Granny dying. Dad's affair. The divorce. You leaving. It feels like my world has suddenly disappeared.'

'Think how I feel,' Carla said quietly.

'I'm sorry, Mum. I really do hope your new life works out for you. You deserve it.'

'It will. I'm already looking forward to you and Sam visiting. How is Sam? I was sorry to miss saying goodbye to him.'

Maddy smiled. 'He's fine. Told me to send you his love and best wishes.'

'Have you introduced him to Dad yet? Or even told Dad about Sam?'

'No. The timing seemed all wrong. I will soon though. Sam, for some reason, is keen to meet him. Almost as keen as he is for me to meet his parents.'

'This sounds serious.' Carla looked at Maddy questioningly. 'Is it?'

'Think so. It does feel as though he could be the one. Don't worry, you'll be the first to know any news.'

Carla glanced at her watch. 'I'd better get ready to board.' They walked together to the entrance to security. Carla gave Maddy a tight hug. 'Don't worry, everything will be all right. Visit soon, promise?'

Maddy nodded, too close to tears again to speak as Carla turned away and disappeared out of sight.

Carla was close to tears herself as she strapped herself into her seat, but as the plane began to taxi down the runway, she felt her spirits lifting. In less than two hours' time, when she stepped back on French soil, her new life would begin. A life where she could forget recent hurtful events and push them into the depths of her mind and she alone would decide which path she'd take in the future. She was determined nothing would spoil her enjoyment of this French adventure. Whatever it took to make Villa Mimosa and her life in France a success, she would do. Nothing from the past was going to be allowed to intrude and spoil things.

PART II

19

Eight o'clock in the evening and Carla was floating on her back in the pool, relaxing, having just swum fifteen lengths. She'd been living in the villa for a fortnight now and beginning to feel more and more content in her new home. Last week, the van had delivered the few pieces of furniture she'd told David she wanted from the marital home, as well as the rest of her clothes and other personal stuff. In a rare moment of generosity, David had told her to take whatever she wanted from the kitchen too, apart from the coffee machine, so she had. All her favourite kitchen stuff – the mixer, the copper pans, cake trays, pasta machine, and lots of small utensils – were all were now installed here in her new kitchen. Alongside a brand-new grain-to-cup coffee machine. She was enjoying using everything in this new adventure of hers.

Her daily routine here in France was so different to the life she'd left behind in England. Shopping in the market, discovering favourite shops, wandering along the bord de mer, swimming every day. She was slowly getting to meet people too – the neighbours on one side had put a welcome card in the post box with an invitation for aperitifs when she'd settled in. The only disappointment so far was that she hadn't found any available French lessons to join. Not that she'd tried that hard yet, there had been so much to do.

Two of the upstairs bedrooms and the sitting room still lacked several items of furniture, but gradually she was finding what she needed, either in local stores or ordering off the internet. And she'd discovered the joy of the French equivalent of car boot sales, vide greniers, last Sunday when Joel had told her about one in nearby Golfe Juan. It was thanks to him that the terrace now boasted a large white wrought-iron table and six chairs with comfy cushions.

It had been strange, at first, living in the house and sharing the kitchen with Joel. Separate lives in the same house – the exact arrangement she'd suggested to David. Carla doubted it would have worked so well with him, but with Joel it did, probably because they'd never been a couple and really did lead separate lives. He was a good housemate and Carla already knew she'd miss him when he found a place of his own again and moved out.

David had rung once to say he'd agreed to everything at the solicitors and their divorce was now underway with no further objections from him. The conversation had been strained and short, but at least they'd been civil to each other.

Maddy had Skyped several times and she and Sam were coming next weekend for a few days. Maddy, never having met her Great Aunt Josette before, sounded excited, saying she was looking forward to meeting Granny's sister at last. Carla doubted somehow that Josette felt the same. Her reaction when Carla had told her about Maddy and Sam coming for a visit had been decidedly lacking in enthusiasm at the prospect. Josette had seemed uncertain, worried even, at the thought of meeting Maddy for the first time, which was perhaps understandable. It wasn't as if Maddy was a baby to be handed around the relatives and be cooed over. That should have happened years ago.

Turning on her front, Carla swam down the pool towards the steps. Climbing out and wrapping herself in a large towel, her thoughts turned to Josette. Carla's own dream of finally getting to know her aunt and spending time with her was failing to materialise. Since she'd moved into the villa, she'd got the feeling that Josette had withdrawn from her, deliberately putting up barriers between the two of them. She longed to show her how different the villa was now. Several times she'd invited her for lunch, a coffee and even a swim now that the weather was so hot, all of which Josette had declined for no real reason as far as Carla could tell.

On the other hand, Josette always seemed pleased to see her when she called in at the cottage and would happily sit and have a coffee or a cool glass of rosé with her, or go for a walk along the ramparts. Carla was beginning to suspect that the villa itself was the problem. Knowing that Josette had planned on selling it and had only reluctantly agreed to let her rent it, Carla was becoming convinced that the real problem was Josette's memories stopping her from making new, happier, ones. Something would have to be done. Precisely what, Carla had yet to fathom out. It would be Amelia and Josette's birthday the weekend Maddy and Sam arrived, the first since Amelia had died. It wasn't a day Carla was looking forward to herself. Perhaps celebrating the day with Josette by treating everyone to lunch somewhere would help ease things.

Once she'd showered and pulled a cotton dress on, Carla took a bottle of wine, a packet of crisps and two glasses out on to the terrace. Joel wasn't home yet, but he was always happy to join her for a small nightcap. In fact, the two of them sitting out on the terrace in the evening was turning into something of a ritual.

The bats were flitting around the hedge at the bottom of the garden in the half-light before Carla heard the gates opening. She smiled at Joel as he appeared on the path at the side of the house. A Joel who didn't immediately return her smile and was clearly upset over something.

'Are you okay?' Carla asked. 'Has something happened?'

He nodded. 'I'm fine but... I'm working over on the Cap. There's a team of us landscaping a garden for some Russian billionaire,' he paused. 'One of the other gardeners found this little chap terrified under a hedge. Reckons the mother was run over up there a couple of days ago. Said if I didn't take him, he'd get rid of it like the rest he'd found yesterday. I couldn't let that happen.' As he spoke, Joel had gently put his hand in a pocket of his gilet and brought out a wide-eyed brown and cream kitten. 'I'm hoping you like kittens?'

Carla held out her hands. 'Oh, the poor little thing.' The kitten settled in the palms of her hands as she cuddled him against her. 'He's all skin and bones. He must be starving.'

'If you don't want to keep him, I'll take him to the refuge tomorrow,' Joel said.

'No, you won't. He's just a baby. It's a long time since I had a cat – my husband was allergic. I'm more than happy to give this little one his forever home.'

Joel flashed her a smile. 'I was hoping you'd say that. I stopped off at the vets and the supermarché on the way home and picked up food and stuff.'

'Come on then, let's get some food and liquid inside him and settled in the kitchen for the night,' Carla said.

Twenty minutes later, the kitten, having eaten and drunk and been the recipient of lots of cuddles from Carla, was happy to curl up in a small cardboard box Joel had lined with one of his old working shirts.

Out on the terrace, Carla poured the last of the wine into Joel's glass while he made short work of the packet of crisps.

'What are we going to call him?' Carla asked. 'Any ideas?'

Joel shook his head. 'The perfect name will announce itself as he settles in and gets to know us. Really,' he said, laughing at Carla's disbelieving expression. 'You wait and see.'

20

Since the day in Monaco with Gordon, Josette had found herself thinking more and more about photography as a hobby at this stage of her life. She did miss the buzz of capturing the essence of a scene, of a person, on film and was increasingly drawn to the idea of picking up her camera again. She could just take photos for pleasure. But definitely not selfies on her phone like everyone seemed to these days.

She'd dusted off the Nikon, even bought a couple of rolls of film and inserted one in the body of the camera, but so far she hadn't ventured out carrying it. But she would soon.

In the meantime, she needed to go through the packets of photographs she and Carla had looked at briefly a few weeks ago. She wanted them bundled back up ready to return to Carla on her next visit. Better for Carla to be their custodian than her. She pushed away the thought: *you could take them round to the villa and give them to her whenever you like.*

Opening one of the packets, she saw the photo of herself and Mario in Le Suquet was still on top of the pile. Maybe she'd keep that one. Frame it and put it in her bedroom.

Dream about what might have been. No, she wouldn't do that. That particular dream had faded away years ago. Josette placed the photo to one side. She would find a frame for it though and simply cherish the happy memories it evoked.

Josette thumbed through the photos, stopping to look at one of Amelia and Robert standing in front of the villa with Carla between them. It was one she realised she herself had taken on that ill-fated visit for their mother's funeral. She remembered how Amelia had been acting oddly throughout the three day visit and looking at her with a strange look in her eyes. As they were leaving for the airport, Amelia had grabbed her by the arm and said, 'I want nothing more to do with you. Stay away from my family from now on.'

Josette had stared at her. 'Amelia, whatever's the matter? What have I done?'

'You know what you've done and, as far as I'm concerned, you're no longer part of my family and I don't want to see you ever again.'

With that, Robert had taken her by the arm, given Josette an apologetic look and shrug and told Amelia to get in the taxi with Carla.

Josette had phoned Robert at work the next day, but he'd been unable to come up with any reason for Amelia's behaviour.

'I'm really sorry, Josette. I tried to talk to her last night, but she said the matter was closed and she didn't want to discuss it.'

'Do you think she's she having a breakdown again? Has the depression returned?' Josette asked quietly.

'No. She's just got some bee in her bonnet about you over something that happened in the past and is adamant she wants nothing more to do with you.'

And all contact with her twin had suddenly and inexplicably stopped from that day. Robert had been coerced into acting as an unhappy go-between for the sisters whenever Villa Mimosa business had to be discussed. Hurt and bewildered by her twin's rejection, Josette had thrown herself into work, accepting far flung commissions that she'd normally have turned down. Before she'd realised it, she'd turned into this nomadic freelance photographer, with no real roots and unable to settle anywhere for long. Returning to Antibes just over a year ago to finally claim back her heritage and settle down had seemed the right thing to do at the time, but now she wasn't so sure.

The fact that Carla was now living in Villa Mimosa had complicated things. In all the years of renting out the villa since she and Amelia had inherited it, she'd avoided going inside – until that day she and Carla had gone in together. Despite the lighter decoration, the new kitchen and the modern bathroom suites, the atmosphere swirling around her, especially upstairs, was a repressive half a century old one she remembered well. And while she longed to see everything Carla had done to the villa, she couldn't face it. She was afraid the tainted atmosphere in the villa would forever be uppermost in her mind. The fact too that the secret from the past, the one she'd sworn she'd never tell anyone, had taken to continually shouting out in her head, 'Tell them and shame the devil', didn't help her peace of mind.

'Josette, can I come in?' Gordon called as he knocked the door.

'Sure – it's open,' and Josette began to scoop the pictures back into their various packages. She'd hand them over to

Carla and if questions were asked about some of the photos later, she'd answer them truthfully.

'This is a surprise,' she said, looking at Gordon.

'Wondered if you fancied a walk, followed by an aperitif in Billy's and possibly supper if he's cooking.'

'Sounds good. Could we walk via the Villa Mimosa?' Josette asked, coming to a sudden decision. 'I'd like to drop these photographs off for Carla.' Having Gordon at her side would make it easier.

'Sure. Any of yours among that lot?' Gordon said, looking at the packet.

'A couple but nothing you'd find interesting, It's mainly family.'

Walking along boulevard Edouard Baudoin, they stopped to watch a couple preparing for a parasail.

'Looks such fun,' Josette said as the pair took off, rising into the sky behind the boat towing them. 'Wish that had been here when I was growing up! I'd have loved to have had a go.' She sighed. 'Too old now.'

Five minutes later, they were almost at the entrance to the villa. 'It feels so weird having family living here. I can only hope Carla has made the right decision and that the house is kind to her,' she said, without thinking.

'I know every house has a unique atmosphere and this one in particular has a bad vibe for you, but it may help if you think of it as just a pile of stones held together by mortar or whatever stuff they used to build it with at the beginning of the last century,' Gordon said.

'It's not just the house,' Josette sighed. 'I think I've forgotten how to be a part of a family. I'm not sure I can cope with my new face-to-face persona of being Tante Josette to

Carla, let alone becoming Great Tante Josette to Maddy and Edward. I've never had an aunt. How do aunts behave?'

'Eccentricity rules,' Gordon said. 'My favourite aunt was Aunt Tilly, she hated her real name, Matilda, and regaled me with tales of the time she ran away to join the circus before she eloped with the local vicar. She told great stories.'

Josette laughed. 'See, I told you I had no idea. I'm not cut out to be an eccentric aunt. I can't compete with that kind of history.'

Gordon stopped walking and, placing his hands on her shoulders, turned her to look at him. 'It's not a competition. Be yourself. You've had an interesting life and I know Carla is already extremely fond of you.'

'The villa holds so many ghosts for me,' Josette said, shaking her head.

'The villa has entered a new era with Carla. You must forget the past and live in the moment. You'll be surprised how easy that can become with practice.'

'Going to take an awful lot of practice in my case.'

'Probably, but you have to try. Come on let's deliver those photographs.'

Carla was sitting on the terrace when they arrived and sprang up with a welcoming smile.

'Josette. Finally you came. I'll make some coffee, but first there's someone in the kitchen you need to meet.'

Josette was aware of Gordon's hand lightly on her back, guiding her forward as she hesitated before following Carla into the kitchen.

The kitten, asleep in the comfortable igloo Carla had bought him, opened his eyes at the sound of voices, yawned, stretched and padded over to Josette, who, after placing the packet of photos on the table, scooped him up with a smile.

'Hello, you. It's been a long time since there was a cat here. The last one was called... Star, I think. So what's your name, little one?'

'He hasn't got one yet. Joel says the right name will arrive,' Carla said, spooning coffee into the cafetière. 'So far it hasn't, any suggestions welcome.'

'I agree with Joel,' Josette answered. 'The cat will tell you what he wants to be called.'

'You're as bad as Joel,' Carla said. 'He'll end up as Cat at this rate. Is that the packet of photos I brought over earlier?'

Josette nodded. 'I thought you might as well keep them here.'

'Maddy didn't get a chance to see them before, so it will be fun going through them with her, especially now you've told me who some of the people are.' Carla glanced at Josette before speaking to Gordon. 'I'm planning on taking us all to Cannes for a celebratory lunch next Saturday – would you like to join us?'

'What are you celebrating on Saturday...?' Josette's voice died away as she realised what the date would be. 'Oh, non, non, non. I don't usually bother with my birthday.'

'Sorry, but this year begins a new tradition and you are definitely celebrating,' Carla said. 'No argument.'

21

The morning Sam and Maddy were due to arrive, Carla was up early. She wanted everything to be perfect for Maddy's first visit. The villa, she felt, was looking good, but she wanted to get some flowers and some special artisan soap from the stall in the market for their bedroom, as well as salad things and a baguette for lunch. Flight delays aside, Maddy had said they should arrive at about twelve thirty by the time they got through Arrivals and picked up their hire car.

Wandering through the market buying the things she wanted, Carla tried to squash the nervous butterflies floating around in her head over Maddy's visit. She so wanted Maddy to like the villa, her new home, be happy for her. To realise Carla had done the right thing in moving here.

Carla bought two coffee eclairs from the patisserie stall and took a short cut through a nearby alleyway to Josette's cottage – a sudden desire to see Josette overcoming the need to return to the villa.

'Your favourite coffee eclairs,' Carla said when Josette

opened the door, showing her the box of cakes. 'Fancy a coffee to go with them?'

Outside in the courtyard listening to the buzz of the bees around the jasmine, Carla tried to relax.

'I can't believe how nervous I am about this weekend,' she said, accepting the demitasse coffee from Josette.

'C'est naturel. Family is important to you.'

'What time are you coming over to meet Maddy?'

Josette shook her head. 'I hadn't planned to come over today.' She waved away Carla's objections. 'The two of you will have lots to talk about. Besides, I'm a little nervous too about meeting Maddy for the first time.'

'Oh, Josette, I'm sorry, I'd forgotten you've never met Maddy – or Ed – in the flesh, only ever seen photos. Please come to the villa and meet Maddy today.'

Josette shrugged. 'All in the past now.' She hesitated. 'Maybe tonight you bring Maddy and Sam here for aperitifs?'

'That would 'be lovely,' Carla accepted quickly before Josette could change her mind. 'Can I bring anything?'

'Non merci. Just my great-niece and her boyfriend.'

Once back at the villa, Carla put the soaps she'd bought in the bathroom and a bunch of fragrant sweet peas in a crystal vase on the dressing table in the bedroom. Downstairs in the sitting room, she placed the sunflowers she'd been unable to resist in a large terracotta pottery vase and stood them to the side of the French doors leading to the garden, where the dappled water of the pool was an inviting oasis in the sunlight.

The terrace table was set for lunch, a bottle of rosé in the cooler, salad in bowls in the kitchen, cheese already at room temperature on the board with a cloche and a selection of cold meats in the fridge.

Carla bent down to stroke the kitten, who was winding himself between her legs. 'Hello, kitten-cat. You planning on being part of the welcome too?' she said, picking him up. 'I wish you'd hurry up and tell us your name. I can't keep on calling you kitten-cat.'

He purred as she stroked his head before jumping out of her arms as they both heard a car arriving and headed for the shelter of the plumbago shrub from where he could keep a watchful eye on people.

'Mum, this is just gorgeous,' Maddy said as she got out of the car and ran to hug her mum. 'I didn't expect it to be like this. And you look much better. Very French. Love the outfit.'

'It's just cool summer stuff from the market,' Carla said. 'White capri trousers and a striped top are almost de rigueur for daywear down here. Sam, it's lovely to see you here,' she said, giving him a hug too. 'Come on, let me show you everything,' she added, leading the way indoors. 'Sitting room, kitchen, sunroom, downstairs bathroom and two more rooms. This is my room, as the plan is to keep the whole of upstairs for guests.' Carla laughed. 'I feel like an estate agent showing you around.'

'It feels funny seeing that here,' Maddy said quietly, looking at the painting of a Provençal market scene Carla had hung on one of the sitting room walls. 'I'm used to seeing it in the dining room at home.'

Carla nodded. 'I expect it does. In the end, Dad insisted I took whatever I wanted but...' she shrugged. 'New things for a new beginning, but I've always loved that painting. Now for upstairs. I've put you in the large bedroom overlooking the pool.'

'Wow,' Maddy said as Carla pushed open the bedroom door. 'Just wow.'

'I'll leave you to freshen up. Lunch on the terrace in ten minutes okay?' And Carla turned and went back downstairs to finish putting lunch on the table.

When Maddy and Sam came downstairs, Carla was in her bedroom fetching her sun hat.

'You said this is another bedroom?' Maddy asked, about to open the door to Joel's room.

'Yes, but you can't go in there – it's Joel's room.'

Shocked, Maddy turned to look at her. 'Joel?'

'He's my gardener and pool boy. He needed somewhere to stay when his landlord gave him notice.'

Maddy was looking at her wide-eyed.

'Josette has known him years, so it's not like a stranger renting the room.' Although, as she said it, Carla realised she'd never got round to discussing the question of rent with Joel. But then, neither had she paid him for all the extra work he did in the garden and keeping the pool clean. She'd talk to him after the weekend, she decided, sort it out. 'It's only temporary anyway, until he finds somewhere else,' she added. 'Come on, let's find Sam. Sam, are you happy with wine – or would you prefer a cold beer?'

'Rosé will be fine. Oh, you've got a cat,' Sam said.

'You're not allergic are you?'

Sam shook his head.

'In that case meet kitten-cat who is in need of a proper name if you have any ideas? Joel rescued him a couple of weeks ago. He seems to like you,' Carla said, watching as the cat made himself comfortable on Sam's lap.

Over lunch, the three of them caught up on their news and Carla told them about their aperitif invitation at Josette's for that evening. When Maddy excused herself for five minutes to get her iPad to show Carla some pictures, Carla turned to Sam.

'You're a good influence on my daughter. I've never seen her so happy.'

'I don't think her father thinks like that,' Sam said. 'He barely acknowledges me when we meet.'

'Don't worry about David. Maddy could be dating a royal prince and he'd still sulk,' Carla said. 'She's always been his little girl and he's convinced he knows what's best for her. He'll be fine once he realises how serious Maddy is about you.'

The three of them spent the rest of the afternoon sitting around chatting and swimming in the pool when they got too hot.

'This is just perfect,' Maddy sighed. 'I can't believe the villa is actually yours and Great Aunt Josette's.'

'Are you happy to spread the word for me then at home? Tell your friends if they want to spend a weekend in Villa Mimosa they can be my guinea pigs, maybe later this year or early next when I'm a bit more organised, and I'll give them a discount.'

'Mum, they're going to snatch your hand off with an offer like that!'

Carla glanced at her watch. 'Talking about Josette, we'd better think about showering and getting ready to go.'

Maddy looked at her. 'Mum, what's she like, this unknown great aunt of mine? Is she as scary as Granny could be at times?'

Carla shook her head and laughed. 'Definitely not. She's so different, it's hard to believe. But she's not easy to get to know. One moment I think we're getting close and the next minute, it's back to square one again. She seems keen to keep part of herself detached and private. I'm not sure why yet. So don't expect an exuberant welcome.'

* * *

An hour later, Carla was leading them along the ramparts in the direction of Josette's cottage. With the temperature still nudging twenty-nine degrees centigrade, it was a lovely summer evening and Carla enjoyed pointing out interesting places as they walked. Passing the imposing old chateau that housed the Picasso museum, she said, 'Well worth a visit – if not this time, the next time you come over.'

Further along, and before turning right down the narrow lane that led eventually to Josette's, she pointed out another landmark, the cottage on the ramparts where the writer Paul Gallico had lived.

Josette's door was on the latch and Carla called out a cheery 'Coo-Coo' as she pushed it open.

'Come on through,' Josette called.

Josette, to Carla's relief, seemed pleased to see them, greeting both her and Maddy with a hug and a smile and a handshake for Sam. Looking at Maddy and Josette happily chatting and tentatively getting to know each other, Carla began to feel optimistic that Josette would eventually relax and become the fond aunt she'd always wanted.

Josette declined the invite to return to the villa with them for supper but, as they left, admitted she was looking forward to seeing them all again on Saturday. 'I've ignored my actual birthday for years and I certainly never expected to celebrate it with family ever again,' she said, her voice breaking slightly as she hugged Carla goodbye.

Maddy was quiet walking back to the Villa Mimosa and Carla looked at her. 'You okay?'

'You were right. Josette is nothing like Granny. She's so much easier to talk to. You don't get the feeling that she's judging you all the time.'

Carla glanced at her, surprised. 'You never said you felt like that. Granny did have funny ways, but she did love you.'

'I know she did, but I'm really looking forward to getting to know Tante Josette.'

When they got back to the villa, Joel was home and executing a fast front crawl in the pool. As he climbed out and grabbed a towel to rub himself down before Carla made the introductions, Maddy whispered to Carla. 'Wow. Who's that?'

'Joel.'

Maddy looked at her. 'Really? When you said Joel was your pool boy, I wasn't expecting him to be like that! Way to go, Mum.'

'Maddy, behave. It's not like that.'

'Why not? Maybe it should be,' Maddy said. 'He looks... nice,' she finished as a smiling Joel began to make his way over to them.

'He is nice,' Carla said. 'And he's a good friend. Friend.' she repeated for good measure. 'I'm still a married woman.' Although, in a few weeks, that wouldn't be true: she'd be single and free again, a state she was determined to enjoy. The days of a woman needing a man to complete her were long gone. Although having a close, special male friend to share things with would be wonderful, she had no intention of deliberately setting out to meet anyone. If it happened, it happened. If not, she'd enjoy her new life in France and work hard to turn the villa into a successful chambre d'hôte.

22

The morning of Josette's birthday, Carla and Maddy were in the kitchen decorating the cake Carla had made ready for the birthday tea. Sam was reading down by the pool, with the cat once again curled up on his lap.

'Sam's got a fan there,' Carla said, glancing out of the window.

'Mmm,' Maddy said.

Something in the sound made Carla turn and look at her daughter. 'You all right?'

'Who'd have thought the first birthday without Granny we'd be here in France celebrating with Tante Josette instead,' Maddy said quietly, glancing at Carla as she creamed butter and sugar together for the icing. 'D'you think Granny is turning in her grave? I mean, she never had a good word to say about her twin, did she?'

'No, she didn't,' Carla admitted. 'And birthdays with her were always such hard work – I'm hoping Josette's today will be fun.'

'For twins they weren't at all alike, were they? Not just in looks. Even when Granny was being nice, there was still something. Tante Josette is much easier to be around.' Maddy said with a sideways look at Carla. 'Has she talked to you about what it was like growing up as a twin here in this house?'

Carla shook her head. 'Not really, but I do think the two of them were close as children – until they were quite grown-up actually and then the feud kicked off. I keep hoping Josette will tell me something of the family's history, but she seems determined to keep the past in the past.' Carefully, Carla smoothed the butter icing over the top of the cake before placing a 'Bon Anniversaire' in the centre and a single sparkler candle behind it. 'There. What d'you think?'

'It looks great, Mum, reminds me of the cakes you used to make Ed and me. I know I shouldn't, but I'm going to clean the icing bowl. Want some?'

'No, thank you,' and Carla watched affectionately as her daughter wiped her finger around the bowl and licked it clean. 'Going back to the thought of Granny turning in her grave – she can't. Her ashes are in my room.'

Maddy stared at her. 'You've brought them here?'

Carla shrugged. 'Nobody could decide where to scatter them at home, so I thought Granny might like to be back in France. I did think about scattering them here in the garden, but when I mentioned it to Josette she went quiet and said she'd think about it. So far she hasn't come back with a yes or a no, or any other suggestion.'

'Why not just do it without mentioning it to her?'

'I'll probably do that, although I don't want to upset Josette and I got the feeling that she's not happy with the idea of scattering Amelia in the garden. Anyway, that's a problem for another day. Now, promise me you won't mention the cake and having a birthday tea here this afternoon. I want it to be a surprise. No giving Josette time to think of an excuse for not coming back here after lunch.'

'Promise. Why are we going to Cannes anyway? Why not a restaurant in Antibes?'

Carla hesitated. 'I've seen a photo of Josette as a young woman with a man in Cannes and I think her happy memories of the place have faded over the years. I want to give her a present day, happy memory. With family.' she added.

* * *

A couple of hours later, sitting around a table in the Garden Restaurant of the Carlton Hotel, Carla picked up her wine and invited everyone to wish Josette, 'a very happy birthday'. Customers on nearby tables overheard and raised their own glasses and smiled congratulations in Josette's direction. An emotional Josette responded with tears in her eyes and a whispered 'Merci.'

Carla started in recognition as a man seated at a table nearer the window got up and began to thread his way through the restaurant towards them. She smiled and stood up to greet him.

'Bruno, how lovely to see you again. Let me introduce you to my tante, Madame Josette Rondeau, her friend Gordon, my daughter Maddy and her boyfriend Sam. I'm sorry, I don't know your full name?'

'Bruno Grimaud. Enchanté to meet you all.'

'Bruno is the man who rescued me from being knocked down on my first visit here,' Carla said. 'I suspect I owe him my life. Will you join us for a drink?'

'Merci, mais non. I must return to my guests, but I am pleased to see you again and to meet your family.'

'I'm living in Antibes now in the old family villa, so maybe we'll bump into each other again,' Carla said.

Bruno glanced at her. 'I hope so. I would like that. Enjoy the rest of your anniversaire, Madame Rondeau,' he said, smiling at Josette before turning away and rejoining his friends.

'I'm not sure you're going to be safe living down here,' Maddy said. 'All these sexy men around. First Joel and now Bruno.'

'Maddy, stop it,' Carla said. 'I've told you, I'm not interested.'

'Maybe not at the moment, but when you are, you're going to be spoilt for choice,' and Maddy, wiggled her eyebrows wickedly at her mother before picking up her wine.

It was gone three o'clock before lunch was finished and Carla asked the concierge to order their taxi. 'Now for your presents and cake back at the villa,' she said to Josette. 'No argument,' she added, holding up her hand. 'It's your day for being spoilt.'

Sitting in the taxi travelling back to Antibes, Josette stared unseeingly out of the window as the car sped along the bord de mer. How could meeting a stranger with the name Grimaud throw her thoughts into such turmoil? It was a common enough Italian name. She knew there were hundreds of Italians living along the French border. But hearing Bruno's surname had been an unexpected shock, sending a tremor through her body.

Today's birthday was turning out to be unlike any she'd experienced in the last fifty years. Carla and the others had gone to so much trouble to give her a special day, making her feel cherished as never before. How could she possibly contemplate telling Carla – and Maddy – the family secret from the past knowing without doubt it would destroy any growing feelings between them and her. But would it be better to get the true story out into the open now before they all got too close?

'Earth to Josette. Are you listening to me?' Gordon said, gently nudging her.

'Sorry, I was thinking about something I should maybe do and can't decide when would be the best time, if I do decide to do it. What did I miss?'

'I was just explaining about your birthday present. You have to wait until Tuesday when you and I have a lunch date and afterwards you will have your present, okay?'

'Gordon, you don't have to give me anything,' Josette said. 'Lunch, though, would be lovely.'

'I get the feeling you haven't had much spoiling in your life,' Gordon said quietly. 'And I, for one, am happy to indulge you,' and he picked up her hand and held it tightly for the rest of the journey.

Josette smiled at him before turning to look out of the window again. Would he still be her friend when he learnt the secret of her past? Her life was in a good place at the moment, by putting the secret out into the public domain, as it were, she would be throwing herself on the mercy of others and it was impossible to anticipate their reactions. It was painful to contemplate being cast aside again.

'D'you truly think living in the moment is the right thing

to do? Or at least try to do?' she asked, suddenly turning to face him. 'What if it causes problems? What if...?

'Honesty is the best policy has always been my motto,' Gordon said. 'It's easier to go forward and build trust when things are based on truth rather than lies.'

'Is that what living in the moment means to you? Living an honest open life?'

Gordon nodded. 'That's what I believe it boils down to.'

Josette leant back against the leather of the taxi seat. 'I wish I had your confidence about that.'

Silently, Gordon squeezed her hand.

Once back at the villa, Carla shooed everyone out onto the terrace while she and Maddy organised the birthday cake and opened the champagne. As they appeared carrying the cake with its lit sparkler, Josette clapped her hands in delight.

'I'm being really spoiled today,' she said. 'Carla, I can't thank you enough.' Josette looked at Carla and Maddy, her family, trying to keep the tears at bay. Was this the right time to break her silence? Perhaps it would be better to wait until she was alone with Carla. Tell her the truth privately.

Suddenly her feelings and Gordon's words in the taxi rushed to the front of her mind. Honesty should be king. She needed to break her pact and tell the secret. Only then would she be free to live a mindful life in the present. She took a deep breath.

'Bien. Gordon has been encouraging me to forget the past and to live in the moment.'

Everyone turned at her words and looked at her.

'I have decided the time has come for me to be brave and tell you a family secret. And to pray for your understanding. But, first, could I please have another glass to boost my courage?' Josette held out her empty champagne flute. 'Have you got that packet of family photographs handy?' she asked Carla, as Sam poured her drink.

Carla fetched the packet from her bedroom and handed it to Josette, who began to riffle through the contents.

'The picture I need you to look at again is... this one,' and Josette pulled it out and handed it to Carla.

'It's me as a baby in my pram here in the garden, with Mum, Dad and Grandmother watching me,' Carla said. 'I don't understand?'

Josette shook her head. 'Non. The baby in the pram isn't you. It's your brother. Robert junior. Always called Bobby.'

'That's ridiculous! I don't have a brother,' Carla said, staring first at the photograph and then looking up at her aunt, puzzled.

Josette held her gaze. 'You did. Amelia was pregnant when she married your father. C'était un mariage de fusil de chasse. In England, I think you would call it a shotgun wedding.'

'So where is he now? This brother of mine?' Carla asked.

There was a short silence before Josette spoke.

'Bobby died just after his second birthday.'

Carla stared at the photograph again. 'Why did neither of them ever tell me about him?'

'I don't know the answer to that, I'm afraid. What I do know is they both adored him and his loss hit them badly. Neither of them could bear to even mention his name.'

'Why did he die? Was he ill? An accident?'

'Meningitis. Amelia blamed herself for not getting him to a doctor quickly enough. She had a breakdown over it.' Josette said.

'Something else I was never told about,' Carla said. 'How long after he died before I was born?'

'I think it was just over a year,' Josette said. 'Your birth changed everyone's lives.'

'How?'

Josette looked away before taking a deep breath to try and stop her voice from trembling. She felt Gordon's hand reach for hers and held it tightly.

'That's the really difficult and important part of the secret I need to tell you. Amelia was not your mother.' Her words fell into a stunned silence that lasted, it seemed to Josette, for an eternity.

It was a wide-eyed Carla who looked at Josette and spoke first. 'Of course she was. Dad would never...' She stopped as she registered the look on Josette's face. 'Oh my god. It's you, isn't it?'

Josette bit her bottom lip as she gave Carla a brief nod. 'Yes. I'm... I'm your mother – not your aunt.'

There, she'd finally got some of the truth out where it belonged. What would happen now, she didn't dare to think. Looking out at the sea of shocked faces, Josette worried she'd let too much wine go to her head and had made a grave error in telling the truth. She knew from the look on Carla's face that they wouldn't be playing Happy Families again for quite some time.

23

'I think I'll make a cup of tea. You two want one?' Carla said, looking at Maddy and Sam. A brief nod from both of them and she stood up and made her way to the kitchen. Shock had kept the three of them sitting in silence on the terrace when an agitated Josette had stood up saying, 'I'm sorry. I think I'd better go. Thank you for today.' Gordon had quietly said his goodbyes, taken her by the hand and left with her.

Carla had never felt less like tea, but she had to do something grounding to reassure herself she had a normal life when it felt like her whole world had fallen apart. Maddy too, she could tell, was struggling to take in the enormity of what she'd been told.

The day had been going so well until Josette had decided her birthday tea was the right time to break the silence of the past. Why had she done it today? The ramifications of admitting her true status in the family would taint her birthday for evermore.

Joel walked into the kitchen as she lifted the kettle to pour the boiling water and Carla glanced at him.

'You're looking serious.'

Joel hesitated. 'I was about to join you on the terrace when Josette dropped her little bombshell. I'm sorry, I couldn't help overhearing.'

'Not sure that "little bombshell" is the right description. More akin to a nuclear explosion,' Carla said, sighing. 'We're being very British and having a cup of tea. Want to join us? There's cake as well.' Carla placed four mugs, plates, knife, milk and sugar on a tray as she sensed Joel's reluctance to intrude. 'Please do join us,' she said quietly as Joel hesitated. 'I'd really appreciate it. We can pretend then it's still a normal Saturday afternoon down on the Riviera.'

Joel took the tray from her and carried it out to the terrace table. The sparkler had burnt itself out and somebody had removed it from the cake and placed it to one side.

Carefully, Carla cut four slices and handed them round, praying as she did so that somebody would say something and break the awkward silence that hung in the air. When nobody did, she gave a strangled laugh and said. 'Well, at least you've been spared my out of tune rendition of "Happy Birthday", so that's something to be thankful for.'

'Mum, do you believe Josette?' Maddy asked quietly. 'It seems such a big lie to have been covered up for half a century.'

Carla sighed and nodded. 'Well, we've always known there had to be some big reason for the feud for it to last so long, and Mum, sorry Amelia, would never talk to or about Josette, so yes, I do believe her.'

'I suppose, too, once your grandparents had died there was no one else to talk to about it,' Sam said thoughtfully.

'There was always me! But none of them seemed to have

ever considered it important enough for me or my family to know the truth,' Carla said.

'D'you think Granny Amelia found she couldn't have any more children after the baby died and Josette offered to be a surrogate?' Maddy twisted her mouth in concentration. 'But then why hide the truth from you – and refuse to speak or see her? Oh!'

'I hope you're not thinking what I think you are,' Carla said sharply. 'Because your grandfather would never...' but Maddy interrupted her.

'Maybe Josette had an affair with Grampa, became pregnant and when she said she was going to get rid of the baby, he implored her to let him and Amelia have the baby to raise.'

Having played with her slice of cake rather than eaten it, Carla now pushed the resulting crumbs around the plate. 'I have no idea what happened. I do know that I'm going to have to confront Josette and ask her to talk to me about the past and tell me the whole truth – as much as I dread hearing the details.'

'Whatever Josette tells you will be one side of the story,' Maddy said. 'It's too late now to talk to anyone else about it and get their version of what happened.'

'One sided or not, it won't alter the truth about my parentage,' Carla answered. 'But it will hopefully explain a...' she hesitated. 'A few things I've wondered about in the past.'

Maddy looked at her, but Carla shook her head.

'I need to talk to Josette about my parents' relationship. Get her to explain a few things I noticed down the years – if she can, of course.'

'Probably more than you want to know,' Maddy said,

standing up. 'I'm going to change and have a swim. Need some exercise to clear my head.'

Sam stood up too. 'I'm going to investigate the Irish bar I saw earlier.' He glanced at Joel. 'Fancy joining me for a drink?'

'Sounds like a plan,' Joel said.

'Supper at about seven,' Carla told them. 'You're invited too, Joel.'

Sitting alone on the terrace after the two men had left and watching Maddy's furious front crawl pounding length after length in the pool, Carla's thoughts naturally centred around Josette's thunderbolt announcement. An announcement that begged the question, if Josette was her mother, who was her father? Was Maddy right with her surrogate theory? Or had she been born as a result of her father and Josette having an affair? Something she found impossible to believe. Tiredly Carla buried her face in her hands and took a deep breath. Josette couldn't drop a bombshell like she had and not expect more questions to be asked. Questions that Carla needed the answers to, even if she dreaded hearing them.

As for Josette, would the acknowledgement of their mother–daughter relationship today, destroy forever the easy comradeship that Carla had hoped and believed had been beginning to develop between them when they'd merely been aunt and niece? More to the point, did she still want to get to know Josette better? What if there were still untold secrets to be discovered?

* * *

Josette was unable to stop the violent shaking that overtook her body as she left the villa. Ignoring her protests that she was fine and just wanted to go home, Gordon took her to his apartment. 'It's about time you saw where I live,' he said. 'I warn you, there are a few stairs involved.'

Gordon's top floor apartment was in one of the four storey houses situated in the old town with a view out over the Mediterranean. As Gordon led her through to the rooftop terrace, Josette ran her hand along the white grand piano that dominated the apartment.

'Do you write your music on this? Getting it up the stairs must have been a nightmare!'

Gordon nodded. 'I do. And it was. Had to come in through the window in the end. I had a lot of apologising to do the next day for the crane blocking the road for so long. Cost me a fortune in chocolates and wine for everybody. Even now I'm extra polite to the local gendarmes.'

While Gordon poured her the small medicinal brandy he insisted she needed, Josette stood on the rooftop terrace getting her breath back after the climb and taking in the view right across the bay to the distant mountains behind Nice.

'It's a lovely apartment. I thought you might live in one of the modern complexes by the marina,' Josette said.

Gordon shook his head. 'All glass and elevators? Not for me.'

Handing her the drink, Gordon watched and waited as she sipped it and the shaking calmed before stopping altogether.

Josette managed a smile and a quiet 'Thank you.'

'You're not going to forget today's birthday in a hurry, are you?' Gordon said.

'It's definitely one of the most memorable I've ever had,' Josette agreed with a wry smile. 'I don't know what possessed me to blurt out the truth today. I'd had such a lovely time with you all in Cannes, being thoroughly spoiled. You talking about honesty in the taxi got me thinking – not that I'm blaming you for anything of course,' she added quickly, looking at him. 'It's just that I realised I wanted a chance to forgive myself for the past and for Carla to know the truth so that we could go forward to an honest, open future together.' She finished the last of her drink before saying, 'But blurting out the truth like I did will not have helped to achieve that. In fact, right at this moment I wouldn't mind betting she hates me.'

'I think right now her mind will be going round and round with several emotions. Love. Anger. Hate. You do realise she's going to want the answers to lots of questions she's bound to ask you?'

Josette nodded. 'I also know the answers to those questions are likely to raise even more difficult, hurtful ones. I'm going to have to dig deep to find the courage to talk to Carla and pray she'll forgive me.'

'I expect Maddy will also want to talk to her grandmother,' Gordon said, looking at her.

Josette sighed. 'What have I done? Talk about Pandora's box. I don't want to be cast as the outsider again.'

'I can understand that. May I ask you a question?'

Josette nodded. 'Bien sûr.'

'You went white and very quiet when Carla introduced Bruno Grimaud. I was wondering why?'

Josette, surprised he'd registered her reaction, hesitated before answering. 'The Grimaud name was very common down here when I was growing up, you rarely hear it now. I suspect the older generation have died out and most of the young people have moved away for work. Hearing it was a shock – it brought back more memories of the past.'

'Good ones or bad ones?'

'Oh, you know what teenage memories are like – a real mixture,' Josette said, hoping that Gordon wouldn't probe any further.

Gordon nodded. 'I do. Now, how do you feel about going to the cinema this evening and then coming back here for supper?'

Josette, about to protest that she'd rather go home and be alone to think about things, changed her mind. She didn't really want to be alone with her thoughts. It was still her birthday, a visit to the cinema would be a treat and she enjoyed Gordon's company.

'Supper out here under the stars?'

'If you want.'

'Sounds like the perfect end to my birthday,' Josette said. Standing on the rooftop terrace looking out to sea as Gordon placed his arm around her shoulders and gave her a reassuring squeeze, Josette sighed. Although the last few hours could never be undone and there would be repercussions, both known and unforeseen, from telling Carla and Maddy the truth, her heart felt strangely lighter. This time she wouldn't be banished as punishment. This time she would stand and face the music.

24

After waving goodbye to Maddy and Sam the next day as they left to catch an evening flight home from Nice, Carla felt her spirits plummeting. What a weekend it had turned out to be. She and Maddy had talked and talked about Josette and the situation they found themselves in. Maddy, still in a daze about the news, had wanted to go round and see Josette and learn more details, but Carla had persuaded her to leave it until her next visit.

'I'll have spoken to Josette by then and hopefully have more of an idea as to what happened,' she'd said.

While Maddy was dazed by the revelations, Carla was stunned and angry. Her whole life she'd been living a lie, believing she was her parents' true daughter. To discover she was Josette's illegitimate daughter – because however you looked at it, that's what she was – had blown her mind. No wonder Amelia had conspired to keep them apart. Or was that Josette's doing? She'd always fought against them having close contact with that 'if it's an emergency' attitude of hers.

There were so many unanswered questions about the

past, her childhood and what, in her own mind, she'd begun to call her false life as a dutiful daughter, that Carla didn't know where to start. Before she went to see Josette she'd have to make a list of questions. Tick them off one by one. Not that she was up to facing Josette yet despite promising Maddy she would go and see her soon.

When her mobile rang, Carla merely glanced at the caller ID, expecting to see David's number. He'd taken to ringing her on a Sunday evening and she'd taken to ignoring it. To her surprise it was Ed. Carla smothered a sigh. Clearly, Maddy had phoned her brother with the news. Carla herself had been hoping to wait until she'd sorted things out in her own mind before telephoning her son.

'What's going on, Mum? I got some garbled version from Mads about Granny not being granny.'

'Yes, that's right. Seemingly Tante Josette is your granny. I'm sorry you had to find out this way. It's been a bit of a shock to Maddy and me,' Carla said before taking a deep breath and telling Ed what little she knew about the family drama that had unfolded. 'I'll be able to tell you more when you come home,' she said. 'I'll have more details from Josette by then.'

Typical of Ed, he was more concerned with how she was than hearing about ancient family rifts. 'Must have been one hell of a shock for you,' he said. 'Is Josette going gaga, blurting it out at the party? She could have at least told you in private.'

'Josette is most definitely in full control of all her faculties, but several glasses of champagne possibly had something to do with the timing of the revelation,' Carla said. 'Tell me your news. Are you still enjoying life over there?'

'Yes, but I'm looking forward to coming home, although

with you and Dad divorcing I'm not sure where I'll be based for a bit.'

'Dad's kept the house, so your room is still there. I know he'll welcome you as usual,' Carla said quietly. 'And, of course, you're more than welcome here at the Villa Mimosa.'

'Mads says it's a real South of France villa. I can't wait to see it, which will definitely be sometime this year.'

After a few more minutes' conversation centred around Ed's work and how much he was enjoying being a locum in South Africa, it was time to say goodbye.

'Don't worry too much about the Josette situation. Probably be a nine day wonder and then fade into the background of our family history. Look after yourself Mum,' Ed said.

'You too, Love you,' Carla said, knowing she could get away with being a bit soppy over the phone. 'Thanks for phoning.'

Carla wandered out through the sitting room to the terrace and sat looking out over the garden. Was Ed right, that discovering her family was not the traditional homogenous one she'd believe it to be, would be a mere nine days' wonder? She supposed, in time, it would stop dominating her thoughts and she'd come to terms with it, simply because there was nothing she could do to change things. But there was an awful lot of talking to be done before that happened.

Joel emerged from his room, towel in hand, ready to for his evening swim. He hesitated, looking at her, before saying, 'Exercise is good for clearing the head. Perhaps you swim too?'

Carla shook her head. 'Not tonight.'

Joel shrugged. 'Okay.'

Carla watched as he walked to the far end of the pool and

dived in smoothly with barely a splash before coming up to the surface halfway down the pool and swimming to the end. She didn't feel like swimming, but Joel's company for supper would be good.

As Joel climbed out of the water ten minutes later, Carla stood up. 'Join me for supper tonight? Nothing fancy. Something with sauté potatoes because I feel like comfort food.'

'Thank you. I'll be about five minutes,' Joel said.

Carla peeled some potatoes and set them to boil before looking in the fridge for inspiration. She pulled out some lettuce, rocket leaves, tomatoes and olives. That was the healthy bit sorted. She found a tray of coquilles Saint-Jacques in the freezer and switched the oven on ready to pop them in as she sautéd the potatoes.

Five minutes later as she strained the potatoes, her hand slipped and she splashed boiling water over a couple of her fingers. Joel heard her anguished cry as he came into the kitchen, took in what she'd done and ran out, saying, 'Hold your hand under running cold water until I get back.'

Seconds later he was back with a broken cactus-like leaf. After gently drying her hand with some kitchen paper, he cut the leaf open and spread the cooling pulp over her hand.

'What is it?' Carla asked.

'Aloe vera – you know, that large plant down by the plumbago. If you're going to make a habit of burning yourself, I'll pot you up a small one to keep on the kitchen windowsill. Good for sunburn as well. Feel better?'

Carla nodded. 'Thanks.'

'Shall I cut the potatoes into sauté-sized pieces and pop them in the pan?' Joel said.

'Thanks.'

Once the coquilles Saint-Jacques were in the oven and the

potatoes were in the pan sautéing, Carla set the buzzer and they both went out onto the terrace with a glass of wine while supper finished cooking.

'Maddy and Sam get off all right today?' Joel asked.

'Yes. They're promising to return within a couple of weeks. Mainly because I think Maddy wants to talk to Josette.' Carla sighed. 'I have to say, she is keener than me. I know I have to but...' her voice trailed away and she shook her head.

'You will 'ave a lot of things you want to say, and ask, Josette,' Joel said. 'For what it's worth, my advice is don't rush things while you're still feeling so emotional. Better to talk when you've got used to, and accepted, the fact that you and Josette are related in a way you never imagined.'

'Right now acceptance is a long way off,' Carla said. 'I've got so many questions that need answering.'

Joel was silent for a few seconds. 'It might 'elp to remember that women's rights in France were a long time coming. They didn't get the vote until 1944 – twenty years after England. Even in the late sixties, women were still very much at the mercy of their families – particularly their papas. Which means that probablement Josette was not given a lot of choice in 'ow her pregnancy was dealt with.'

'I can understand that, but what I can't get my head around is why wasn't I told the truth after my grandparents died or when I was eighteen?' Before Joel could answer, Carla stood up. 'That's enough of my problems for now. Let's see how supper is doing. Have you seen kitten-cat today by the way?'

Joel pointed in the direction of the cherry tree. 'He likes to hide up there. Probably sitting on a branch out of sight right now watching us. He's definitely un chat who likes to climb and be le roi of all he surveys!'

'Le roi means king doesn't it?' Carla said thoughtfully.

Joel looked at her, startled. 'Oui.'

'We could call him king, but it sounds too English,' Carla said. 'But I think the name Leroy will be perfect. Yes?'

Joel burst out laughing. 'Je adore your pronunciation! Leroy it is.'

25

When Josette phoned Gordon to cancel her Tuesday lunch with him, he refused to let her.

'And leave you to wallow at home? No. Besides, I've told you, I have organised your birthday present for afterwards.'

'I'm not exactly good company at the moment, I warn you,' Josette said, wincing inwardly at the memory of her birthday.

'I'll risk it,' Gordon said. 'I'll pick you up at twelve thirty. Wear sensible shoes.'

Too tired to argue, Josette had given in. Since her birthday she'd barely slept. Even when Gordon had escorted her home exhausted at one o'clock on Sunday morning after the cinema and supper on his rooftop terrace, she'd not slept. Last night, she had tossed and turned, going over and over things in her mind until she heard the sounds of the town waking up as the sun rose and then she'd perversely fallen asleep, only to be woken a mere hour later by the strident boom of the town hall clock at seven.

As the night-time hours dragged by, Josette berated

herself for even thinking about breaking the pact she'd made all those years ago. She should have taken the secret to her grave like she'd always planned to. All she'd done now was ruin the good relationship she and Carla had been building as aunt and niece. She'd already realised there were uncontrollable consequences of her action which were going to reverberate for a long time. But as she'd released the whole sordid mess out into the world, it was up to her to try and repair things. If only she could think how.

Going upstairs to get ready for lunch with Gordon, she wondered where they were going. Remembering his instruction about wearing comfortable shoes, she decided to team her favourite blue capri trousers with her deck shoes and wear a white long-sleeved T-shirt. Looking at the bags under her eyes, she reached for the concealer and did her best to banish the 'Je n'ai pas dormi depuis des jours' look.

Gordon knocked the door as she rubbed some gloss into her lips and she ran downstairs.

'Will I do for whatever you've got planned?' she asked as Gordon greeted her with a kiss on each cheek.

'You're dressed perfectly, both for lunch and afterwards.'

As they walked along the bord de mer, Gordon said, 'I thought we'd have lunch on the beach. It's such a perfect day.'

Ten minutes later, sitting at table under a large parasol a metre or two away from the waves lapping the shore, Josette looked around her. Out on the horizon, the Îles de Lérins were bathed in sunlight, boats of all sizes were sailing in the bay. Overhead, hang-gliders drifted past and, higher above them, aeroplane vapour trails criss-crossed the sky. Josette sighed. She realised, in that moment, whatever the future might hold, she was glad to be living back here.

To Josette's surprise, instead of asking for a bottle of rosé to go with their food, Gordon simply ordered a glass each. 'I want us both to be fully compos mentis to enjoy the afternoon. Too much wine could take the edge off,' he explained. 'So make it last. We'll celebrate afterwards.'

'Are you going to give me a clue before whatever it is happens?' Josette said.

'Well, I'm fairly certain you're going to like what I've planned. It's something to lift you out of yourself that's for sure.' Gordon raised his glass in a mock salute.

'I like surprises normally, but I'm getting concerned about this particular one, you're being so cloak and dagger about it.' Josette said.

'Relax. We've got over an hour before our appointment.'

Three quarters of an hour later, the obligatory beach meal of mussels et frites eaten, Gordon stood up and held out his hand to Josette.

'Come on. A short walk along the beach and then it's time for your birthday treat.'

Fifty metres on, he stopped by the kiosk for boat trips out to the Îles de Lérins.

'We're having a boat trip out to the islands?' Josette queried.

'Not a boat trip as such,' Gordon said. 'But we will see the islands,' and he led her down to a boat waiting by the pontoon.

'We're not going parasailing, are we?' Josette asked, suddenly realising what the boat was. She laughed with delight when Gordon nodded. 'Oh, what fun.'

Minutes later, the pair of them were sitting on the back of the boat, pulling on life jackets and doing up numerous safety harness catches. Josette squeezed Gordon's hand as the boat engine started and they moved away from the shore into open water. As they gained speed, one of the crew let out the cable and the parachutes began to pull them up and up until they were flying high above the sea.

'I love flying and this is so good,' she said. Excitedly, she clutched Gordon's arm. 'Look. I can see Villa Mimosa. How wonderful is that.'

Gliding above the islands before the boat turned and took them back towards the coast, Josette wished she could just stay up in the sky forever – or at least until her family problems had solved themselves. Something she knew that was unlikely to happen without her helping things along. What and how, though, still eluded her.

Older people might be expected to know how to deal with things through the wisdom of age, but personally, she had no idea how to make things better between her and Carla. Hell, these days there were times when she felt as mixed up and indecisive as she'd ever done.

Sometimes being old really was the pits. Age didn't arrive complete with guaranteed common sense – especially if you'd never possessed any in the first place. This current debacle with Carla proved that point beyond any doubt. Josette sighed. She should have stayed silent, kept the secret – or died first. Because sure as hell Amelia wouldn't have spoken out.

Mentally, she shook herself. She would not spoil this birthday treat thinking negative thoughts. As the boat headed along the coast back to the pontoon, Josette gazed at the old Provençal hotel.

'When I was growing up here that place was still open. So many stories around town about the famous people who stayed there, then and in the past. Imagine the tales it could tell.'

'On my first visit to Juan-les-Pins back in the late sixties, I stayed there – think it was the year it closed. Nobody dreamt when it shut for refurbishment it would never again open,' Gordon said.

'You lucky man to have been inside. I've always wished I'd had the chance,' Josette said, turning her head to look at him. 'The late sixties was when I left. I wonder if we'd have met all those years ago if I'd stayed around.'

'Possibly,' Gordon said.

As the boat slowed and neared the pontoon, the winch on board slowly brought the two of them down until suddenly their feet were dangling in the sea, before they were safely back on board and undoing the harnesses before climbing off the boat.

'That was wonderful,' Josette said, standing on tiptoes to kiss Gordon's cheek. 'A true breath of fresh air. Thank you.'

* * *

While Josette and Gordon were floating over the coast, Carla was busy in the villa's garden. She loved pottering about, pulling up the occasional stray weed, trimming back something that was overgrowing, picking a few flowers for the sitting room. She'd checked with Joel he didn't mind her doing this and he'd laughed at her.

'Carla, it's your garden. You can do what you like.'

'I know, but you're the real gardener and do all the hard work making it look so good. I'm an amateur in comparison.'

She'd found three lovely tall terracotta pots during her last foray to the hypermarket on the edge of town and had been itching to fill them with plants. Yesterday in the market she'd bought trays of white daisy plants, trailing ivy, lavender, geraniums and a couple of passion flowers she hoped would climb over the pillar at the end of the terrace. Today she was spending the morning planting everything and trying not to think about Josette. Something that was proving impossible.

It had been three days now since her world had been shaken to the core with Josette's announcement. Days during which she'd avoided going anywhere near Josette's cottage or any of the cafes she knew she favoured around the market in case she bumped into her. She'd half expected Josette to visit or even phone, wanting to talk and tell her more. Instead, there had been silence. Maybe she was regretting letting her shameful secret be known? Perhaps she was waiting for Carla to do the contacting.

Carefully, Carla upended a plastic pot and pulled a well-grown daisy plant out and placed it in the centre of one of the tall terracotta pots, bedding it in as deep as she could. Should she make the first move? Or stay with Joel's advice about not rushing things and let her emotions cool down so she could view things rationally? If that day ever came.

Thinking about Joel, Carla smiled. She couldn't ask for a better housemate. Considerate, kind and good company, she really liked having him around. Occasionally, sitting on the terrace having had supper together, she'd catch an unguarded look of sadness on his face but he'd nodded and smiled when she'd tentatively asked if everything was all right and inevitably started to talk about something that had happened at work. She never pushed him at these times, figuring that he'd talk to her if and when he wanted to. She hoped he regarded her as a friend he could turn to, like she did him.

Placing three trailing ivies at equidistance around the daisy, Carla watered everything and moved down the terrace to the last pot placed close to the column she hoped the passion flowers would climb. As she picked up her hand trowel and the last of the compost, her glance fell on the wild bit of garden to the side of the pool house. White roses and blue daisies were even more prolific than the first time she'd seen them and thought about scattering Amelia's ashes there. It really was a lovely, quiet spot. Goodness only knew what Josette had against it.

Deep in thought, Carla planted the two passion flowers, looped them around the pillar and watered them in. There. A couple of weeks and the pots would look lovely.

After tidying up and washing her hands, Carla went into her bedroom. She smiled as she saw Leroy curled up on her bed in a patch of sunlight. 'No cherry tree this afternoon, Leroy?' she said, giving him a gentle stroke before she picked up the urn from the floor in the corner by the bed.

Out in the garden again, she surveyed the wild area. Would Amelia appreciate being scattered here? Or would she rather be a thousand miles away? Carefully, Carla trod between the roses and the daisies until she reached the hedge at the back. Picking up a stone, she scraped a flat spot and placed the urn on it, pressing it into the earth until it was standing steady. This way, Amelia's ashes could be scattered at a later date if Josette suggested another, better, place. Something else she needed to talk to her about. At least the ashes were now out of her bedroom where she'd begun to resent their almost malevolent presence.

Walking back towards the house, she remembered she hadn't checked the post box for the day's mail. Still getting used to the fact that she had a box attached to the main gate at the end of the drive rather than a letter box in the front door, she often forgot to check for post. Now, unlocking the box, she pulled out a handful of promo brochures and a letter with an Italian stamp – addressed to Madame Josette Rondeau, care of Villa Mimosa, Antibes.'

Carla sighed. Was this a sign that she had to make the first contact or just bad timing? Would Joel deliver it for her perhaps? No, she wouldn't ask him. She'd deliver it herself; she didn't have to knock and hand it over to Josette, she could just post it in the letterbox and walk away.

Idly, Carla turned the letter over, wondering who Josette knew in Italy. The 'posted from' section on the back of the envelope had been filled in with a name and a postcode. Carla frowned as she saw the name. Why was it strangely familiar?

26

Despite the rolls of film Josette had bought for her Nikon, she hadn't taken a single photograph yet. Her birthday revelation and the reactions to it had driven everything else from her mind.

Taking her camera out of its case, she couldn't believe how casually she'd given up the very thing that had always made her feel alive. For years, taking photographs had been her raison d'être as well as her living. Once upon a time she'd never left home without her camera hanging securely from a cord around her neck. Looking at things through the lens of a camera, capturing the very essence of someone on film, recording a disappearing world, the joy of taking photographs had held her captive as much as she'd captured the images she'd aimed her lens at. So why had the passion disappeared? Had age simply drained her energy and turned it into apathy?

She could still list all the reasons she'd used to convince herself it was time to stop. She was tired of finding herself in a pack of paparazzi all clamouring for that one shot which would shoot them into the big time. The constant travelling had taken its toll; staying put in one place had become increasingly attractive. It was easier too, to make way for youngsters less than half her age and their burning ambition rather than compete with them. But to give up taking photographs altogether when it had always given her such pleasure? Why had she done that when she returned to Antibes? There was no logical answer to that question. A camera in her hand had always been her life force. Nor was there any logical reason why ten minutes ago she'd fetched her camera bag from the bedroom, filled with the sudden desire to take photographs again.

Out in the courtyard, Josette held the camera up to her eye and focused the lens on a bee industriously harvesting nectar from a honeysuckle flower high on the wall. The bee buzzed away out of the flower and over the wall before she could press the shutter and capture the moment. Josette sighed with annoyance. Her fault, she'd been too slow but now she'd finally picked up her camera again, there would be plenty of opportunities.

That evening, when she and Gordon went for a stroll along the Cap d'Antibes and out to Juan-les-Pins, Josette picked up her camera as she left the cottage. There might be a chance to take a few snapshots of the sea, or the pine trees silhouetted against the night sky, something to at least reassure her she still had a good eye, remembered how to frame a photograph and knew instinctively the right second to press the shutter. Basically, she needed to discover if she still possessed the skill of making art out of the everyday. That something in her life was still reassuringly the same. If Gordon noticed she had her camera hanging from her wrist, he didn't mention it.

She'd forgotten jazz festival time was approaching, but as she and Gordon neared Juan-les-Pins, they saw the stands being erected ready for the concerts and already the atmosphere was starting to build, with amateur musicians busking on the street corners.

Josette breathed contentedly. She'd be sure to wander around here when the festival started. In the past, she'd taken photographs of so many of the stars: Dizzy Gillespie, Sarah Vaughan and, in later years, Jamie Callum and Norah Jones, to name but four. She'd even met her idol, Ella Fitzgerald, one memorable evening at an after-concert party.

'I love festival time,' she said, lifting her camera to take a photograph of a young dark girl playing bongo drums on the corner by Pinède Gould. Further along, a couple were gently crooning a duet as the man strummed a guitar. Raising her camera again, Josette said absently to Gordon as she looked through the lens, 'You've never told me what kind of music you like or the type of songs you write.'

'I like jazz and, old-fashioned it may be, swing. As for the type of stuff I write,' he shrugged. 'A couple of mine made it into the hit parade.' Gordon glanced at her, before quietly humming the melody of a well-known hit.

Josette turned to look at him, her eyes opened wide in surprise. 'Wow. That's one of yours? It's one of my favourites. It seemed to speak to me, give me hope. Those words – where there's life, there can be love – became my mantra for a long time.'

'Oh Josie, why didn't you and I meet years ago, when we were young?' Gordon said, putting his arm around her shoulders and drawing her against him for a hug.

Josette stilled in his arms at the shortened version of her name. Gordon's Scottish lilt, not unlike a certain Italian one years ago, made it sound like an endearment. An endearment she realised she liked. Despite not knowing a lot about his past, she knew her feelings for Gordon were running deep. Did his words mean he felt the same way? She looked up at him and took a deep breath. Her new living in the present philosophy might have a lot to answer for again if she got this wrong too. 'Maybe now is our right time?'

Gordon gave her an unfathomable look before smiling and taking her by the hand. 'Come on. We need to celebrate finding us.'

Josette laughed. 'Okay. Where are we going?'

'Back to my apartment, of course. There's a bottle of champagne in the fridge that will serve us very nicely.'

Josette overslept the next morning, waking to the sounds of the town hall clock striking eight. For several moments after the noise of the bells had died away, she lay there with her eyes closed remembering the delights of the previous evening.

Gordon had opened the champagne and they'd sat out on the rooftop terrace in the twilight, drinking and gently flirting with each other as they watched the moon rise. The bottle was still half full when Gordon stood up, placed his glass on the small table, held out his hand and led her to his bedroom.

Josette's lips curved into a smile as her thoughts drifted back to the rest of the night.

It had been gone three o'clock when Gordon had walked her home through the deserted streets, kissed her tenderly and said, 'See you later.'

'Would you like to come in?' Josette had asked.

Gordon had shaken his head. 'Best not. I have a breakfast meeting with someone – if I stay with you, Josie, I'll never make it.' Another kiss and he'd gone.

Fleetingly Josette wondered if his breakfast meeting was with someone she knew, before dismissing the thought. It wasn't any business of hers. Today was a good day; the beginning of new things. She had no intention of spoiling it by overthinking things. Pushing the bedcovers back, she got out of bed and made for the shower.

Ten minutes later, as she switched on the coffee machine and pushed a couple of pieces of bread into her toaster in lieu of a fresh croissant, she heard the rattle of the letterbox. She glanced at the kitchen clock. The post was coming earlier and earlier these days, but this early was a first. She'd have her coffee before she even opened the box to take the contents out, which was probably only piles of promotion leaflets and bills. She was going to sit in the courtyard, eat her breakfast and think happy thoughts. But as she took her first sip of coffee, the rift with Carla surfaced in her mind and her happy mood was torn apart.

She'd been hoping that Carla would turn up and force the issue, demanding to be told the whole sordid story, something which Josette acknowledged was her right, but even just thinking about having to say the words out loud made her feel ill. She'd give it a couple more days and if Carla hadn't called round by then, she'd have to go to the villa, tell her the full story as best she could and plead forgiveness.

As she spread some butter on her last piece of toast, Josette heard the flap on the letterbox again. It was nearer the normal time for post to be delivered so perhaps it had been the wind earlier blowing the flap. She got up and made her way to collect the post. As expected, she found a pile of promo leaflets, but underneath them was an envelope addressed to her at the villa. Josette's heart sank a little as she realised Carla had obviously delivered it without bothering to knock and give it to her personally. Clearly, she still wasn't ready to talk.

Josette, glancing at the Italian postmark on the envelope, gasped in shock at the address written in handwriting that had once been so familiar to her and turned it over with a shaking hand. Seeing the name on the back confirmed her fears and her breath stalled. Why get in touch now? And why did she have to receive the letter on the first day in years when she felt blessed and happy, with a sense of belief bubbling up inside her that, despite her worries over the future, things would work out?

27

Earlier, standing in front of Josette's cottage, Carla had hesitated for a moment and almost knocked on the door before resolutely pushing the letter into the wall box. Despite it being nearly a week since Josette had blown her life apart with her confession, she wasn't ready to face her and demand answers. Besides, there wasn't time this morning, she needed to get back to Villa Mimosa.

On the way home, she stopped to buy croissants and three almond slices in addition to her daily baguette. Joel would have left for work, she knew, but she'd keep an almond slice for him.

Once back at the villa, Carla set the coffee up, put the croissants and a couple of the almond slices in the round bread basket and placed it, along with plates and coffee cups, on the terrace table, trying to quell her nervousness. Arranging a secret breakfast meeting, even with a friend, had such a clandestine feel.

She suspected if Josette had talked to anyone about her outburst at the birthday party, it would have been Gordon. It had been an impulsive decision to ask Gordon if she could talk to him sometime soon and he agreed but suggested an early breakfast meeting would be best if she didn't want to mention it to Josette. Whether he would talk to her this morning remained to be seen.

When Gordon arrived, Carla couldn't help remarking how well he looked. 'You've got a proper spring in your step today,' she said after they exchanged air kisses.

He gave her a smile. 'Life is good.'

Carla fetched the coffee and the two of them sat at the table.

'Your garden's looking beautiful,' Gordon said. 'How are you getting along with Joel living here?'

The unexpected question made Carla blush. 'It's fine. We get on well. I like having him here. Definitely going to miss him when he moves out.' She pushed the croissants towards Gordon. 'Not that we see that much of each other. He's always out working and when he's here he likes to potter in the garden.'

'Josette speaks highly of him,' Gordon said. 'Now, my dear, as delightful as it is to be here, I know you want to talk to me about Josette, so come on, fire away.'

'I could do with some advice,' Carla said. 'I don't know what to do. Should I go and see Josette – or wait for her to come and talk to me? I need her to tell me the whole story because sure as hell there is more to it than she's told us. I also need to know why she decided after all these years to simply baldly announce to the world the fact she's my mother, not my aunt?' She pushed her untouched croissant away. 'I'm finding it so hard to take in the enormity of what she's been hiding all these years.'

Gordon took a drink of his coffee.

'Has Josette said anything to you? Would you tell me if she had?' Carla asked. 'If she's told you things in confidence, of course I don't expect you to break that, but if there's anything you can tell me? Anything to help me understand. Have you seen her since her birthday?'

'Yes, I've seen her a couple of times.'

When Gordon didn't expand on that statement, Carla said, 'How was she?'

'Worried about the effect the news has had on you. Worried about if she's done the right thing. Worried that she's ruined any chance of building a proper relationship with you. Worried she didn't take the secret to the grave. Let's just say, she's worried.' Gordon glanced at Carla. 'She's not had much practice at being a part of a family for the last fifty years. She's very fond of you, despite not being in your life for so many years.'

'You see, that's the kind of thing I need to know. Surely she could have insisted I was told the truth when I was old enough?'

Gordon shook his head. 'I don't know. Like you say, you need to talk to her. Maybe give it another week and then if she hasn't come to see you, you'll have to be the brave one. I do know she hates the thought of being outside the family again.'

'D'you think she's ready to talk to me? To tell me about the past? A past she clearly wishes she'd left buried.'

'I think she's braced for your questions but frightened about your reaction to the answers.'

Carla sighed. 'A letter came here for Josette this week. I popped it into her box this morning. It had an Italian stamp. The family name on the back rang a bell with me, but I can't place it. I nearly knocked on the door to give it to her, but I chickened out.'

'Was the name Grimaud by any chance?' Gordon asked.

'It was.' Carla looked at Gordon in surprise. 'How did you know that?'

Gordon shrugged. 'Just a guess. It's interesting though. That's your friend Bruno's name. Apparently there were a lot of Grimauds down here years ago.'

'Of course,' Carla said. 'I'd forgotten his surname. But why would he be writing to Josette. He only met her for the first time in the Carlton.'

Gordon shrugged. 'Who knows? We'll both have to be patient on that one and wait for Josette to tell us all. Now, I must go. I have a plane to catch later.

Josette placed the letter unopened on the table and poured herself another coffee. Sitting there sipping her drink, she couldn't stop herself looking at the envelope with her name on it in bold writing, taunting her. What sort of letter would she find inside?

If it was from the person she already knew deep down it was, would it be demanding answers about her actions of over fifty years ago? Or would it be conciliatory in a 'let bygones be bygones' kind of way? Would a meeting for old times' sake be suggested?

Should she even open it? She could tear it into pieces and drop it in the rubbish. Deny ever receiving it if she had to. No, she couldn't do that. That would just be adding more lies to an already sorry life story. But she didn't have to open it. Unopened, she could live in ignorance of its contents.

Cautiously, she picked it up from the table and half rose to go and put it in the drawer, before sinking back down onto her seat. However painful it was, she had to open it.

Carefully, she peeled the flap open and drew out an expensive piece of notepaper, a name and address printed on top. The name was the one she'd been expecting, hoping, to see. Mario Grimaud. The address was one she didn't recognise. Somewhere in San Remo. It wasn't a long letter. It was direct and to the point. Like the writer himself had always been. His voice said the words in her head as she read.

Mio Caro Josie,

I barely know where to begin this letter, other than to say I'm very happy to have news of you from my nephew, Bruno. My dearest wish is for us to meet again, for me to learn something of how your life has been – I hope it has been a happy one. I've never understood why you left without a word, but I accept you must have had your reasons. Your parents refused to tell me anything and never spoke of you to me again. I kept hoping you'd return and tell me what prompted your unexpected departure. But life goes on and one learns to accept that certain things were never meant to be. What I've never truly accepted in all these years has been your absence in my life as the friend you always were, if not as the wife I'd wanted you to be. Perhaps you missed me too a little? Can we meet as friends? It would make me very happy to see the love of my life once again.

Amore, Mario. xxx

Under his signature was an Italian telephone number.

Josette placed the letter on the table and brushed away the tears that were falling down her cheeks. No recriminations, no blame, just a declaration of a love that had never died despite her cruel desertion of him all those years ago. The letter didn't tell her anything about him. Had he ever married? Did he have a family? She knew no more about his life than he did hers. Could she bear to meet him? See the man he'd become. Welcome him into her life again? Would he be disappointed in her? Could friendship alone bring a satisfactory closure to their long-ago love?

Mario's letter was stirring other memories in her, transporting her back to her youth, to the consequences of the night she'd promised to meet him but instead had been forced to run away. To memories of Robert and Amelia. Amelia. How had she ever been naive enough to expect her twin to accept and understand her action? Meeting Mario again would mean telling him the truth about why she'd left without a word. The truth that had driven a wedge again between herself and Carla, instantly joining the one that Amelia had fuelled for years.

Josette closed her eyes and took a deep breath. Would it make any real difference were Mario to learn the truth after all these years? The truth wouldn't change the effect her actions had had on both their lives. Meeting up with the man she'd left behind to avoid hurting him with her betrayal was a risk, but it would at the very least give her closure on that particular part of her past. But any meeting would have to wait until after she and Carla had talked.

Standing up and moving into the kitchen, Josette opened the dresser drawer. The original 'Private and Confidential' package Carla had brought over all those weeks ago was still on top of the bits and pieces that filled the drawer, unopened. Taking it out, Josette scrabbled around the contents of the drawer and found a rubber band. Placing Mario's letter on top of the package, she joined the two of them together with the rubber band. She would reply to Mario one day soon and agree to meet him, but not yet. The timing was all wrong.

28

The day after her breakfast meeting with Gordon, Carla found a picture postcard in her post box. Before she threw it in the kitchen bin, thinking it was a piece of junk mail she'd missed earlier in the week, she glanced at it quickly.

The picture was of the harbour in Cannes and it was simply addressed to 'Carla at the Villa Mimosa, Antibes' followed by the 06 postcode. The message was short and to the point. 'I'd love to buy you dinner one evening. Ring me if you think you'd enjoy it too. Bruno Grimaud.' His number was written clearly at the bottom.

Sitting on the terrace, Leroy on her lap, Carla thought about the postcard and its invitation. She'd never told Bruno her surname or her address. Was he the Grimaud who'd written to Josette? If so why? She did remember telling him she was living in the family villa now and had he simply assumed that something addressed to her there would reach her? And why did he want to buy her dinner?

She'd liked Bruno from the moment he'd saved her from certain injury all those months ago, but she knew nothing about him other than he lived in Cannes. He could be married for all she knew, and if that was the case there was no way she'd agree to have dinner with him. Carla's innate good manners rose to the surface. She couldn't ignore the invitation. She'd have to phone him, if only to say thank you but no thanks.

While the phone rang, Carla worried whether she should speak English or struggle with her French. Bruno solved that problem when he answered the phone in English.

'Bruno Grimaud. Can I help you?'

'This is Carla. I got your card today.'

'I was hoping you'd ring,' Bruno said. 'When can you have dinner with me?'

Carla hesitated. It seemed rude to simply launch into the questions she wanted to ask him before she agreed to his request. 'I'm not sure. Why do you want to have dinner with me?'

'Because I like you,' was the instant reply. 'Isn't that enough reason for a man to ask an attractive women out?'

Carla ignored both the compliment and the question, saying instead, 'How did you find my address?'

'Learning your aunt's name that Saturday in the Carlton made it relatively easy. I will explain more over dinner if you would like me to. Any more questions?'

'One important one. Are you married?'

'Not any more.'

Carla took a deep breath. 'Okay, I'd love to have dinner with you if we can make it somewhere in Antibes?' That way she'd be able to get home easily if it all went horribly wrong.

'Of course. Are you free this Saturday evening? I'll make a reservation and pick you up at seven thirty. And, Carla? I'm

really looking forward to the evening and getting to know
you better.'

As she said goodbye, Carla realised she was already
looking forward to Saturday and Bruno's company. It would
be interesting to hear his explanation too about how learning
Josette's name had made it easy to find her address.

* * *

Carla made a big bowl of pasta that evening and when Joel
came home they sat on the terrace eating supper together.
Joel, Carla sensed, had something on his mind as he was
quieter than usual.

'Busy day at work?' she asked as she dished him up a
large helping of pasta liberally covered with pesto sauce. She
pushed the salad bowl and the parmesan grater towards him.
'You still working out on the Cap d'Antibes?'

Joel nodded. 'Different villa, mais oui, still up there. Not
sure for how long though. Rumour has it that the company I
mainly work for is in financial trouble.' He picked up the
parmesan grater and grated some cheese over his pasta
before looking up at Carla. 'Which means it will be even
harder for me to find a permanent place to rent. They were
the main payers that proved I had a regular income big
enough to be a reliable tenant. I've got a couple of other
private clients but...' Joel shrugged.

'I know you want to find a place of your own again, but
you have a room here for however long you need it,' Carla
said.

'Merci. I don't want to impose, but I do love it here with
you.' Joel's voice was quiet, his gaze intense as it locked on her
own. 'But you're not going to want me living in your spare

room for ever – particulierement when you have your chambre d'hôte.'

'Not sure that will happen this year now,' Carla said. 'I need to talk to Josette and to come to terms with not being who I thought I was before I'll be comfortable enough in myself to be civil to complete strangers.' Blinking, she broke the gaze between them and reached for her wine glass. Was she reading more into that intense gaze and the 'love it here with you' remark than he'd intended?

'You know, years ago it wasn't uncommon for a woman to raise her sibling's child as their own, whether it was because they were illegitimate or born as part of a surrogate pact,' Joel said. 'Families stuck by each other in times of trouble.'

'But mine fell apart,' Carla protested. 'Even if that was the case in the beginning.'

'Peut être the falling out wasn't about you. There could have been different, deep seated reasons for that to happen,' Joel said. 'Don't let the knowledge that your mother is a different woman to the one who raised you tear you apart. Trust me – you are luckier than some who discover their family is not as united as they've always been led to believe.'

Carla looked at him, struck by his serious look. 'That sounds like personal experience?'

Joel nodded. 'Maybe I'll tell you about it one day. You, though, do need to talk to Josette soon.'

Carla helped herself to some more salad. 'Gordon says she's worried she's done the wrong thing in telling me, that she's alienated me forever. I need to see her and assure her she hasn't, but...' Carla shook her head. 'I have to know the truth about how exactly I was conceived before I can think about even being just friends with her again.' She looked at Joel. 'Sadly, I don't think there is a quick fix to this situation.'

29

Joel was in the sitting room when Carla came out of her room on Saturday evening. She'd dithered over what to wear for dinner with Bruno. In the end she decided on a creamy coloured summer dress printed with blue cornflowers, a scooped neckline, and a hanky point skirt. Wedged espadrilles on her feet and a blue bolero in case it turned chilly completed her outfit. She hoped she was dressed suitably for wherever Bruno was taking her.

The look Joel gave her as she walked into the sitting room was unexpected, as were his words.

'You look lovely,' he said. 'Going somewhere nice?'

'Hope so. I'm having dinner with Bruno.' When Joel looked at her blankly, Carla realised he didn't know who Bruno was and quickly explained. 'He's the man who pulled me out of the way of a car in Antibes. We bumped into him in Cannes the day of the disastrous birthday lunch. I'm not sure where we'll be going. Oh, he's here. I'll see you later. Enjoy your evening.' And Carla went out to greet Bruno.

'I know you said dinner in Antibes,' Bruno said, opening

the passenger door of the silver Jaguar convertible he'd parked in the driveway. 'I hope that includes the outskirts of town? I've booked a table at one of my favourite restaurants in Juan-les-Pins.'

Carla, sliding into the passenger seat, managed to nod. Bruno's car was a serious top-of-the-range model and as they drove westward along the bord de mer, she had this feeling she knew exactly to which particular restaurant he was taking her. One of the most prestigious in the area, it was a favourite with the A-listers who crowded into the area for summer. As Bruno drew up outside and the valet opened her door, she took a deep breath and tried to squash the intimidated feeling welling up inside her. She wasn't used to places like this. Although Bruno clearly was.

Giving the keys to the valet to park the car, Bruno took her by the hand and ushered her inside. The maître d' greeted him by name and led them directly to a window table. Carla looked around her with interest. Still early evening, the place was half empty, but Carla was sure she recognised a couple of famous faces at a nearby table.

'You're very quiet,' Bruno said. 'Are you all right?'

'When you asked me to have dinner with you, I wasn't expecting to be taken to a Michelin starred restaurant,' Carla said. 'Or to arrive in such a luxurious car.' She smiled at him, anxious to show him she was happy. 'You're spoiling me.'

The sommelier arrived then, poured two glasses of champagne and discreetly left them. Bruno raised his glass to her. 'To new friends.'

'To new friends,' Carla echoed before taking a sip of the ice-cold drink. Could she and Bruno really be friends? The Jaguar he drove was the kind of car Carla could only imagine owning in her wildest dreams. And this restaurant? It was so obvious that he was completely at home here, whereas she, well, she almost pinched herself when a well-known French singer and his young companion were shown to a table near them. This place was a world away from her normal life. Would their different backgrounds prove to be a barrier to friendship?

She took another sip before placing her champagne glass on the table and looking at Bruno. Time to get a grip.

'You were going to explain how you found my address so easily?'

'Meeting your aunt at the Carlton was the big clue.'

Carla waited while Bruno looked at his glass reflectively, as though weighing up his words before saying, 'You should have received a letter addressed to Josette, care of the villa, last week.'

Carla nodded. 'Yes. I... took it around to her cottage.' No point in telling him that she and Josette weren't currently talking. 'I noticed the name on the back of the envelope was Grimaud. Was the letter from you?'

'No, but your aunt has always had a shadowy presence in my life. When you said her name as you introduced us that day, I was stunned. I could barely believe I was actually shaking the hand of the woman whom my family talk about with sadness. And, it also gave me a dilemma, deciding what to do about it.'

'Why?'

'I had to decide whether to tell my family that I'd met Josette. That she'd returned to Antibes. I was afraid the news would upset people – particularly my uncle. In the end I spoke to my father about it and we decided I had to tell everyone.' Bruno shrugged. 'There's unfinished business between our two families.'

Carla looked at him. 'That sentence, coming from someone with Italian connections, is worrying.'

Bruno looked at her, puzzled, before realising what she meant and laughing. 'I promise you we're not the mafia.' He took a drink of his champagne before continuing. 'The letter you delivered to Josette was from my uncle Mario. Fifty years ago, your aunt and my uncle were expected by everyone to marry, they were inseparable, but then Josette simply disappeared from his life without saying goodbye. Her family cruelly told him she'd left Antibes for a new life and nothing else. All these years later, Mario longs to know the truth about what happened.'

Carla looked at him with a growing sense of unease creeping through her body. Was her birth responsible for tearing another family apart?

'But so far, Josette, she has not replied. Maybe you could persuade her to write?' Bruno said. 'It would mean a lot to my uncle to know the truth, even at this late stage.'

Carla was thankful the waiter arrived with their starters at that moment, sparing her the need to answer Bruno. How could she tell him that she suspected she was the reason his uncle's life had been shattered all those years ago? She smothered an inward sigh, acknowledging what she couldn't put off any longer. Tomorrow she would go and talk to Josette.

She came to with a start as Bruno's hand covered hers on the table and he asked anxiously. 'Carla? Are you well? You've gone very pale.'

Carla managed a reassuring smile. 'Not sure why because I'm fine. This looks delicious,' she said, looking at her starter of scallops in a rich creamy sauce and picking up her cutlery.

Bruno studied her for a few seconds before saying, 'Bon

appétit,' and doing the same. For a few moments they both ate their food in silence before Bruno said, 'Now you know how I found you, can I assure you it wasn't just because of the connection between your aunt and my uncle that I wanted to see you again. I'd like us to be friends.'

Carla smiled at him. 'I think we are already are, aren't we?' She kept the thought, *even if we do inhabit vastly different worlds*, to herself. Bruno was excellent company and she was enjoying her glimpse into his privileged world.

By the end of the evening, she'd managed to put all thoughts of Josette and the impending conversation about family dynamics out of her mind.

After the meal, Bruno suggested a walk along the beach. When he reached for her hand as they strolled along, Carla happily left her hand entwined with his. It was nearing midnight before he drove her home and parked in the driveway under the main outside light that Joel had thought-fully left switched on.

'Thank you for a lovely evening,' she said.

'My pleasure. We will do it again soon,' Bruno said. 'Next week?'

Carla smiled as she shook her head. 'I'm a bit busy next week. I'm planning a small party soon – maybe you'd like to come? I'll phone you nearer the date, shall I?'

He leant across and kissed her cheek. 'I look forward to it.'

As she went indoors Carla heard Joel's bedroom door closing. He was normally in bed by ten because of early starts. Had he been waiting up for her to be safely home? If so, why hadn't he called out goodnight?

30

Carla wandered through the market a day later, trying to get her thoughts and the questions she needed to ask Josette into some sort of order. And trying to convince herself that today was a good day to go and talk to her.

Not yet eight o'clock, the market was quiet with some stallholders still setting up. Carla bought a couple of pains au chocolat and croissants from the boulangerie for breakfast as Josette would hopefully offer her coffee. Near the boulangerie, the florist was busy unloading her van of flowers bought earlier from the large Nice flower market along the coast. Carla stood watching for a moment as lots of different coloured roses, lilies, daisies, freesias and sunflowers were grouped together on the trestle table. Sunflowers. One of Josette's favourite flowers.

Five minutes later, Carla was standing in front of Josette's front door, clutching a bunch of sunflowers and waiting with trepidation for her knock to be answered. As the door opened, Carla thrust the flowers towards Josette. 'These are for you. May we talk? I've brought breakfast.'

Josette nodded. 'That would be good. Thank you for the flowers.'

'I'll put the croissants on a plate shall I, while you make coffee?' Carla said. Fetching the plates, she cast a surreptitious look at her aunt, trying to gauge the kind of mood she was in. Impossible to tell, but she could see that Josette looked tired, with bags under her eyes.

'How are you?' Carla asked quietly.

Josette shrugged her shoulders. 'Ça va. Been better. Lots on my mind.'

'Same here. I've not been sleeping well either,' Carla said.

In the deepening silence between the two of them, Josette poured the coffee and pushed a cup towards Carla. For several moments both women sat and sipped their coffee, deep in their own thoughts, neither willing to be the one to start the difficult conversation they both knew had to be faced. In the end it was Carla who took a deep breath and spoke.

'I had dinner with Bruno the other evening. He told me the letter I delivered to you last week was from his Uncle Mario, an old friend of yours apparently, hoping to catch up with you now you're back in Antibes. He was saying you hadn't replied yet?'

Startled, Josette shook her head. 'No. I will reply when... when things are sorted.'

'Would those "things" you say you want sorted include my illegitimacy?' Carla said. 'I've been in turmoil ever since your birthday. Dazed, shocked, angry, with so many questions I need answered. The obvious first question being – why break your silence of fifty years and tell me you are my mother now?'

Josette regarded her steadily. 'Because you are living here

and for the first time ever our lives are becoming entwined. And because Amelia is no longer alive to be hurt by learning the whole truth. I want our relationship to be based on honesty. I want people to know our true connection is as mother and daughter. Even if you decide, now I've told you the truth, you cannot forgive me and no longer want me in your life, I want to be able to say to people, yes, I have a daughter.'

'A daughter you got by betraying your own sister,' Carla said.

'I didn't think of it as betraying anyone. I thought I was helping my beloved sister's husband to recover after a tragedy.'

Carla caught her breath. 'So if Dad is my real father you must have had an affair with him?"

Josette nodded. 'Yes, he was your father but it only happened the once, so it wasn't an affair as such. I didn't set out to sleep with Robert. I would never ever have done that to my sister. Jamais. Besides, I was so happy with Mario. We were getting married. What I did robbed me of everything I loved. It was something that... that happened, and you were the unexpected result,' Josette sighed. Her hand shook as she picked up the coffee pot and topped up both their cups.

Carla stared at her. 'So, tell me how this unexpected affair, liaison or whatever you want to call it, happened.'

'It's a long story and one I wish I didn't have to tell you,' Josette said, taking a deep breath. 'After Bobby died, Amelia had a breakdown. Thinking it would help her to recover, Amelia came home alone for several months. Robert came over as often as he could get time off work, which wasn't often, maybe three times in six months. The pair of them were in a terrible place emotionally. Amelia could barely look

at Robert when he visited, let alone share a bed with him,'
Josette said. 'Eventually, our parents decided that it was time
for Amelia to go back to Robert and England and try to get
on with her life. Amelia protested she wasn't well enough yet,
but our parents insisted. Robert was duly summoned to come
and collect her.'

Josette was silent for a moment, remembering the
weekend that Robert had arrived to take his wife home. She'd
driven Amelia in the late evening to meet him off the last UK
flight for the day at Nice airport. She remembered how
shocked she'd been at his appearance that night. Several
weeks since his last visit, the haggard lines of sorrow on his
face were etched even deeper, his hair, unkempt and streaked
with grey, hung over his collar, while huge bags made his dull
eyes appear sunken into his face.

'Your poor husband looks terrible. I think Mama and
Papa are right – he needs you at home,' Josette had said,
turning to Amelia.

Her twin had stared at her. 'It's not me he needs, it's
Bobby. And I can't help him when that is what I need too.'

Amelia had been unable to stop herself flinching away
when Robert had leaned in for a hello kiss and he'd closed
his eyes in anguish before stepping back with a sorrowful
shake of his head.

Once in the car, both Amelia and Robert had stared
unseeingly out of opposite windows as Josette drove along
the bord de mer. Things were no better when they arrived
back at the villa. Amelia told Robert the bed in her room was
all his – she was sleeping in the spare room. For the next
twenty-four hours, Amelia and Robert were overly polite to
each other when in the parents' company, otherwise they
ignored each other.

Josette glanced across at Carla. 'It was a terrible weekend. I had a date with Mario that Saturday evening and was glad to get away from them both. It was quite late when I got home. We'd been to a party in Cannes. Walking along the upstairs landing, I saw the door to Robert's room was ajar, a feeble light coming from his bedside table. When I glanced in, Robert was standing with his back towards me looking out over the dark garden, his body wracked with shakes as he sobbed.' Agitatedly, Josette pushed her untouched croissant around the plate while Carla looked at her and waited.

It was a minute or two before Josette spoke again.

'I walked in, leant against his back and put my arms around him to hug him tightly and told him how sorry I was.' Josette closed her eyes, trying to stop the tears that were welling. 'I didn't expect him to grab me, thinking I was Amelia finally coming to comfort him.'

'He mistook you for Amelia? And you didn't tell him?'

Wearily, Josette nodded. 'I could have stopped him, pushed him away, but I took a conscious decision not to, he was a man on the edge of grief. He needed comforting.'

'You decided to comfort – to sleep with – your sister's husband because he was grieving, just like that?' Carla struggled to keep her voice neutral, to stop the incredulity she was feeling from sounding in her voice.

'I felt so sorry for him. Amelia seemed to be reaping all the sympathy over the loss of Bobby. It was like she and other people had forgotten, even ignored, the fact that Robert too, had lost his son. He was expected to keep that British stiff upper lip in place at all times. If I'd realised the consequences my action would cause, the harm it would unleash,' Josette choked back the tears. 'I thought just the once wouldn't hurt and it would help him.' She glanced at Carla. 'I do know how

naive I was before you say anything.' Josette brushed the
tears away with her hand before standing up and pushing
her chair back. 'Help yourself to more coffee if you want. I'll
be back in a moment.'

Carla, realising how upset her aunt was, nodded as
Josette disappeared indoors. Sitting there trying to analyse
the things she'd just learnt, Carla felt close to tears herself.
True, some of her questions had been answered, but the
answers had only served to raise even more questions. The
answers to the new questions were likely to be as devastating
as the previous ones. Learning and dissecting fifty year old
family history and knowing that it was unalterable didn't
make it any more acceptable or easier to bear. Carla sighed.
She was floundering in a sea of emotions that threatened to
drown her if she gave in to them.

Josette, when she returned ten minutes later, seemed
more composed. 'Shall I make some more coffee? Tea?'

Carla shook her head. 'No thanks, I'm awash with the
stuff.' She gave Josette a concerned look. 'Are you okay to
continue? Or shall I come back another time? There are still
things I need and want to know.'

When Josette nodded wearily and said. 'Let's get it over
with,' Carla took a deep breath.

'When did Dad realise you weren't Amelia?'

Josette hesitated before saying quietly, 'I think he probably knew within the first thirty seconds, but when I made no
attempt to stop him...' she shrugged her shoulders. 'But afterwards it was awkward.'

Carla looked at her and waited.

'Robert cried as he held my hand and asked me to forgive
him, saying it would never happen again, and imploring me
never to speak of what had happened to anyone. "Nobody,

especially Amelia, must ever know, it has to be our secret," he said. I promised him that not only would it never happen again, I'd never tell anyone. Of course, five weeks later when I realised I was pregnant that turned out to be a promise I couldn't keep.'

'But you did,' Carla said. 'For fifty years, you kept the secret from me. Pregnancy, though, was something you couldn't hide.'

'When I told my parents I was pregnant, they took charge. There was no way they were going to allow the fact that they had another unmarried pregnant daughter to become common knowledge and bring disgrace to the family name.' Josette fiddled with her coffee cup for a second or two before continuing.

'My parents gave me three choices. If I kept the baby, I would no longer be their daughter and I would have to find somewhere else to live. I could have an abortion,' Josette paused. 'Or I could leave immediately for England, have the child in due course and give it to Amelia and Robert to bring up as theirs.'

'They actually instigated you giving me to Mu— Amelia? Didn't you protest? Try to keep me?'

Josette shook her head. 'Back then you still did what your parents told you – particularly if you were still living in their house with their rules. Besides, how could I keep you? I had no money, nowhere to live and no prospects. Going to live with the father was a fourth suggestion at one point but...' Josette gave Carla a weary smile. 'Abortion was never a real option,' she added quietly. 'They also believed giving the baby to Amelia would help her get over Bobby's death and help her to heal. For me it became the obvious decision.'

Josette was silent for several seconds. 'I was dispatched

immediately to England, to live with Amelia and Robert, told to stay there until you were born and then I could come home if I really wanted to – but I was never to mention having had a baby to them. As far as they were concerned, you were always treated as truly Amelia's and Robert's child.'

'Did you tell them who the father was?'

'No.'

'What about Dad? He knew he was my father, didn't he?'

Josette nodded. 'Yes, and we decided together it was best never to tell anyone else. Amelia would have felt betrayed by both of us if she'd known. Initially she did promise I could tell you I was your mother "when the time was right". Sadly that time never came. She also tried on several occasions to make me tell her the father's name, but that was never going to happen,' Josette said.

'How did Amelia feel about all this in the beginning? Did she really want me? Or was it another case of the grandparents forcing her to agree?'

'I think at first Amelia did feel a bit resentful and that I was using her. But the look on her face the moment she met and held you was one of wonderment and love. She and Robert did love you – you helped them heal and become a family unit again.'

'In that case why don't I have any younger brothers and sisters?'

'Amelia couldn't have any more. Something had gone wrong at Bobby's birth. That in itself was a huge part of their problem,' Josette said. She stood up and walked over to the honeysuckle and began fiddling with a long tendril that was flapping around. 'Once you were born and handed over, I left Amelia and Robert. I did visit a few times every year and was always made welcome. They were difficult visits for me though. Made me realise what I'd given up. Every time I visited I hugged you tight, dreaming of a day in the future when I would be allowed to tell you I was your true mother. Then I'd leave on another freelance assignment – the further away from England and France, the better, for a few months. Gave me time to get myself together before the next visit. But then the year your grandmother died, it all fell apart.'

Agitatedly, Josette snapped the last few centimetres of the honeysuckle off as she glanced at Carla.

'When grandma died,' Carla said. 'I do remember Mu— Amelia being in a terrible mood with Dad when he insisted I should come to France with them. She thought I was too young and it wasn't necessary for me to attend.'

Josette nodded. 'The day of your grandmother's funeral was the day Amelia told me she wanted nothing more to do with me and banned me from contacting her or you. She broke my heart that weekend. It was the last time I saw you until we met in Paris years later. I have no idea to this day why Amelia turned on me so suddenly. Robert tried to find out, but Amelia refused to tell even him.' Josette glanced at Carla uncertainly. 'From then on, Robert kept me up to date with your life despite Amelia trying to cut all contact. Even though it was second-hand information, I heard about all the big moments in your life, birthdays, exams, wedding, the twins being born. Everything in fact a mother longs to be involved in, I was there for in spirit. I just wasn't allowed to participate – even as your aunt.'

'I wish Dad had told me he was still in touch with you – I could have written to you in secret too. I always longed to get to know you better.'

'Well, now you know the whole sorry story about how my one stupid, impulsive act changed the lives of everyone involved,' Josette said. 'How do you feel about things now? Do you still want me in your life having learnt the truth?'

'Like you said earlier, our lives are becoming more entwined,' Carla said thoughtfully. 'What you've told me today is going to take time to sink in, but at least we now have things on an honest footing. I have no idea how long it will take me to stop thinking of you as Josette, my idiosyncratic renegade aunt, and accept you as my mother instead. It's going to take months to get to know each other properly.' She gave Josette a serious look. 'The one consistent in my life story is the fact that Dad is still Dad. I just wish he was still alive and I could talk to him about everything.'

Josette reached out for her hand. 'I'm glad you finally know the truth.'

Carla squeezed the hand holding hers hard before leaning in and gently kissing Josette on the cheek. 'I'm glad too. I love living here in Antibes and having you in my life, but we do have a lot of bridges to build.'

31

Carla wandered through town in a daze after leaving Josette, trying to absorb and accept the things she'd just learned. She had no doubt that Josette regretted the way her actions of that long-ago night had changed the course of her life, but she wasn't bitter about things. She'd got on and lived her life as best she could, keeping silent about the truth of Carla's conception, the knowledge of which could only cause her twin more heartbreak.

Josette wasn't bitter, but Carla realised Amelia had been. With due cause, as Carla now knew. Losing Bobby, a beloved son, and unable to have more children was reason enough to make any woman bitter. But as a little girl she'd naturally loved her mummy without question and taken for granted the love shown her in return. Until one day she realised the love had become one-sided – Amelia had changed towards her.

She'd wanted a birthday party... it had to have been her ninth birthday, the one before her grandmother had died. Amelia had refused outright to organise one for her, telling her, however many tantrums she threw and however much she sulked, it wouldn't make any difference and there would be no more parties. Carla remembered crying to Robert, but he'd been unable to make Amelia change her mind.

On the day, he'd taken her and a friend to the zoo, followed by a pizza in town. She'd enjoyed every minute of it and had told Amelia so when she'd got home. 'I've had a lovely day with Daddy. I'm glad you didn't come with us. You'd have spoilt it.' Amelia had glared at her tight-lipped before turning away with an almost indiscernible shrug.

Looking back on it now, forty-one years later, Carla realised that particular birthday had been the turning point of her relationship with the woman she'd called Mother all her life. It was the beginning of never being able to do anything right however hard she tried and coincided with what Josette had told her about the funeral weekend.

Josette saying that Amelia had promised they would tell her the truth together when she was old enough raised the question, why had Amelia changed her mind? Josette must have been upset by her twin's behaviour towards her and hurt beyond measure, being forbidden to tell Carla the truth, as she'd been promised. Once again the position she'd found herself in must have been unbelievably hard. No wonder she'd come up with the 'emergency only' contact ploy to try and keep Carla at a distance when she longed to tell her who she really was.

Deep in her thoughts, Carla had paid no attention to where she was walking and was startled when a woman jogging bumped into her, calling out a polite 'Desolé' as she carried on without stopping. Looking around, Carla was surprised to find herself near the small cafe where she'd first met Bruno. She hadn't realised she'd come so far. Turning, she began to walk in the direction of Villa Mimosa. Time to go home and try to come to terms with the whole story of her birth.

* * *

After Carla left, Josette splashed her face with some cold water in an effort to try and calm the redness and puffiness the tears of the morning had caused. A swift glance at her watch told her if she didn't hurry she was going to be late meeting Gordon.

He'd phoned her a couple of times since their night together, checking how she was and apologising that he was having to go away for a couple of days but he'd meet her in their usual place for lunch today. Quickly, she tidied her hair back into its customary neat chignon, a quick spray of perfume and she was ready.

Gordon was already sitting at the table that was fast becoming 'their' table in the restaurant when she arrived.

'I've really missed you for the last few days,' she said, smiling at him, as he stood up to greet her with a kiss. 'I'm so glad you're back.'

'I've ordered us a couple of aperitifs. I hope that's all right? You okay?' Gordon asked. 'You look...'

'Tired? Washed out? I am a bit,' Josette admitted. 'Last week I had an unexpected letter and then, this morning, Carla came to see me.'

'Who did the letter from Italy turn out to be from?' Gordon said.

'How did you know it came from Italy?' Josette asked, certain she'd not mentioned the letter to Gordon before.

'Carla told me. She talked to me before I went away about

you being her mother – she wanted to ask if I knew more than she did. Which, of course, I don't,' he said. 'I'm glad you've talked to each other.'

'At least she knows the truth about how it happened. How easy she will find it to accept and forgive remains to be seen.' Josette sighed. 'I can only wait and hope we can build a new relationship.'

Gordon took hold of her hand. 'Sometimes the things one dreads the most turn out to be blips – large blips maybe, but blips in the scheme of things. Give it a few weeks and I'm sure you'll be surprised how far you and Carla have progressed along the mother–daughter relationship road to recovery. Together you'll find a way through.'

Josette smiled at him, grateful for his support and inwardly praying he was right. 'As for the Italian letter. It was from an old friend, Mario Grimaud. A relation of Bruno's. We lost touch years ago and he'd like to meet up. I haven't replied yet.'

'Why not?'

Josette was silent for several seconds before saying quietly, 'Because Mario is my "l'esprit d'escalier". The ghost on the stairs of my life.' She looked at Gordon. 'For the moment, at least, I think it's best if he stays there. Things are complicated enough.' She picked up a piece of bread from the basket on the table and pulled a piece off. 'I will write to him eventually. I can't be rude and ignore it. Especially as coincidentally, Carla and Bruno seem to have struck up a friendship.'

The waiter arrived at that moment with their aperitifs and to take their food order.

Once they were alone again, Josette said, 'So tell me, where did you disappear to so unexpectedly?'

'London. The agents finally found a buyer for my house there and I had to return to sign the papers, get rid of some stuff and let various friends know. All done and now France is officially my home.'

Josette raised her glass. 'In that case, congratulations and welcome to a happy and long life in France.'

Gordon touched his glass against hers. 'Vive la France.'

32

Carla realised as she put the phone down after ordering pizza for her and Joel's supper, that summer evenings at the Villa Mimosa had, without conscious effort, slipped into a comfortable routine for the two of them. It was a rare day that didn't end with them sitting out by the pool, eating supper and enjoying a nightcap together. One of them would cook supper, or order a takeaway, and they'd sit there talking until twilight, watching the occasional bat flit around the garden and the eaves of the house. Other than the May Day party with Gordon and Josette, and her dinner date with Bruno, Carla hadn't been out in the evening since she'd moved in. As for Joel, he didn't seem to have much of a social life either. Neither of them could be said to be 'living the life' on the Riviera, but Carla knew, until Josette had opened up about her past, she personally hadn't felt so happy for years.

Waiting for Joel to arrive home, Carla's thoughts were still whirling around the things Josette had told her. She knew talking things through with Joel, that his sane, common sense approach to life, would help her get things in perspective. Sitting down by the pool with Leroy on her lap, she thought about Josette coming home that fateful evening and trying to comfort Robert. Glancing up at the bedroom windows at the back of the villa, she briefly wondered which... No, she wouldn't let her thoughts dwell on that aspect of things. On a need to know basis that information was way below zero.

Joel was later than usual. He and the pizza delivery arrived at the same time. Knowing that Joel liked a swim as soon as he got home, Carla put the pizza in the warming oven and organised the glasses and plates while he did his evening routine of twenty lengths.

Twenty minutes later, as they both tucked into their supper, Carla said, 'Josette's told me more about my family history.'

Joel looked at her. 'Vraiment? I'm listening.'

'Behind the bald fact that Josette is my mother lies a multitude of hidden heartbreaks and complications. My birth tore several people's lives apart – not least Josette's,' Carla said and told Joel everything she'd learnt. 'It's a sorry tale, isn't it?' she concluded.

'It is, but it's also in the past – it will only tear your present life apart if you let it,' Joel said.

Carla chewed a piece of pizza before sighing and saying, 'I don't want my life torn apart any more than it has been lately, but I'm currently struggling with a real bag of mixed emotions, trying to accept the truth after a lifetime of being told lies.' She glanced at Joel. 'I do feel incredibly sorry for Josette, the way her life was changed so dramatically when all she intended was to give my father some comfort for what he was going through.' She pushed her plate with its unfinished pizza slice away. 'She does say that not admitting she was the wrong twin when things got out of hand was a very naive thing to do.' She picked up her wine glass and drank a mouthful. 'Which, of course, brings me to Dad's part in all this. He can't be accused of forcing Josette against her will because she didn't push him away, but he certainly wasn't innocent. Oh, I wish all this had come out years ago and I could have talked to him... to everyone involved. Heard their sides of the story.'

'It wouldn't change anything though, would it?' Joel said. 'Josette is the person at the cœur of all this and I believe she's told you honestly what 'appened that night.'

Carla sighed. 'I'm sure she has and I realise she found it hard when Amelia reneged on her promise of telling me who my true mother was, but I still find it difficult to forgive any of them for not telling me the truth years ago.'

'I think the least Josette deserves is a happy ending with her daughter,' Joel said quietly.

'What about a happy ending for me?'

'From what you've told me, I don't think the woman whom you've always regarded as your mother gave you a particularly happy childhood. Vrai?'

Carla nodded. 'True. I was closer to my father. Mum... Amelia was always telling him off for spoiling me. Now I think he just wanted me to know how much he loved me, even if Amelia didn't – or couldn't.'

Joel looked at her. 'Establishing a mother–daughter bond with Josette would give you your happy ending, n'est pas?'

Carla closed her eyes and took a deep breath. 'Yes, it would, but whilst Josette has had years and years of knowing the truth, I've only just learnt about it. These deceptions have formed the basis of my whole existence and they're going to be on my mind for some time. Moving forward, embracing the new family dynamics is going to take time.'

'Agreed, but it only will take as long as you let it,' Joel said.

Carla opened her eyes and turned to looked at him. 'Maddy will be here for a holiday at the end of the month for my birthday. That's going to be hard. I know she knows the basic fact that Josette is her grandmother, but learning how it came about and dealing with it will be hard for her.'

'Sam coming with her?'

'Hope so, I like him. I have high hopes for that relationship.'

'Spoken like a true mother,' Joel said with a grin.

The house phone rang at that moment and Carla ran indoors to answer it.

When she returned, Joel was sitting there, glass of wine in hand, lost in thought, an unfathomable expression on his face.

'You all right?' she asked.

Joel shrugged and pointed to his mobile on the table. 'Just got a text. Remember that landscaping company I told you I do a lot of work for? Finally gone bankrupt. As of now, I officially have five paying private clients. About ten less than I need to stay solvent, and twenty less if I'm ever going to make any real money and get back on my feet.'

'Oh, I'm so sorry,' Carla said. 'At least your room here is yours for as long as you want it. And if I can help in any way, just shout.'

'Merci, Carla.'

'Some of the clients left in the lurch will be looking for gardeners, won't they? Perhaps you'll be able to pick up a couple of accounts.'

'Nice thought, but most of them live either on the Cap

d'Antibes or out on Cap Ferrat where appearance is everything.'

Carla looked at him puzzled. 'Meaning?'

'Meaning that even a humble jardinier is expected to arrive in a suitable vehicle. We were always taken to jobs in one of the firm's up-to-date 4x4s which, although usually covered in earth and in need of a wash, still maintained an expensive look. My ancient van wouldn't be allowed through the gates of most of the villas.'

'That's ridiculous.'

'Maybe, but that's the way it tends to be down here. You have to at the very least give the appearance of being success-ful. It's a materialistic society where money talks.' He took a long drink. 'Maybe it's time for me to give up. Find something else to do.'

'Have you always been a gardener?'

Joel shook his head. 'Non. In another life I was an officer in the French Navy. When my final commission finished, I followed my lifelong dream of working on the land. I did a horticultural degree course as a mature student and, five years ago, I became a gardener.'

'That's quite a change of direction,' Carla said.

'C'était merveilleux. My first job was at a chateau along the coast. As one of six under-gardeners, I did a lot of weeding and trimming hedges. Which gave me a lot of time to think about the way my life was unravelling.' He looked at Carla. 'I should tell you that at the time I was married.'

'What went wrong?'

'Miranda couldn't handle the transition from being the wife of a naval officer to being the wife of a jobbing gardener. The drop in income was bad, but the loss of status was the real killer for her. She'd always wanted to live behind a set of those posh electronic gates up on Cap d'Antibes.' He looked at Carla ruefully before picking up the bottle and pouring another drink. 'The last I heard she was with an IT million-aire and enjoying life in Switzerland.'

'Did you have any children together?'

'Non, which was good as things turned out. Miranda swore she wanted them when we married, but she was always too busy and too worried about losing her figure to actually commit to having a baby. I'd have loved a family of my own. C'est la vie.'

Carla, sensing the unspoken sadness behind his words, was about to sympathise with him, when Joel spoke again.

'Was that Maddy on the phone? Keeping tabs on her mother, is she?'

'No, it was Bruno. He wanted me to have dinner with him again, but it's impossible this week – until after my birthday, in fact. I've invited him to the evening do. I don't know enough people to call it a party. Oh, maybe I should have checked with Josette first. I didn't think.'

'Josette will be fine about him coming,' Joel said. 'What date exactly is your birthday?

'The thirtieth, so make sure you keep that day free. Luck-ily, it's a Sunday.' Carla said. 'I'm planning on a family lunch – just the six of us, and then a low-key party in the evening.'

Joel looked at her. 'I'm invited to the family lunch?'

'Yes, of course,' Carla said. 'I can't imagine you not being there.' Which was the truth, she realised. 'Think of it as being my plus-one for the occasion, levelling up the numbers, if that makes you feel better,' she said, worried she was asking too much of him. 'Of course I'll understand if you've got plans, but I really hope you haven't.'

Joel burst out laughing. 'Plans? When did I last have

plans at the weekend? Non, do not answer that, s'il vous plait. If it makes you happy then I'm more than happy to be your plus-one for the day. Merci.'

Carla smiled at him. 'Good. That's settled then.'

33

The days flew by almost without Carla noticing to the end of the month and her big birthday. She was looking forward to Maddy and Sam coming over then for a holiday. She was loving her new life in France. She felt healthier, which she put down to swimming every day, walking more and mostly eating a Mediterranean diet of lots of fresh vegetables and fish. Her French was improving too, thanks to Joel. Every evening as they sat companionably on the terrace, Joel made her talk to him in French for a few moments.

Joel. He was a big part of her life these days and she really liked having him around. Telling him she couldn't imagine celebrating her birthday without him being involved had been the truth. The evenings he worked extra late for his private clients and didn't get home until nine or even ten felt lonely and empty without him there.

And despite all the family revelations from Josette, Carla felt in a good place. Far better than at the beginning of the year. Moving to France had been the right thing to do for her.

Twenty-four hours later and just an hour before Maddy

and Sam were due to arrive, Carla ticked the last item off her to-do-list. Everything was organised for the next week. The food fridge was bursting with staple food items and there were more delicacies and luxury treats on the shelves than she cared to think about. The small wine fridge was crammed full of rosé and white wine, plus several bottles of champagne. Time to relax, swim, shower and dress.

Carla swam a few lengths before clambering onto the floating sunbed. Lying there on her tummy, drifting around the pool listening to the sound of the unseen cicadas somewhere high in the trees around the garden, was sheer bliss. For some reason, a memory of last year's non-birthday came into her mind.

David had been away on a business trip. Something she'd had no right to be as happy about as she had been. The obligatory large bouquet of roses had arrived and she'd duly placed them in the ugly cut glass vase David's mother had given her on a long ago birthday and stood it on the dining room table, visible to all. The twins had both sent her cards – Maddy's with a spa voucher enclosed and Ed's wrapped up with a silk scarf.

The weather had been foul – an 'orage' the French would call it. Roads had been flooded, hailstones as big as marbles had bounced off cars and windows. The lightening during the five hour storm had been spectacular and it was late afternoon before she'd braved the last of the rain and walked to Amelia's. The air when the storm finally blew itself out was cool. Much like her reception from Amelia.

Already suffering health problems and in the early stages of Alzheimer's, Amelia had been less than welcoming. Her weekly home help would have been in yesterday, Carla knew, but already the sitting room was untidy and the kitchen work surfaces were strewn with spilt breakfast cereals, toast crumbs, plates, dirty cutlery and broken pieces of china. As her shoes had scrunched across the linoleum, Carla had realised the broken china was the remains of the sugar bowl.

'Mum, you could have swept up the sugar after you dropped the bowl,' Carla had said, sighing and getting the dustpan and brush out. 'You'll have trodden it everywhere.'

'Knew you'd do it when you got here,' Amelia had said, shrugging before pointing at the paper bag on the table. 'What's in there?'

'Two cakes for us to have with a cup of tea. As it's my birthday today, I thought we'd treat ourselves.' Carla had looked at her mother. Surely now she'd wish her happy birthday?

'Hurry up and make the tea then, I'm starving,' Amelia had said and went back into the sitting room and sat laughing at the cartoon channel on the TV.

Carla had put the cakes on plates, poured the tea into a china cup for Amelia and a mug for herself and carried it through. 'I'll just turn the sound down a bit,' she'd said, reaching for the remote.

Amelia had glared at her and picked up one of the cakes.

'You going to wish me happy birthday then, Mum?' Carla had asked.

Amelia took a bite of her cake before saying, 'No, and you're not my daughter.'

'If I'm not your daughter, who am I?'

'Don't know. Social Services?'

'Oh okay,' Carla had said. Futile to argue with Amelia.

'This cake is delicious. You should have bought me more.'

An hour later, as she left, Carla realised that the afternoon marked a turning point in both their lives. There was no way Amelia could continue to live alone. Her mind was clearly deteriorating. It was time to find a retirement home for her, which Carla acknowledged in her own mind was the beginning of the real end for her mother.

Thinking about that birthday afternoon now as she drifted around the pool on the sunbed, it struck Carla how different things were just one year later. How different she herself was.

Climbing out of the pool to shower and get ready to meet Maddy and Sam, Amelia's voice rang suddenly in her head again. 'No, you're not my daughter.' Had that been a true Alzheimer's moment? Or had a befuddled Amelia simply been stating the truth? Impossible to know, but, whatever the truth, it was all so sad.

Ten minutes after their arrival, Maddy and Sam were sitting on the terrace, Maddy with a glass of ice-cold rosé and Sam with a beer.

'It's so good to be back,' Maddy said, sighing happily. 'Can't tell you how much we've been looking forward to this holiday.' She took a sip of her wine. 'Dad been in touch?'

Carla shook her head. 'No, thank goodness. Did you tell him you were coming here?'

'Yes. He phoned and wanted to know where you were spending your birthday, so I told him.'

'How is he?'

Maddy shrugged. 'Okay, I guess. He's been working out and lost a ton of weight. I hope you and Josette have talked?' she said, changing the subject and looking at Carla.

'Yes, we've talked,' Carla said. She knew she had to tell Maddy everything Josette had told her, but she'd been hoping to put the moment off for a couple of hours at least.

'Good. You can fill me in with all the gory details later,'

Maddy said as though reading her mind. 'First I need a swim. Sam?'

'I'll join you in a bit,' Sam answered. 'Quite happy here for now.'

As Carla and Sam watched Maddy swim a few brisk lengths before turning onto her back and drifting, Carla said. 'Maddy seems to be accepting our changing family dynamics. First me and David divorcing, me moving to France, then all this business with Josette's revelation.' She turned to Sam. 'I think you being there for her has helped more than a bit. Thank you.'

Sam shrugged her words away. 'I mainly listened to her. Having divorced parents myself, I was able to understand some of what she was going through. As for Josette – I think Maddy's hoping to get to know her better this holiday – she figures she'll be a great granny. Have you seen much of Josette recently?'

'Not since she told me the story behind my birth. I think we both decided we needed some breathing space to let things sink in. I hope she and Gordon will be spending the day here on Sunday though.'

'I want to see her before then,' Maddy said. Unnoticed, she'd floated close to the side of the pool and was now holding on to the edging stones and regarding them both. 'I think we need a day out, the three of us. A spot of granny-mummy-daughter bonding.' She smiled up at Sam. 'You'd enjoy a day of mooching around Antibes by yourself, wouldn't you? Good, that's what we'll do then. We can walk round to Josette's later and organise the day. If we go to Cannes, we can indulge in a spot of retail therapy too. I'm dying to explore all the shops everyone talks about in rue d'Antibes.'

34

Josette was taken aback when she'd opened the door to find Maddy and Sam standing on her doorstep.

'Bonjour,' she said, kissing Maddy on both cheeks before turning to Sam to do the same. 'Bienvenue et entre.' She gestured for them to come in.

'Thank you, but we won't come in. I've come to invite you for a family bonding day,' Maddy had said. 'Which means, Mum, you and me going to Cannes for lunch and a spot of shopping. Please say you'll come. You can choose a day to suit you?'

'Any day,' Josette said in a daze.

'Tomorrow then. Come to the villa about ten and we'll go to the station together. Ciao,' and Maddy had grabbed Sam by the hand and left.

Now, sitting on the train as it made its way along the coast on the short journey to Cannes, Josette looked at the two women sitting opposite her and smiled. She was with her daughter and granddaughter on a family outing. Something a short time ago she would have placed money on being as likely to happen as a snow storm in Antibes in August. She leant down and took her camera out of her bag. 'May I take a quick photo of the two of you? This is such a special day for me. A day out with my daughter and granddaughter.' Before either of them could protest she looked through the viewfinder, focused and clicked. 'Thank you.' Putting the camera back in the bag, she asked, 'So, what are your plans for today?'

Maddy shrugged. 'No real plans, although rue d'Antibes is a must. And somewhere really nice for lunch – off the tourist trail if possible, where we can chat and get to know one another. You'll know the easiest route around town so you can tell us which way to go.'

'D'accord,' Josette said, having a quick think. 'We'll make for the Palais des Festivals first, a spot of window shopping in the really posh designer shops down there, a walk along the Croisette and then make for the top end of rue d'Antibes. I know a good restaurant up there. After lunch we can go shopping.'

'Sounds perfect,' Carla said. 'Come on, we're here,' she added as the train drew into the station.

The three of them wove their way down through the streets crowded with locals and tourists to the front and crossed the road to the Palais des Festivals. Maddy instantly struck a pose on the famous flight of steps and Josette took her camera out of her bag again.

'No red carpet but, hey, everybody will recognise the steps I'm standing on,' Maddy said. 'To think Chris Hemsworth was standing on these very steps a few months ago,' and she feigned a swoon.

Josette clicked away until Maddy stopped posing and they all walked across to drool at all the luxury items in the shop

windows of Chanel and Hermès, to name two of the designer
labels they could all only dream of. They'd strolled past both
the Carlton and the Martinez Hotel before Josette had them
turning left, away from the Croisette, and heading into the
back streets. Ten minutes later, Josette stopped outside a
restaurant with the most delicious aromas drifting towards
them on the air.

'Voilà! This is the place I was thinking of. There's a
secluded garden with lots of shade.'

'It looks good,' Carla said. 'And eating lunch al fresco is
obligatory down here.'

Sitting in the restaurant garden, under the shade of a
huge lime tree, an attentive wine waiter discreetly hovering
with the bottle of champagne she'd insisted on ordering,
Josette raised her glass. 'Here's to dysfunctional grandmoth-
ers, daughters, and granddaughters everywhere, but particularly to us! Santé. May this family outing be the first of many.'

Maddy took a sip before saying. 'Family names. We need
to sort out what we call you. Are you happy with Josette? I
can't get my head around Gran just yet and I'm pretty sure
Mum is going to stumble over calling you Mum for a while.'
She ignored Carla's sharp intake of breath and smiled at her
grandmother.

Josette slowly nodded. 'I'm happy with that. Now, tell me
about you and Sam. Are you in love with him? Is he about to
put a ring on your finger? Don't look at me like that, Carla, as
a grandmother I claim the right to ask embarrassing
questions.'

All the embarrassing, caring, questions she'd longed to
ask Carla down the years but was never permitted to. Would
she and Carla ever be close enough in this new family order
for them to talk to each other properly? She knew Carla was

treading on eggshells around her, but Maddy was uninhibited, openly saying things as she thought them and she appreciated that.

Josette dragged her thoughts back to the present as she heard Maddy say: 'I don't need a ring on my finger, but I definitely think he's "The One" that Mum has always insisted I'll meet,' she said. 'Even if Dad doesn't agree. Having screwed up his own marriage, it's not as if he's the expert on relationships.'

'There are two sides to everything,' Carla said quietly.

'Why are you defending him?' Maddy demanded.

'I'm not defending him. He's still your father and I don't want the fact that we're divorcing to change your relationship with him. He's always adored you.' Carla took a deep breath. 'And, to be honest, I'm not happy discussing this in front of Josette or in public.' She glanced around at the other diners.

'Josette is your mother. There are things she deserves to know about you. Like how unhappy you've been for years, how Dad cheated on you and why the family fell apart.'

'Josette already knows most of that. Can we just not discuss it in detail here please?'

'Did you know Gordon took me paragliding for my birthday treat?' Josette said, deciding a change in the conversation right now would be a good thing.

Both Carla and Maddy turned to look at her, surprise on their faces. 'Way to go,' Maddy said, smiling.

Carla looked at her in disbelief. 'But—'

'If you're about to tell me I'm too old for things like that, don't. You should have a go. It's wonderful. Invigorating and life-affirming. We're going to do it again soon.' She registered the speculative look on Maddy's face and guessed what she was thinking.

'We're just friends,' she said. 'You, young lady, can stop looking at me like that. Now, shall we order lunch?' and she picked up the menu the waiter had placed in front of her earlier.

Once lunch had been ordered and the waiter had topped up their champagne glasses, Maddy jumped up and insisted on taking a selfie of the three of them.

'I know you'll have lots of photos,' she said to Josette, 'but I want one of the three of us on my phone. A souvenir that will come everywhere with me.' Sitting back down with a happy smile on her face, she said. 'Let's talk about Sunday. Family lunch for the four of us, plus Gordon. How many for the party in the evening, Mum?'

'I've invited Joel to join us for lunch, so there will be six of us,' Carla said, ignoring the look on Maddy's face. 'For the party, and out of politeness, I've asked the neighbours on either side,' Carla turned to Josette. 'You'll know them better than me. Heléne and her husband have said they'd be delighted to come, Marcus and Joan are sailing all day but have said they'll pop in when they get back. And I've asked Bruno, so we'll be eleven.'

'Bruno Grimaud is coming?' Josette said, startled.

'I invited him when I had dinner with him the other evening,' Carla said. 'It's not a problem, is it?'

Josette shook her head. Not yet. But remembering the unanswered letter from Mario at home in the bureau drawer, she wondered whether the nephew would take the opportunity to try to champion his uncle's cause.

'Having both your boyfriends at the party could be risky,' Maddy teased.

'I've told you – Joel and Bruno are friends. Friends who happen to be male. Not my boyfriends in that way,' Carla answered. 'I like them both, but Bruno, with all his money, lives a very different life to mine. Joel is very much more down to earth. I know I'll miss him when he moves out of the villa.'

'It's a good job you don't have to introduce either of them to Dad,' Maddy said. 'You know how materialistic he is. Joel wouldn't impress him, but Bruno, especially if he's as rich as you think he is, would. It's why I'm keeping Sam away from him as much as possible,' she added quietly. 'Makes life so much easier.'

Their meals arrived at that moment and conversation stilled as they tucked into the food with appreciative sighs.

'Is there any particular kind of retail therapy you two are after when we finish here?' Josette asked. 'It's a long time since I treated myself to anything new. As well as your party, I'm going out to dinner with Gordon and his god-daughter sometime soon and feel the need to glam myself up. I'm relying on the two of you to help me buy the right dress.'

'Not sure what I'm going to buy,' Maddy said. 'But I'm sure I'll be able to justify spending a few euros.'

'I'm not intending to buy anything, so I'll be happy to help you both.' Carla said.

'Mum, that is totally the wrong attitude. The fact that it's your birthday party demands you buy a new dress with the 'wow" factor. And sexy shoes. Only too easy at your age to play it safe.' She wagged a finger at Carla.

Watching and listening to the two of them, Josette felt a tinge of envy for their easy daughter-mother relationship. Was she ever likely to achieve that with Carla? She could already feel a bond growing with Maddy. Maybe it was the skipped generation making it easier? Had Amelia had a good relationship with her granddaughter? Giggled and played games together? All the things she'd missed out on.

Josette pushed the insidious thoughts away. She wouldn't allow regret to cloud the day – or the future. Her new mantra of living in the present was the only way to cope with the changes in her life.

35

The morning of her birthday, Carla woke early and lay thinking for several moments, enjoying the tranquillity of her room in the early morning sunlight. Today she was fifty years old. She didn't feel fifty – not that she knew how fifty was meant to feel. If she was lucky, those fifty years represented half of her life and she could live to be a hundred. What could she expect from the rest of her life if she was fortunate? Probably best not to expect too much of anything and then she wouldn't be disappointed.

This time last year, life had seemed so simple. Her marriage was no great shakes, but then she suspected very few of her friends were still in the red-hot glow of romantic love after nearly twenty-five years. It had become second nature to ignore the state of things between her and David, push it into the background of her life and concentrate on caring for her mother. Knowing David's past track record for affairs, maybe she should have realised the inevitable would happen. But her reaction of running away had been totally out of character. For once in her life she'd found the courage from somewhere deep inside her to fight back. If she'd realised it was going to start a game akin to knockdown dominos with her old life, would she still have reacted in the same way?

The answer had to be a big yes. She loved everything about living in France. The weather, the food, the villa – especially the villa. It was home. She felt more alive than she had done for years and was even coming to terms with the shock of hearing Josette's confession. Maddy's idea of a day out in Cannes had certainly helped there. It had been a fun day and, by the end of it, the three of them were starting to relax around each other. Maddy, she could see, was already forming a bond with Josette, having seemingly decided her new grandmother was cool and hip.

Carla, pleased they were getting on so well, felt an unexpected tinge of sadness for Amelia. She had never been the cuddly granny, spoiling the twins with treats, with a whispered *'don't tell your mum'*. She'd never taken any nonsense from either of them, demanding good manners from them all the time. Carla guessed that Josette would be a much more laid back grandma even at this late stage and would spoil the grown-up twins in different ways at every opportunity she got.

'Mum, are you awake? I've brought you breakfast,' Maddy pushed open the bedroom door and came in carrying a tray. 'Happy birthday,' she said. 'Prosecco and croissants okay?'

'Perfect,' Carla said. 'You're spoiling me.'

As she clinked glasses with her daughter, Carla thought how lucky she was to have both Maddy and this new life she'd created for herself in France. She was adjusting to Josette's different role in her life and she had no reason to doubt that the two of them would eventually work things out between them – especially with Maddy's help. The only person missing was Ed and he'd be back in Europe sometime soon – in time for Christmas anyway.

Maddy shooed her out of the kitchen when she went downstairs after a leisurely bath. 'It's a no-go zone for you today, Mum. I'm doing lunch and organising stuff for tonight's party. Sam and Joel are in charge of the barbecue. Sam's giving me a hand right now, so there's nothing for you to do. Sit down and relax until Josette and Gordon get here for lunch.'

It felt strange sitting out on the terrace listening to the activity in her kitchen and not being involved. Maddy and Sam had given her tickets for a ballet at the Grimaldi Forum in Monaco as well as a coffee table book filled with glorious pictures of gardens in the south of France. Looking at the book now, she couldn't wait to show it to Joel. Joel. Where was he this morning? She hoped he hadn't forgotten he was invited to lunch today.

Sam appeared with a cup of coffee for her. 'She who must be obeyed sent me out with this.'

'Thanks. And thank you for the ballet tickets and this wonderful book.'

'Our pleasure. Can't stop. I've got to go and skewer chunks of lamb and cherry tomatoes ready for tonight. Your daughter can be incredibly bossy, you know.'

Carla laughed as Sam disappeared back indoors. Oh yes, bossiness was second nature to Maddy. She was surprised it had taken Sam so long to realise it.

Josette and Gordon arrived shortly afterwards. With a twinkle in her eye, Josette handed Carla an envelope. 'From Gordon and me. Joyeux anniversaire ma chérie.'

Carla opened the envelope carefully and took out a voucher for a paragliding trip for two people.

'You need to do it before you're too old,' Josette said, laughing at the expression on Carla's face. 'Trust me. You'll enjoy it.'

'Oh! You're incorrigible. Thank you.' Giving Josette a quick thank you hug, Carla couldn't help but think how different Josette's attitude to life was from Amelia's and how hard it had always been to get Amelia to laugh.

Joel was home from wherever he'd been just before lunch.

'I thought you'd forgotten about lunch today,' Carla said. 'I'm so glad you hadn't,' she added, smiling at him, realising how disappointed she'd been feeling at his absence.

'Joyeux anniversaire, Carla,' Joel said, kissing her on the cheek and quietly saying, 'I have a small present to give you later.'

Lunch, a mixture of cold meats, cheeses, salads and fresh baguettes, was accompanied by ice-cold rosé. To Carla's surprise, Sam poured everyone a glass but himself.

'Would you like a beer instead?' she asked.

Sam shook his head. 'No thanks. I'm driving this afternoon. I'll make up for it this evening.'

'Oh. Where are you off to?' Carla said, surprised. She'd been expecting him and Maddy to spend the rest of the day at the villa with her.

'He's taking me to Saint Paul de Vence,' Maddy answered. 'One of my clients has a holiday home there and has invited us over. Late afternoon is the only time she has free.'

'I would ask if I could come with you – a visit to that perched village is on my list – but obviously if it's a client...'

'Sorry, Mum. We'll take you another time,' and Maddy

pushed a plate full of charcuterie towards her. 'Have some roast pork – it's delicious.'

Carla took a piece of meat and placed it on her plate. She didn't for one moment believe Maddy had a client with a home over here. She knew instinctively her daughter was up to something. Why hadn't she mentioned earlier that the two of them were going out for the afternoon? Something in their story didn't add up.

'Impossible for you to go anyway. I'm going to need you to help me with the garden lights for this evening,' Joel said, breaking the silence that had fallen.

'Solar lights? I thought you said they were bad for the insects?' Carla said.

'Not solar. A string or three of battery operated bulbs and tea lights in jars.'

The rest of lunch flew by in a mixture of laughter and chat. Gordon had them all crying with laughter as he recalled a particular birthday of his, when he'd ended up being besieged by a group of women determined to find the answer to that age-old question, what does a Scot wear under his kilt?

'In the end, I jumped into the river and swam to the other side to escape them. My problem then was the twenty-five-mile trip to get home with no money and soaking wet.'

It was gone four o'clock when Maddy and Sam stood up and said they had to go. Josette and Gordon also said their goodbyes.

'See you back here at seven o'clock,' Carla said, walking to the driveway with them.

Joel had disappeared when she went back out on the terrace and she started to carry the dirty plates and glasses into the kitchen. As she closed the dishwasher door, Joel came into the kitchen, holding a small box.

'Happy birthday again.' And he handed the box to her.

'Joel, you didn't need to buy me a present. I know how difficult things are for you at the moment,' Carla said, touched that he'd bothered. Unwrapping the box, she found a glass pot nestled in amongst a layer of tissue paper. A glass pot like she'd never seen before. So many colours swirled together creating a riot of colours all nudging up against each other.

'It's from the local glassworks, what they call their end-of-day creations,' Joel told her. 'All the leftover chips of glass are reheated, fused together and blown into various shapes. I thought this one was the right size for your basil plant on the kitchen windowsill.'

'I love it. And you're right, it's perfect. Thank you so much,' Carla said, impulsively leaning in to give him a thank-you kiss. Time seemed to stand still for several seconds before Joel moved back and Carla was left wondering what had just happened.

'Glad you like it.' Joel smiled at her. 'Come on, we've got work to do in the garden.'

Carla was quiet as she followed Joel out into the garden. She hadn't meant anything special by the kiss, she just wanted him to know how much she loved the little pot. The unexpected feelings it had flipped inside her were a surprise. Joel on the other hand didn't seem disconcerted in the slightest.

Together they strung one set of lights around the cherry tree and stood close together, untangling a second set.

'What is it with strings of lights? Every New Year I carefully tidy the Christmas tree lights away and eleven months later they're tangled up as if I'd just thrown them in the box,' Carla said, laughing. 'Which is something I'd never do.'

'I can vouch for that. You were always the Queen of Tidy.'

Carla dropped the lights as she spun round. 'David. What the hell are you doing here?'

'Come to wish you happy birthday.' He held out the large bouquet of roses he was holding. 'It is a big birthday, after all.'

Carla stared at him as she silently took the flowers.

'You're looking good,' David said. 'Life in France clearly suits you.'

'You've lost weight,' Carla said, thinking, but not putting it into words, how gaunt he looked.

'Where's Maddy? She here with that boyfriend of hers?'

'Yes, she and Sam are here. Except they're not at the moment. Did she know you were planning to come?' Carla asked, feeling flustered. Was this why Maddy had elected to disappear for the afternoon?

David shook his head. 'No. I was at a loose end and fancied a weekend in France. See, I can be impulsive too.' He turned to Joel and held out his hand. 'I'm the ex-husband. You are?'

'Joel, the gardener.'

Carla stared at him. Why had he said that? He was more than the gardener.

'Working on a Sunday? There's devotion to duty for you,' David said.

'Joel is a good friend of mine and he lives here,' Carla said, a sharp edge to her voice.

David looked at them both, before he nodded and gave her a knowing smile. 'Oh, having a bit of a Lady Chatterley moment, are we?'

'That is extremely rude of you and I think you should apologise to Joel, if not to me. And then leave.' Carla stared at him furiously and refused to be the first to look away. The seconds ticked by as David tried to outstare her and she knew he was planning his next move.

Finally he held up his hands. 'I apologise to you both. Unreservedly. I was out of order. There, happy?' He looked at the lights Joel was still holding. 'Are the lights for a party this evening? Am I invited?'

'You seem to have forgotten the bit about leaving, so I'll make it easy for you. No, you're not invited. Goodbye, David,' Carla said.

As David made no attempt to move, Joel stepped forward and said quietly, 'You know the way out.'

David glared at Joel and turned on his heel to leave at precisely the moment Sam came up the driveway and parked.

Carla watched in astonishment as Maddy got out of the car followed by...

'Ed. What a wonderful birthday surprise,' and she flew across to hug her son.

'Not the kind of welcome I got,' David muttered as Maddy joined him.

'You didn't really expect to be made welcome did you, Dad? Why are you here anyway?' Maddy demanded.

'Big birthday for your mum, thought we were all supposedly being civilised about the divorce,' David shrugged. 'Realise now it was a big mistake. I was about to leave when you arrived. I'd like to say hello to Ed before I go though.'

'Not sure he'll be pleased to see you either. Like me he's pissed off with you over the way you've treated Mum.'

'You know what? I'm pretty pissed off with myself,' David said. 'I keep making things worse too.' He glanced across at

Joel, who was stringing a second set of lights around the garden with the help of Sam. 'Mum tells me he lives here. Are they an item?'

'No. He needed somewhere to live and Mum offered him a room. He's nice. Helps Mum around the villa. Means she's not lonely living here on her own.'

David nodded. 'That's good. She's looking really well.'

'Mum's changed a lot recently. I think she's enjoying her new independence and living in France.' Maddy glanced at him. 'In fact, every time we come over, she seems happier than ever. Especially now all the business with Josette is settling down.'

'Okay, I get the message,' David said. 'No need to rub it in. But just so you know, I do have regrets. Can we have a truce please? I've missed you not being around too. Come and see me at home soon?'

'Promise you'll be nice to Sam? No sarky comments about his work.'

David nodded. 'I promise to try. Will you go and put in a good word for me with Ed now?' He looked across to where Carla was talking animatedly to their son.

'I'll try, can't promise anything though,' Maddy said, starting to walk away.

'Oh, hang on a minute. What did you mean – business with Josette?'

'I'm sure Mum would have told you if she'd wanted you to know,' Maddy said and continued to walk towards her mother and brother.

'Ed, Dad wants to talk to you. I've warned him he's not our favourite person right now, but he does seem to want to try and put things right between us.'

'Hmph. How d'you feel about that, Mum?'

'Whatever I feel isn't the issue. He has always been a loving father to you two, cutting him adrift on my behalf will really tear the family apart. I don't know why he came today, but I'm guessing it was more a case of him wanting to be part of the family unit rather than causing trouble – although he managed to be very rude earlier.' Carla said, looking over to where David cut a lonely figure, standing by himself watching them.

She sighed. It was her birthday. And not any old birthday. A big one. She didn't want the day marred by unpleasantness and she and David had been together a long time. They had definite history that couldn't be ignored. Her life now was good. She could afford to be generous.

'Go and talk to him. You two are all he's got now and it's actually because of his philandering that I'm the happiest I've been in years. He asked earlier if he was invited to the party and I said no. Go tell him he can come if he would like to. Seven o'clock. But tell him he has to lose the snide remarks.' And she pushed Ed in the direction of his father.

36

A couple of hours later, Carla came out of her room wearing her new chiffon maxi dress that both Maddy and Josette had insisted she buy from the trendy boutique they'd found in Cannes, along with the pair of high-heeled sandals that were already killing her.

'You look great, Mum,' Ed said, coming out of the kitchen with a tray loaded with food for the barbecue. 'I'll just get this over to Sam so he can start cooking, then I'll be back to pour you a glass of champagne.'

Joel was busy lighting the tea candles in their jars hanging from various trees and shrubs around the garden, as well as standing alongside the pool and down the paths. So many flickering candles. Carla was looking forward to dusk descending when the candles and the lights would come into their own, casting long shadows over the garden, creating a mysterious, magical atmosphere as they did so.

Joel had exchanged the shorts and coloured T-shirt she was used to seeing him in for dark jeans and a white shirt, the sleeves of which he'd rolled up, leaving his suntanned muscular forearms exposed. A pair of sunglasses were pushed back on his head. She laughed as she saw Leroy stalking him around the garden. Nothing new there. Whenever Joel was home, the cat could always be found close by.

She wished Joel hadn't told David he was the gardener the way he had. Surely he regarded himself as a friend first and foremost? She knew that was how she thought of him – a good friend too.

'Here you go, Mum, one glass of bubbly,' Ed handed her a glass of pink champagne. 'Your lodger seems a nice bloke,' he said, following her gaze.

Carla nodded, still watching Joel as he switched on the lights in the trees. 'He is. He's a good friend.'

'Nothing more?' Ed asked quietly. 'He seems very fond of you.'

Carla turned to look at him. 'No. I'm barely divorced from your father and happy enjoying the single life. Santé.' Ed looked at her quizzically, but the arrival of the neighbours, Heléne and her husband, prevented him from pursuing the subject, to Carla's relief. David arrived soon after, carrying a magnum of champagne.

'I had the hotel keep it in their fridge for me, so pop it back in yours for half an hour and we can drink it later. Happy birthday by the way.'

Dutifully, Carla did as she was told. Coming back out, she smiled at Josette and Gordon, going across to greet them and make sure they too had a glass of bubbly.

Josette looked over to the barbecue, where Sam was turning the meat. 'Who's that talking to Sam and Joel?'

'It's...' Carla stopped. 'Of course, you've never met him have you? That's David. Come on, I'll introduce you.'

'David as in ex-husband? What's he doing here?'

Carla shrugged. 'Said he wanted to wish me happy birthday, but really I think he wants to mend bridges – particularly with the twins.' As she headed over, she called out. 'David, come and meet...' for a second she was almost tempted to say 'meet my mother' but knew David would think she'd flipped and demand an explanation. An explanation she'd give him another time, but not tonight. 'Meet Josette. And this is her friend, Gordon.'

'Hello, Tante Josette, the mysterious unknown aunt,' David said, holding out his hand. 'Good to meet you after all these years. Gordon, pleasure to meet you too.'

Carla gasped. 'Oh, I've just realised. Ed's here too. You're meeting all my family today. Come and sit on the terrace and I'll bring him over.' Carla grabbed Josette by the hand and started walking quickly towards the terrace, leaving Gordon to talk to David. 'David doesn't know you're actually his mother-in-law yet – well ex-mother-in-law now. I'd rather not have to break the news to him tonight, so promise you won't say anything, will you?'

'Promise,' Josette said. 'You'd better tell the twins to be careful to not mention it as well.'

'Gordon won't say anything, will he?' Carla asked, anxiously glancing back at the two men.

'Non. Gordon's a very discreet man,' Josette assured her. 'Now, where's my,' she dropped her voice to a whisper, 'grandson?'

By the time Carla had introduced Josette and Ed and made both twins promise not to breathe a word of Josette's story to David, the other neighbours and Bruno had arrived. Five minutes later, Sam and Joel shouted, 'Food's ready.'

Dusk was falling by the time Maddy appeared, carrying a birthday cake ablaze with candles. After everyone had sung

'Happy Birthday' and Carla had managed to blow out all the candles, Maddy took the cake back into the kitchen to cut it up. In the lull that followed before the slices were handed around, Carla overheard Bruno quietly ask Josette why she hadn't answered his uncle's letter.

Josette looked at him before answering equally quietly. 'Because I'm not sure what to say to him after all this time,' and she'd moved closer to Gordon and caught hold of his hand. Bruno watched her thoughtfully before accepting a slice of cake from the plate now being offered by Maddy. Ten minutes later, he made his way across to Carla to say goodbye.

'I'm sorry to leave, but I have an early morning flight to catch tomorrow,' he apologised. 'May I call you when I get back next week? Maybe we can have dinner again.'

Smiling, Carla agreed. 'That would be lovely.'

An hour or so later, sitting next to Joel on the terrace, sipping a last glass of champagne, Carla sighed happily. It had been a good evening. Bruno leaving had been the signal for the others to drift away, including David, who'd said he'd see them all in the morning before he left for the airport. Carla resisted the urge to ask 'why?' Ed had taken himself off to bed, muttering about jet lag, but Josette and Gordon had said they were in no hurry to leave.

Now, quite dark, the garden was bathed with a romantic glow from the candles and lights. Someone – she suspected Maddy – had put some 'music to smooch to' on and she and Sam were gently swaying together by the side of the pool. As were Josette and Gordon, Carla saw with delight.

Carla closed her eyes and let the gentle music float over her. The past year had been fraught with problems and stress, but things were on a more even keel now, despite everything. A new year stretched ahead of her. A year she was determined to make the most of. She sensed someone standing in front of her. She opened her eyes to see Joel looking at her.

'Would you like to dance with me?' He held out his hands and gently pulled Carla to her feet when she took hold of them.

Standing in the circle of Joel's arms, her head resting on his shoulder, as they moved slowly together to the rhythm of the music, Carla's only thought was, *This is the perfect ending to my birthday*, and she unconsciously snuggled in closer to Joel.

37

The next morning, Carla and Ed were having a late breakfast out on the terrace when David arrived to say goodbye before heading off to the airport.

'Great party last night,' he said. 'Really enjoyed myself. Maddy not up yet? I was hoping to see her before I left.'

Carla shook her head. 'Afraid not.'

'Any coffee left in the pot? Just got time for a quick one,' he looked at Carla hopefully.

'I'll get an extra cup,' Ed said, before Carla could offer.

'Didn't get a chance to ask you yesterday, but Maddy mentioned something about you having to deal with all the "Josette business". No problems with this place I hope?'

Carla shook her head. 'No. Something else entirely.'

'You going to tell me?' David looked at her expectantly.

Carla sighed. She had to tell David the truth sometime and, as he had a plane to catch soon, he wouldn't be able to stay and plague her with questions. 'Josette told me, she, not Amelia, was my mother,' she said quietly.

Speechless for once, David stared at her.

'Which, as you can imagine, was a huge shock.'

David still hadn't spoken when Ed reappeared with a cup, poured a coffee and handed it to him. 'Thanks.' He took a long drink. 'You told the twins and not me?'

'I would have told you soon,' Carla said. 'But, to be honest, it's taken me time to get my head around things. What with the divorce and settling in here, telling you about Josette slipped way down the list. And, really, it doesn't affect you in the same way.'

'Does she know who the father was? I mean, according to Amelia, Josette was always a bit of a hippy. Free love and all that in the sixties.'

'You are totally out of order with that remark,' Carla snapped at him. 'I might have guessed you'd jump to conclusions and make some crass insinuation. Josette told me who my father was. It's the man I called Dad all my life.'

'Robert?'

'Yes.' Carla held up her hand. 'There isn't time today for me to tell you the full story, but Maddy and Ed know it and have my permission to tell you more. Right now you have a plane to catch.' She stood up. 'Have a safe trip home,' and Carla picked up the remains of breakfast and made her way into the villa, leaving Ed to see his father off.

She was busy wiping down kitchen surfaces when Ed came back.

'Dad said to apologise. He'll ring you later.'

'He's had to do a lot of apologising this weekend,' Carla said. 'And I really hope he forgets to ring.'

'You probably don't want to hear this, but yesterday he seemed really sad, admitting everything was his fault and saying he knows he totally screwed up things. He never wanted a divorce.'

'Of course he didn't. He wanted to have his cake and eat it. Hoped I would forgive him and the status quo would return.'

'So no chance of the two of you getting back together again?' Ed said. 'Like Dad was hinting he wanted yesterday to me and Maddy.'

'NO. That little episode this morning confirmed I've done the right thing for me. Going back to a marriage that in truth died many years ago would be a backward step in so many ways. Not least it would mean giving up the life I'm creating for myself here, and I'm not prepared to do that.'

* * *

Josette was in the courtyard deadheading and generally tidying up the shrubs and the pots when there was a knock on the door.

Opening the door, expecting it to be Gordon, she stared in shock at the man standing on the doorstep and held on to the door in an effort to steady herself.

'May I come in please, Josie?'

Silently, she stood to one side and for the first time in fifty years she and Mario Grimaud were within touching distance of each other. He followed her into the sitting room, where Josette looked at him, trying to take in the enormity of him and the situation. Why had he come? Silly question. She knew why he'd come. He wanted closure, to know the truth about the past, and she knew she owed him that at least.

'It's good to see you again,' Mario said. 'When Bruno told me he'd met you and was sure you were my long lost Josie, I couldn't believe it. After all these years, to see you again is wonderful. You look...'

'A lot older,' Josette interrupted.

'You still have those wonderful eyes. I know when you're over the shock of me turning up and you finally smile at me again, your smile will gladden my heart as much as it ever did. And I love your white hair.'

In spite of herself, Josette laughed and smiled at him. 'You always could make me smile.'

'I thought we'd planned to spend our lives together making each other smile,' Mario said quietly. 'So many years I've waited to ask you – why did you leave me?'

Josette shook her head, close to tears at the intensity in his voice. 'I had to leave. There was no choice.'

Mario looked at her, waiting for her to continue.

Josette closed her eyes. This was turning out to be harder than she could ever have anticipated. She took a deep breath, opened her eyes and, looking at Mario, said. 'The truth is I was pregnant with another man's child.'

Her words fell into a silence that was heartbreaking in its intensity. Long seconds passed before Mario said. 'Who's baby was it?'

Josette managed a gallic shrug before saying. 'Does it matter?'

'Yes, it does,' Mario answered with an edge to his voice.

'Robert, my brother-in-law.'

Josette registered the shock in his body and the pain in his eyes as her words sunk in.

'Shall I make us some coffee?' Without waiting for an answer, she went into the kitchen. Spooning coffee into the cafetière, she called out, 'Did you marry? Do you have children? Grandchildren?' Questions she wasn't sure she wanted to hear the answers to, if she were honest. They would only serve to tear the scars that had taken years to heal, wide open again. But she needed to turn the conversation back onto

Mario, away from her own heartbreak. Stop him asking questions she dreaded having to answer.

Mario followed her into the kitchen. 'A year after you left, I met Concheta. Antoine was born a year later.' He paused before continuing, 'Now Antoine is married with a daughter, Stephanie, who is at university in Rome. And Concheta...' he sighed. 'She died a year ago.'

'I'm so sorry,' Josette said. 'I expect you must miss her.'

Mario gave a slow nod as he looked at her. 'Almost as much as I missed you in the beginning. You never married?'

'No. Obviously not meant to be.'

'What happened to Robert's baby?'

'Robert and Amelia adopted her.'

'Is she the "niece" Bruno tells me who has come to live down here?'

Josette nodded, watching as Mario ran his hand distractedly through his grey hair. He was still a handsome man who'd turned into a real silver fox.

'So, for her whole life she's thought of you – known you – as her aunt. Didn't that make you unhappy and want to tell her the truth?'

'It's only since Amelia died that I've got to know Carla. I was never allowed access. Over the years, Amelia turned me into this rogue aunt.' She poured the coffee and handed a cup to Mario. 'Carla does know the truth now. I'd had a couple of glasses of champagne on my birthday and couldn't stop myself. She's still coming to terms with the shock of me being her mother.'

Mario drank his coffee. 'Did you have feelings for Robert?' he asked, a tremor in his voice. 'I'm sorry I have to ask, but I thought I was the only one...' He stopped and looked at her, an unexpected troubled look on his face. 'Robert didn't force himself on you, did he?'

Josette shook her head. 'No is the answer to both your questions. It was me being naive and trying to comfort him which made it all go wrong. Although my parents did accuse me of leading him on at one stage, I truly didn't. It was them who came up with the adoption plan to help Amelia recover after Bobby's death – you remember how ill she was – and to save the family name of course. The thought of any scandal attaching itself to them couldn't be tolerated. Never mind the cost to me.'

'I hated your parents for a long time,' Mario said. 'I think I still do, hearing all this. But after you'd had the baby, why didn't you come back to Antibes? To me?'

'I longed to do just that, but I knew it wasn't possible. I couldn't face seeing you and knowing it was all over between us. You know what it was like down here in the late sixties. I was second-hand goods and I convinced myself you wouldn't want me. Besides, my parents weren't keen on me coming back.'

'How did you survive? And where?'

Josette looked at him before saying, 'Come with me. I want to show you something.' At the top of the stairs, she stopped and pointed to her framed photos. 'I became a free-lance photographer. I travelled the world. These are some of my more popular photographs.'

'You were seriously good,' Mario said. 'I'm not surprised though, you always did have a camera in your hand.'

'Thank you.'

'Why have you come home after all the years away?'

Josette shrugged. 'It seemed like a good idea at the time. Antibes has always held a special place in my heart.'

Mario reached out and took her hand. 'Do I still have a special place in your heart too?' he asked, looking searchingly at her.

She bit her lip and nodded. 'Yes. Always.' She gently pulled her hand back and started downstairs. 'What have you been doing for the past fifty years? Did you ever get those tourist boats? You were so right about the growing tourist industry down here. It's unbelievably busy compared to way back when.'

Mario followed her back downstairs. 'No, I didn't. I went into the family business. I know, I know, after all I said, but in the end I didn't have much option. I managed to put my own stamp on things though. I eventually left Alexandro to run the pizza cafes and I opened a couple of ice cream parlours. You may have heard of them?' and he named one of the most famous glacé outlets on the coast.

'That's yours? I love the ice cream from there.'

'I sold it all last year to an international conglomerate,' Mario said. 'And I've finally got my dream boat. You must come out on it. We could go to Corsica. You'd love Corsica.'

'Peut-être,' Josette said.

'Bruno tells me you have a friend, Gordon? Is it serious between you?'

'I think it could be very serious, which is something I never expected to happen to me again,' Josette said quietly. 'But at our age...' she shrugged. 'New, and old, relationships can be equally difficult.'

'If we were to begin a new relationship, it would be firmly anchored in the old Mario and Josie.' Mario caught hold of her hand. 'I've loved you forever. I was planning on trying to find you when Bruno said he'd thought he'd met my Josie.'

Josette gazed at him. She felt as though she was dreaming. Was it possible after all this time, that she and Mario could be in each other's lives again?

'Were you going to reply to my letter?' Mario asked.

'Yes, when I found the courage. I was going to apologise for ruining your life and to say being friends again would be rather wonderful.'

'Good. Let's start by having lunch together today. Yes?'

Josette smiled and nodded, not trusting herself to speak.

'And, by the way, you don't have to apologise for anything. You didn't ruin my life,' Mario said gently. 'I've not had a bad life – I just lived a different one to the one I'd anticipated. If you ruined anyone's life it was your own, but judging by those photographs upstairs your life wasn't ruined either. Like me, you just didn't live the one you thought you would.'

Josette pulled a face. 'I definitely lived a different life to the one I was expecting. Whether it was any worse than the one I longed for,' she shrugged. 'Who knows. I do regret not marrying and having a proper family.' The words 'with you' hung unspoken in the air between them.

'It's too late for us to have children together, but we can enjoy our own families together. Maybe we are being given a second chance at happiness in our later years?' Mario said. 'You were my first love and seeing you, being with you, hoping to have you as a real presence in my life again as a friend if not a lover, is, my darling Josie, absolutely wonderful. I'm hoping you will feel the same now we are back in touch.'

Josette stared at him in silence, not trusting herself to speak. Did he really think it would be that easy?

38

Josette could never remember the details of the lunch she ate that day with Mario, or even the restaurant he took her to. Details like that were driven from her mind by the events that happened afterwards.

Over lunch, Mario told her again how happy he was to have her back in his life. Now the initial shock of him turning up at the cottage and the hit of euphoria she'd experienced at the sight of him had eased, Josette waited for the happy contentment she'd always felt in Mario's company to arrive. But it didn't. She was such a bundle of mixed emotions, with everything going round and round in her head. Looking at him, she realised this version of Mario was a very grown-up, sophisticated one. The boy she'd loved so wholeheartedly had disappeared.

When Mario actually suggested she might think about coming to Italy to make it easier for them to see each other with the words, 'Be easier for you to move with no real family,' she protested quickly.

'No, I can't do that. Carla's my family now. The twins are

my grandchildren. I need to get to know them all. Besides, Antibes is my home.'

'It was just an idea,' Mario said. 'We can always discuss it again later. When we're more established as a couple.'

Josette had sipped her wine thoughtfully. Mario was taking it as a foregone conclusion that they would soon slip back into their old relationship. Had he always been this bossy? Or had she been so enthralled before that she'd always fallen in with his plans? Fifty years of independent living had changed that though. The meek, pliant young girl no longer existed.

When Mario walked her home, Gordon was knocking on the cottage door. Josette, surprised at how pleased she was to see him, quickly introduced him to Mario. The two men exchanged polite handshakes and muttered greetings at each other before Mario turned to Josette.

'Thank you for today. Give me a call later? You've got my number now.'

Josette nodded. 'Will do. And thank you for lunch.'

Mario turned to Gordon. 'Good to meet you.' And he left them both standing on the doorstep of the cottage.

Silently, Josette unlocked the door and pushed it open.

'You didn't say you were having lunch with Mario,' Gordon said.

'I didn't know I was. He just turned up here this morning, wanting to talk and suggested lunch,' Josette explained. 'We do have a lot of catching up to do.'

'Is he married?'

'He's a widower – his wife died a year ago. He has a son and a granddaughter.'

She shook her head and sighed. 'It was really strange. I've spent years dreaming about what might have been, blaming myself for ruining his life by leaving him. Turns out I didn't ruin his life and now he wants me back in it. Having met him again, I have no idea whether I want that or not. I mean, I think I can sense underneath he's still the same kind Mario that I knew, but we've both been changed by the stuff life has thrown our way. My head is telling me one thing and my heart another. Je ne sais pas – I have no idea what to do.'

It was Gordon's turn to sigh. 'Josette, I don't think I'm the best person to give you relationship advice. Conflict of interest, as the saying goes.'

'I'm sorry. I've got so used to you being my go-to friend for advice, I didn't think,' Josette said. 'Consider the subject closed.'

'Before I can do that, I have to say something,' Gordon said. 'I'm sure you know how I feel about you – about us. But you have to decide what you want for the rest of your life. With whom you want to spend it. I know what I think you should do – and what I want you to do – but it's a decision only you can make. Let me know when you've decided. Ciao.' And, to Josette's dismay, he opened the front door and left, the door closing behind him with a definite click.

Josette squeezed her eyes closed in an effort to stop the tears that were close. The last thing she'd intended to do was to hurt Gordon. He was more than her best friend these days. He was her rock. Shakily, she made her way to the kitchen and sat down.

She'd carried the belief inside her for so many years that the only thing that would give her true happiness would be to be reunited with Mario. Now they'd found each other again, she was full of doubts. To learn he'd married a mere year after she'd left and started a family almost instantly had hurt. Surely that had been too quick if he'd truly loved her?

She, fool that she was, had clung to the memory of her lost love all her life. If they'd married as they'd planned to do, would they still have been together now in their later years?

Meeting Mario today, there had been no instant flaring of pent-up feelings on her part, not even when he'd told her how much he'd loved her. Instead, the wonderful feeling of closeness she'd experienced the other evening dancing with Gordon at the party, the overwhelming sense of belonging in his arms, crept into her mind and dominated her thoughts, whispering that's what true love felt like. Not childish dreams of long ago. Josette sighed. Sometimes, even at seventy-four, she didn't feel capable of making grown-up decisions.

She was starting to wonder too, if the decisions she'd taken earlier in her life had been thought through seriously at all. All those hours in her life she'd spent agonising over which way to go before she'd caved in and allowed frightening events to simply swallow her up and change her life.

She knew instinctively, though, that getting together with Mario would signal the end of her relationship with Gordon. The thought of that happening didn't bear thinking about. She couldn't let Gordon go. It was time to jettison the past and truly live in the present. She'd write to Mario and try to explain how she felt and why it was impossible for the two of them to recreate what they'd once had. And pray that he would understand.

Opening the kitchen bureau drawer, she found her writing pad and a pen underneath Mario's letter and the original package that Carla brought with her. Maybe it was time to open the package. Taking everything out to the courtyard, she sat at the small table and thought about what she was going to say to Mario. First thing would be to emphasise the fact that going back rarely worked. There tends to be too much baggage on both sides and while the central figures can explain away, apologise and even understand the mistakes made, other people on the borders of the relationship often fail to hide their irritation and hurt.

She'd tell him she wasn't sure their shared history was strong enough to withstand the pressures of the present and the future. They'd both changed – it would be better to remember what they'd had, rather than try to recapture it. The years of separation had taken their toll. She'd try to phrase everything as diplomatically as she could.

So many reasons to list, but as she made mental notes about them, she realised the most important one was the fact she was no longer enthralled with Mario. She'd be happy to be in his life as a loving friend but together again as a couple? No, that was impossible. Thoughtfully, she picked up his letter and re-read it. One sentence leapt out at her: *But life goes on and one learns to accept that certain things were never meant to be.* She'd quote those words back at him at the end of her letter.

Ready to write to him now she had things straight in her head, she reached for the writing pad. Her hand knocked the 'Private and Confidential' packet Carla had brought with her at the beginning of summer. Hesitantly, she picked it up. If it contained, as she suspected, Carla's original birth certificate, she would need to give it to Carla.

It was, indeed, the certificate, but there was another envelope, with the words 'The Truth", followed by a large exclamation mark. Intrigued, Josette opened it and drew out two pieces of paper. A letter from Amelia. And an official looking certificate.

Sitting there reading her last letter from Amelia, Josette, blinded by tears, her breath coming out in great rasping gasps, fought to stop herself from collapsing in a heap on the floor. She wished she'd done what she intended to do months ago and burnt the package without opening it. Too late now. The words she'd just read could never be forgotten – forgiveness never given. And she should never, never, NEVER have told Carla the truth about her birth.

The letter slipped through her fingers to join the other piece of paper on the table as Josette stood up in a vain effort to try and calm herself, control her heart palpitations. Amelia's letter had opened a Pandora's box full of sad, unhappy thoughts that would stay forever in Josette's mind, blotting out everything else. There was no way now the past could be pushed back and the box closed, ever again.

PART III

39

Josette dialled Gordon's number and prayed as it clicked through, 'Please, please answer.' But it went straight to voicemail. She took a deep breath. 'I need to see you and talk to you desperately. Something awful has happened. Please come.'

Two minutes later, a text pinged in:

On my way.

Josette heaved a deep sigh of relief. She spent the next half-hour alternating between pacing up and down, re-reading the letter and trying not to cry. Wishing Gordon would arrive. She sprang to answer the knock on the cottage front door the second she heard it.

'I would have been here before, but I was in Villeneuve Loubet,' Gordon said. 'What's happened? It's not Carla, is it?'

Josette shook her head. 'No. I was about to write to Mario and give him various reasons why we couldn't turn the clock back fifty years. That I couldn't be in his life the way he wanted. And then,' she took a deep breath. 'I opened a package Carla had brought over for me after Amelia died.

This is what I found,' and she handed him the letter. 'Read it and tell me what I do now please.'

Josette,

Sorry, I'm not going to address you as My Dear Sister, because quite honestly I've not thought of you in that way for a number of years.

I was so happy when you gave us Carla to adopt and we became a real family again for several years. I loved her dearly, as did Robert (ironically, Robert never lost that love). As she grew up though, we started arguing over when to tell her she was adopted and that you were her true mother, like we originally promised you. Robert argued against it for years, saying she'd only ask who her father was and he was reluctant for that to happen, saying we didn't know the answer. Only he did, didn't he? The rows increased and finally Robert yelled the truth at me one horrendous night, that he was Carla's father because you and he had slept together just the once.

I didn't believe him at first. I swore at him my sister would never betray me in that way. He said he'd never intended it to happen, but when you fell pregnant it seemed providential as I couldn't have any more children and you were in no position to keep a baby. Carla being Robert's meant that we'd at least have a child who was blood related. I slowly accepted the wisdom behind his reasoning but could never bring myself to forgive either of you. The betrayal gnawed away at me for years until I decided I wanted proof and I organised a DNA test. The result of which I've never disclosed to anyone until now.

The naked truth is this (see what I did there?), Robert may have slept with you, but he was not Carla's father. I have no idea who her father is but would guess at the Italian you were infatuated with at that time, Mario somebody or other, I've forgotten his surname.

You, my husband and, I guess, our parents connived in the decision to ruin my life by plotting together to make me bring up a child that wasn't Robert's so you could preserve your reputation. I know you loved Carla from the moment you gave birth, in the same way I loved Bobby. By breaking off your 'aunt' contact and depriving you of involvement in our lives, I wanted you to feel something of the pain felt when a child you love dies.

I have never forgiven you for the deception and leaving this letter for you to read after my death is deliberate – you finally get to deal with the consequences of your action when you tell Carla the truth that neither of the people she believes to be her parents are and that her whole life has been based on a lie. I wonder how she'll react. I hope she hates you as much as I did.

Amelia.

Gordon looked at Josette. 'That was one bitter and twisted woman,' he said, putting the letter down on the table and drawing Josette close to hold her in a tight hug.

'Carla told me when we talked about me being her mother that at least the one constant in her life now was the fact that Robert, who she adored, was still her father. And now I have to tell her he isn't. She'll be shattered.'

Josette closed her eyes and struggled to stop shaking. Amelia was right, of course. Mario had to be Carla's father – he was the only other man she'd slept with at the time. An image of a young Mario flitted into her mind. How could she not let the older Mario back into her life now? Not only had she walked away from him, she'd unknowingly deprived him of his child.

'Did you ever think Mario could be the baby's father?' Gordon asked gently.

'No.' Josette shook her head. It had never occurred to her that the baby could possibly be Mario's – they'd always taken precautions because she'd been determined she wouldn't end up like Amelia, pregnant before she married. At the time, she'd taken for granted that Robert had to be the father of the baby because of that one brief unprotected mistake. Learning the truth after all these years, knowing that she could have kept the baby, secure in the knowledge that Mario would have stood by her, was heartbreaking. For everyone concerned.

'Not only am I going to have to tell Carla that Robert wasn't her father after all, but I'm also going to have to tell Mario about her. And knowing Mario, he's sure to want to meet her.'

'Carla will have to agree to that. Maybe she'll decide she doesn't want to,' Gordon said. 'The first thing you do is tell Carla, then, depending on her reaction, you either tell Mario or you don't. At least for the time being.'

'Don't you think he has the same right to know that Carla has?'

'Yes, eventually, but right now Carla is the vulnerable one. She's had a tough year already. The woman she thought for fifty years was her mother dies, her marriage falls apart, her aunt turns out to be her natural mother, and she's also moved countries,' Gordon said softly. 'She needs more time to adjust and acclimatise to the new order of things. Don't forget the twins in all this either.'

'I could, of course, keep quiet about everything,' Josette said. 'Write my own letter and leave it for them to find when I'm gone. Or would that make me a coward?'

'Yes, it would and you know it's not the answer. Talking of letters, did you say you were writing to Mario to tell him there was no going back?'

Josette nodded. 'Mario did ask me if I thought things

between you and me were serious and I told him they could be. I realised I didn't want to jeopardise what you and I have for the sake of a resurrected dream that might or might not be true. I'm definitely living in the present with this. Even if it's all a big nightmare at the moment.' She glanced at him, still secure in the circle of his arms. 'I honestly can't imagine living the rest of my life without you in it.'

'You don't have to. I fully intend to be at your side.'

'Will you come with me when I talk to Carla?'

'If you want me to,' Gordon said without hesitation. 'When d'you want to go?'

Josette bit her lip and said. 'No time like the present.'

40

The weekend of her birthday had thrown up some confusing emotions in Carla regarding Joel. Since 'that dance', she'd seen very little of him as he'd been busy working, but he'd said he'd be home early tonight and she was looking forward to having supper on the terrace with him. She was pleased that he was picking up more clients for his gardening business now that he had decided to go it alone but missed him when he worked late.

He'd become such an integral part of her new beginning in France, slipping into her life unobtrusively. She knew life without Joel living in the villa would have been a lot lonelier over the past few months. Visualising the place in the future without his presence in the garden, in the kitchen, was impossible. Selfishly, she found herself hoping it would be a long time before he found a place of his own and moved out.

Carla had poured herself a glass of rosé to enjoy sitting on the terrace before starting to prepare supper, when Josette and Gordon arrived. The look on Josette's face told her this was no ordinary social visit and she jumped to her feet.

'What's happened? Are you ill? You look terrible,' she said, pulling out a chair for Josette. 'Sit down. Tell me what's wrong.' She threw a worried glance at Gordon. 'As long as nobody's died, we can deal with it.'

'Mario Grimaud came to see me today. He wanted to know why I hadn't answered the letter you delivered?'

Carla nodded. 'I remember.'

'I had lunch with him. We did a lot of catching up. When I got home, I knew what I was going to say to him. Basically, that there was no going back and the reasons. But then...' Josette took a deep breath before taking an envelope out of her bag and holding it out to Carla. 'Remember the package you brought me? I finally opened it today and there was a last letter from Amelia inside. I'm so sorry,' she choked on her words. 'It's a horrible letter, but you need to read it.'

Carla took the envelope and pulled out the letter. And once again felt her whole world shift on its axis as she read. Swallowing the nauseous feeling at the back of her throat, the colour drained from her face and her hand shook as she handed the letter back to Josette.

She picked up her wine and downed it in one. 'So, tell me – was she right? Is Mario Grimaud my father? Or was it someone else?' Carla asked, shaking her head slowly in despair at Josette.

'Mario was my first love. There was no other man in my life at that time.' Josette could barely get the words out. 'He and I were in love and planning to marry.'

'And he doesn't know?'

'No. We thought you had the right to be told first.'

'We?'

'Gordon and I,' Josette said. 'We don't have to tell Mario if you don't want to.'

'Why not? Is he likely to deny everything?'

Josette shook her head. 'No, he is more than likely to demand to meet you, and his grandchildren. To be part of your life from now on.'

'What if I don't want them involved?'

'I doubt that will be an option if Mario learns of your relationship to him. He'll insist on meeting you and the twins.'

Carla looked from Josette to Gordon and back to Josette. 'I think I'd like to be alone now. Would you leave please?'

'Carla, please, we do need to talk about things,' Josette protested, as Gordon took her arm.

'I think Carla needs time to get her head around this,' he said gently. 'You can talk another day. Come on, let's do as Carla asks.'

Josette sighed. 'D'accord, I will leave you, but please believe me when I say how deeply sorry I am for all the pain I've caused and am causing. Believe me, if I'd known Mario was my baby's father all those years ago, the lives of everyone concerned would have been so different. So different.'

Gordon silently handed her a handkerchief as the tears fell before putting his arm around her shoulders. The look he gave Carla was full of sympathetic compassion for her as he gently led Josette away.

Carla watched them go before her primeval scream of sheer despair rang through the air and she collapsed in a flood of tears. Her marriage was finished, the people she'd known as her parents were dead, her aunt was her mother and now some unknown Italian turned out to be her father. The twins were the only people she knew with absolute certainty she could claim as her own family. Everything else she'd held dear for so many years had been destroyed.

She was still sitting on the terrace absently stroking Leroy, who had curled up uninvited on her lap, when Joel came running out onto the terrace some twenty minutes later.

'Carla, are you okay? Josette rang me.'

Carla jumped. 'I wasn't expecting you home so early.' Gently, she lifted Leroy up and held him in her arms as she stood up. 'What d'you mean, Josette rang you?'

'She said you'd had some devastating news and she was worried about you.'

'She told you the truth there then,' Carla said, placing the cat on the ground and starting to walk into the villa. Joel caught hold of her. 'I haven't started supper yet.'

'Supper can wait.' Joel hugged her tightly. 'What's happened? Talk to me.'

'I will. But I need to be doing something. And I need another drink.' Carla moved out of his arms and carried on walking.

Joel followed her into the kitchen, watched her pour another glass of rosé and shook his head when she offered him one.

Carla took a long drink and felt the alcoholic kick. Carefully, she placed the glass down on the work surface. Taking a couple of onions and green peppers out of the vegetable basket, she picked up a knife and began to attack them.

'Pasta and vegetable sauce okay? I forgot to take the mince out of the freezer.' As Joel nodded, she said, 'Amelia left a vile letter to Josette, which she read for the first time today. I can't believe I delivered the bloody thing months ago when I first came over.' She sighed. 'You already know Josette is my mother, not Amelia. Now it turns out that Robert wasn't my real father either, which, according to the letter, is why

Amelia was so vile to Josette. And to me actually, for most of my life.'

'So who is your biological father?'

'Bruno's uncle. Mario Grimaud. But he doesn't know.'

'Josette's first love?'

Carla nodded. 'Yes. He came to see her today, which prompted her to open the letter from Amelia. Pass me a couple of carrots will you please.'

'How is Josette?' Joel asked quietly as he handed the carrots over.

'Shocked and upset.' Carla shrugged. 'How can she be any other way? She knows the problem is all down to her behaviour fifty years ago when she did something that changed the course of several peoples' lives. Plus the fact that everyone banished the truth from their memories – until now. Talk about the past coming back to haunt her.'

'Des souvenirs chuchotés,' Joel murmured.

'Sorry, my French isn't up to that. What does it mean?' Carla asked, looking at him.

'Whispered souvenirs. Whispered memories from the past, if you like.'

Carla nodded. 'Ones that would have been better staying hidden if you ask me.' As she hacked the carrots into small pieces, Carla said. 'For years I considered my family to be the most boring unit on earth. And now look at us. We're like a derelict building where the foundations have crumbled and all the faults are being exposed.'

'Lots of families have shaky foundations,' Joel said quietly. 'These days it's almost impossible to find a family that doesn't have its black sheep, or its share of rows, fallouts and petty jealousies.'

'I suppose you're right. All part of life's rich tapestry as someone famous once said. No idea who though. You sure you don't want a drink while supper cooks?'

'No thanks. Are you going to meet Mario?'

Carla shrugged. 'I suppose so. He hasn't been told about me yet. Josette says it's up to me when – *if*, she tells him. Right now I can't stand the thought of all the complications it's going to cause. But she has to tell him – the same as I'll have to tell the twins and David. I can just see David's superior reaction to the news now – because, of course, there's never been any scandal in his family.' She glanced up from the tin of plum tomatoes she was opening to add to the sauce. 'Talking of David, why did you tell him you were the gardener rather than a friend?'

'I didn't want him making any crass remarks about me living here and jumping to conclusions about us and upsetting you, but he managed to do that anyway.'

'I was cross on your behalf actually,' Carla said. 'Not mine. I didn't want him upsetting you.'

Joel smiled at her. 'He didn't.'

41

Five thirty the next morning found Carla creeping out of the house so as not to disturb Joel and making for the pool. The night had been hot and sticky and she'd barely slept. She was hoping a few lengths of the pool would banish her niggling headache and clear her mind. Météo-France had been promising an orage for days now, but while she could hear the thunder rumbling away in the mountains behind Antibes, nothing had yet arrived down on the coast. Carefully, she stepped into the shallow end and waded into the water until it was deep enough for her to start swimming a slow breaststroke.

Tossing and turning during the night, phrases from Amelia's vindictive letter had kept popping into her mind. What kind of woman set out to try and inflict the kind of pain felt when a child dies on another woman? A twin sister you'd once been close to. Amelia, knowing the truth for years, had cruelly decided to keep it hidden from her husband, her sister and Carla, intent on causing maximum pain to Josette when the truth was known. If it had been a recent decision, then one could perhaps be charitable and say she was losing her mind and didn't know what she was doing. Only she clearly did.

All those years when she'd barely been able to look at Carla, let alone treat her like a beloved daughter, made more sense now. As did the way Robert had tried to make up for her mother's indifference to her. Her bond with him had held fast. As hard as it was, she was glad he'd died before Amelia and missed this explosive exposé of the truth. It would have destroyed him. At least she had happy memories of her dad. Because he had been her dad in all the ways that mattered. Nobody could take his place in her heart.

She didn't believe for one minute that Josette had connived to ruin Amelia's life to preserve her own reputation. If she'd known Mario was the father of her baby, she'd surely have fought to keep the child and marry Mario rather than obey her father and hand the baby over to Amelia and Robert. Her grandfather had a lot to answer for. From the little Josette had said, he'd forced her to give up her baby and then imposed so many conditions if she wanted to return home, he'd driven her into virtual exile.

Turning onto her back and floating, Carla though about Josette and Mario. How different her life would have been as their daughter. Would she have become the same person she was, living in a different environment? Instead of growing up in England she'd have grown up in France – or possibly Italy – enjoyed a Mediterranean lifestyle full of sunshine. With Italians being renowned for their love of family, she'd probably have had a couple of siblings too. English would have been her second language, she wouldn't have married David and the twins wouldn't exist. The twins.

Carla sighed. How were they going to react to this latest

bombshell? They'd taken the news about Amelia not being their real grandmother well and had started to form a friendly, rather than grandmotherly, bond with Josette. Maddy had admitted to finding her easier to get along with than Amelia. At least they were all grown up, could discuss things rationally and keep things in perspective, even if they were shaken to the core like she was by this latest development.

Josette herself was the big worry. Fifty years ago she'd done what she thought was the right thing, had learnt to live with the sorrow it had caused her, only to discover, half a century later, that it had been an empty gesture. She had lost everything she held dear unnecessarily. Would she follow in Amelia's footsteps and become bitter and vindictive?

Slowly turning onto her front, Carla swam to the shallow end of the pool and climbed out. Amelia had been unbelievably cruel in her actions. It was time to try and make amends. There was no way she was going to react with hate the way Amelia had wanted. Josette had made a monumental mistake but she hadn't deserved the hatred Amelia had harboured against her. She'd been lied to and her life manipulated in much the same way as Carla's by the woman with whom they should both have had a loving relationship. Wrapping herself in her towel, Carla decided she'd go and see Josette and talk to her. Reassure her that she and the twins were her family and nobody could take that away even if they wanted to. Adjusting to their different roles in each other's lives would be difficult but not impossible.

Carla pushed away the thought about Mario Grimaud's reaction when Josette told him the truth. That was another question all together. And not one she relished finding the answer to.

* * *

There was no reply when Carla knocked on the cottage door later that morning and she stood there undecided as to what she should do. Part of her feared that Josette was in there and deliberately not answering. Another part worried that she'd fallen over and was lying injured in need of help. Mentally, Carla shook herself. There would be a perfectly rational explanation, like Josette had gone out with Gordon. That would be it. Gordon would be looking after her. Carla rapped her knuckles on the door one last time just in case, before turning and coming face to face with Josette.

'Thank goodness. I was worried you were in there, injured or something,' she said.

'I stayed with Gordon last night,' Josette said, unlocking the door. 'He didn't want me to be on my own.'

'That was thoughtful of him. Can I come in?' Carla asked. 'I'd like to talk to you.'

Josette nodded and pushed the door open. The two of them walked through to the courtyard where Josette looked at Carla and waited for her to speak.

'Can I give you a hug?' Carla asked softly, moving towards Josette. When a surprised Josette nodded, Carla wrapped her arms around her and held her tight. 'I can't begin to imagine the hell you've been through in your life. I'm sorry my coming to France triggered such distressing revelations for you.' Hugging her, Carla realised how thin Josette was. She'd been slim at the beginning of the year, but now she was so thin Carla could feel her bones. 'There's nothing of you,' she said, concerned. 'Are you eating properly?'

Josette shrugged. 'Gordon insists on feeding me breakfast and I eat again in the evening, but I haven't felt much like eating anything recently, I admit.' She looked at Carla. 'What did you want to talk about?'

'Us. Family. And how to hold it all altogether,' Carla hesitated. 'What Amelia did to you, to us, was undeniably cruel. As for that vindictive letter.' She bit her lip. 'The fact that I was the person who delivered it to you just makes it worse. I wish I'd thrown it away unopened.'

'I was going to burn it rather than open it,' Josette admitted. 'But I guessed your original birth certificate was in it and I knew I couldn't destroy that.'

'Learning you were my mother was a shock, but I'm so glad I had time to get used to the news before yesterday's revelation,' Carla said.

Josette closed her eyes and took a deep breath. 'I'm still struggling to come to terms with Mario's reappearance in my life let alone that particular bit of news.'

'Can I ask why I have such an Italian-sounding name?' Carla asked. The question was one of the many that had been floating around in her head for hours. 'It seems a strange coincidence.'

'Amelia and Robert agreed I could name you and I've always loved the name.'

Carla looked at her, hoping what she was about to say, the questions she was about to voice, wouldn't distress Josette further, but she had to ask. 'You didn't subconsciously suspect that you were pregnant with Mario's baby not Robert's? Did yesterday's news simply confirm something you'd suspected deep down fifty years ago?'

Josette stared at her. 'Mon dieu, non. You can't think that. If I'd had the slightest suspicion you were Mario's, I would never have given you up. Jamais, never, never. You have to believe that.' She clutched Carla's hand. 'You have to.'

Carla nodded. 'I do.'

'As for your name,' Josette said. 'I simply liked it – still do. Amelia and Robert did too. It was unusual in England at that time, which appealed to them.'

'I know you think Mario will want to meet me and the twins when he hears, but maybe he doesn't need to know straight away?' Carla said. 'I promise I'm not about to go and knock on his door and say "Hi Dad"'.

Josette sighed. 'As much as I dread telling him, I think he does need to be told the truth as soon as possible. The longer I leave it, the more it will gnaw away on my conscience. I never did write the letter I planned to send him and I certainly can't tell him about you that way. I have to see him face to face. I'll ring and arrange a meeting.' Josette rubbed her forehead agitatedly. 'Not a meeting I shall look forward to though.'

'Ring him now and organise a day for next week,' Carla said. 'You'll feel better knowing you've done something definite towards telling him.'

Five minutes later, Josette turned to Carla. 'Mario is thrilled I want to see him. Insists next week is too long to wait, so I'm having lunch with him in Ventimiglia the day after tomorrow. Thrilled is not the word to describe my feelings though. Sick and terrified would be nearer the mark.'

'Would you like me to come with you for moral support?' Even as the words left her mouth, Carla wondered what on earth had possessed her to offer. She didn't relish the idea of meeting Mario face to face one little bit. Or seeing his reaction to the news that he had an unknown daughter.

Josette nodded. 'Are you sure? It's not too soon for you? That would be wonderful.'

'Like you said, the longer we leave it, the more difficult it will be when we do tell him,' Carla said. But it wasn't a meeting she was looking forward to – or felt at all prepared for.

42

The following evening, Carla and Joel were sitting on the terrace enjoying the balmy late summer evening.

Carla sighed when she heard her mobile in the kitchen ringing. She got up reluctantly. 'I'd better answer that. Might be Josette about tomorrow.'

Glancing at the caller ID, she saw Bruno's name, not Josette's.

'Are you free this Saturday?' he asked. 'I have tickets for a concert in Nice and I was hoping you could join me? If I pick you up at seven, we could have dinner first.'

'I'm sorry, Bruno, I'm not free this Saturday,' Carla said.

'That's a pity.'

Carla heard the disappointment in Bruno's voice.

'Are you sure you can't cancel whatever it is you've planned?' he continued.

'Quite sure,' Carla said. 'Besides, I don't think it's a good idea for us to see each other at the moment. I'm really sorry about... about everything,' and she ended the call quickly before he could ask what she meant.

After tomorrow he'd know the truth when his uncle Mario told him she was his daughter. A fact that made them close cousins, so there could never be anything other than friendship between them from now on. Once her relationship to Mario was out in the open though, perhaps she and Bruno could become friends.

Joel looked at her quizzically as she sat down again. 'Bruno?'

Carla nodded. 'Wanted me to go to a concert with him. Strange to think he and I are related.'

'Did you tell him?'

'No, of course not. Mario has to be the first to be told.' She sighed. 'This time tomorrow night, Bruno will know and understand why I couldn't accept.'

'If you hadn't turned out to be related, would you have...?'

'Had a relationship with him?' Carla interrupted, she needed Joel to understand how she felt about Bruno – and him. 'No. He's fun. I like him as a friend and he's taken me to a restaurant I could only dream about eating in, but I couldn't live in his world full time.' Leroy jumped on to her lap just then and she stroked him, glad of the diversion and the chance to hide her face from Joel.

Even if it was far too soon after David to feel the way she had on her birthday when she and Joel danced, she knew that she was increasingly attracted to Joel and could only hope that given time he might begin to feel the same about her. She wanted to make quite sure he understood how things were between herself and Bruno.

'Bruno and I were never going to be serious,' she said. 'He's far too rich for me. But I do like him. I'm hoping once everything settles and life gets back onto an even keel, we can be friends as well as cousins.'

Joel smiled at her. 'Good plan. How d'you feel about tomorrow?'

'Nervous, if I'm honest,' Carla said. 'For Josette rather than me. I don't much care if Mario doesn't want to acknowledge me, but Josette will be hurt if that's his reaction and she so doesn't deserve being punished any more. She's terribly fragile at the moment.'

'D'you think Mario is likely to refuse to accept you as his daughter?'

Carla shrugged. 'Who knows? From what Josette says, he seems very keen for them to be in each other's life again, so hopefully he won't upset her with a negative reaction to the news about me. Personally, I don't care one little bit if after tomorrow I never see him again. I don't need or want another father. And I'm sure the twins can live without a new, old, grandfather appearing in their lives.'

43

Josette didn't appear to want to talk as the train travelled along the coast the next day towards Ventimiglia and Carla was happy to sit in silence enjoying the changing view as it flashed between the stations. Biot. Cagnes-sur-mer. St Laurent de Var. Nice. Èze. Villefranche-sur-mer. Monaco. Menton. Station names of places she had yet to visit that sounded exotic to her English ear. Every now and again she glanced across at Josette, concerned that she was stressing about Mario's reaction, but she seemed relaxed, if deep in thought. Finally, the train pulled into Ventimiglia at the end of the line and everyone got off.

The seaside town was busy and they struggled to make their way through the crowds to the coastal road and the restaurant Mario had suggested for lunch. Luckily, Josette had said she'd eaten there in the past and knew where it was.

'At least we'll get a good lunch,' she said. Once inside, Josette gave Mario's name to the maître d' and they were led to a table on the balcony at the front of the restaurant. Not yet twelve o'clock, lunchtime had scarcely begun and only one or two tables had people sitting at them.

Mario saw them as they approached, the smile on his face fading as he saw Josette was not alone. Carla shivered as she felt the intensity of his gaze on her face before he remembered his manners and moved across to welcome them.

'Josette. I hope you are well? I didn't realise you were bringing a friend.' He held out his hand to Carla. 'Nice to meet you, Josette's friend. Please sit down. They will bring the aperitifs I ordered in a moment.'

Numbly, Carla sat as the waiter deftly pulled out her chair. Shock waves were cruising through her body. She felt she already knew this man. He seemed so familiar to her. How could that be possible? She glanced at Josette. Was she going to introduce her? Or keep up the pretence she was a friend? There was a short silence as Josette settled herself on a chair before looking directly at Mario.

'Mario, this is more than a friend. This is Carla, my daughter,' Josette said softly.

Mario nodded. 'I suspected you were more than a friend,' he said finally, smiling at Carla and looking at her thoughtfully. 'You have inherited your mother's eyes, but you remind me of...' he shook his head. 'Someone I can't quite place. Ah, here come our aperitifs.'

Josette waited until the waiter had moved away before putting her hand on his arm. 'I need to finish the introduction. Mario, she's not only my daughter – she's yours too. Perhaps it is yourself she reminds you of,' she added quietly.

Mario stilled. His body stiff. 'It was only the other day you told me Robert was the father. Did you lie to me then?' He stared at Josette, his gaze hard and unforgiving.

Carla registered his hands gripping the edge of the table, his knuckles white, and prayed things weren't going to get out of hand. Had it been a mistake to come with Josette today? Perhaps it would have been better for Josette to have been alone to break the news. For her to meet Mario at a later date.

'No. I have never lied to you. I thought it was the truth – when I left you all those years ago and also last week when I finally confessed to you the reason I had to leave.' Josette took a deep breath. 'I've lived through the last fifty years believing Carla was Robert's child. This week that belief was cruelly shattered. Amelia left me a letter and the results of a DNA test which show conclusively that Robert was not the father of my child. She kept it secret in order to punish me.'

Mario looked at her silently for several seconds. 'Not just you, Josie. She punished the three of us – as well as Robert. All four of us have been treated harshly and denied the lives that should have been ours.'

Josette returned his gaze sadly. 'I'm so, so, sorry. If I could wave a magic wand and change things, I would.' She shrugged helplessly.

A waiter arrived at the table ready to take their main course orders just then and several minutes passed while they decided which of the many pasta dishes on offer each of them wanted.

As the waiter left to take their order to the chef, Mario turned to Carla, the previous intensity in his eyes replaced with a softness as he looked at her. 'So I have a daughter. I'm sorry not to have met you before. Did you have a good childhood in spite of all the secrets? Was Robert kind to you?'

'Robert was more than just kind. He was the best dad in the world as far as I was concerned,' Carla said. 'I miss him dreadfully.'

Mario just looked at her, an unfathomable look in his eyes for several seconds before he spoke, 'I'll take it from your reply that Amelia wasn't the best mum in the world?'

'I think she did her best for a long time,' Carla said. 'But now I know all the details surrounding my birth, I understand more why she was like she was with me.'

'And how about you and Josie?' Mario gestured with his hand at them both. 'Have the two of you formed an instant bond?'

Carla and Josette glanced at each other and smiled. It was Carla who answered. 'Not instant, no. But we're working on it.'

'What about you and me? How do you feel about me being in your life?' Mario asked, looking at Carla.

'Honestly? Yesterday I didn't care whether you were in my life or not. Today I can sense there is a connection between us, but I can't envisage a time when I will ever regard you as more than a friend – or maybe an uncle. You need to know,' Carla paused, 'Robert will always be my dad. I'm sorry.'

Mario nodded. 'Don't be. I understand your feelings. I only met Robert a couple of times, but we got on well on those occasions. I am happy and pleased he was in your life as the loving father I would have been had circumstances been different. Now, I shall simply hope to become a good close friend. The kind you can turn to in any sort of emergency and know they'll be there in an instant.' Mario picked up the untouched glass of wine the sommelier had poured earlier to accompany the aperitifs. 'A toast to old and new friends. And a united future,' he added.

The next hour passed quickly, with the three of them telling each other about their different lives and generally getting to know one another. Carla could sense Josette relaxing more and more as the lunch progressed. As they waited for their desserts Carla picked up her wine glass and absently looked at Mario and Josette – and felt a jolt when the phrase 'these are my parents' floated uninvited into her mind. It was going to take a long time for that reality to sink in.

When Bruno's name came up in the conversation, Carla laughed.

'I can't believe the man who saved me from under the wheels of a car turns out to be my cousin.'

'I will have to give him my sincere thanks for that act of gallantry,' Mario said. 'To think I might never have met you if he'd failed in that moment. Now, when will you come to Italy to meet the rest of your Italian family?'

'How will your family feel about a long lost daughter turning up?'

'They'll be thrilled to meet you. As thrilled as I will be to meet my English grandchildren,' Mario said. 'And I can't wait for Alexandro's reaction when he sees Josie again. He remembers how devastated I was when I lost her.'

'I promise I'll tell the twins about you and ask them to visit again soon.' Carla stood up. 'Excuse me for a moment, I need the cloakroom.'

Mario watched Carla walk across the restaurant towards the cloakroom before catching hold of Josette's hand as she went to pick up a glass.

'Josie, mia cara, thank you for giving me Carla.' Gently, Mario stroked her fingers for several seconds, his eyes misty with unshed tears.

'I know you told me things could be serious between you and your friend Gordon, but that was before I knew Carla was my daughter. I know this isn't the right place to say this, but I want you to forget about Gordon and marry me. It's not too late for the three of us to be a proper family for the rest of our lives. I promise I will do my utmost to make you happy and I want to take care of you both from now on. Please say yes and marry me, Josie.'

44

Josette knew Carla was startled when she returned from the cloakroom to find her in tears and Mario staring morosely into space.

'What's happened?' Carla said, standing there uncertainly looking at them both. 'You haven't rowed already, have you?'

Mario looked at her and shook his head. 'No, not a row as such. I just asked your mother to marry me... and she turned me down.'

Pushing her chair back and standing up, Josette whispered, 'I'm so sorry, Mario. I think it better if we leave now. May I call you later? I'd like to try and explain my reasons better.'

Mario nodded wearily. 'Please.' He stood up and kissed Josette on both cheeks before turning to Carla and, to her surprise, giving her a tight hug, rather than kisses on her cheek. 'See if you can persuade her to change her mind, will you?' he whispered in her ear. 'Please ask the twins to come over as soon as possible. A Grimaud family get-together soon is a definite must.'

As the two of them left the restaurant, Josette said, 'Can we take a walk along the esplanade before we get the train? I fancy some sea breeze.' Without waiting for an answer, she set off at a determined pace.

'Are you okay?' Carla said a few minutes later as she struggled to keep up with her.

'Oui merci,' Josette said before unexpectedly stopping and turning to face Carla. 'So, how d'you like your father?'

'That's hardly a fair question,' Carla protested. 'It's the first time I've met him, but yes, I like him. I think he likes me too. Whether we'll ever bond and be the family unit he seems so keen on when he's met the twins...' she shrugged and looked at Josette. 'Isn't marrying Mario the one thing in life you've always dreamt of doing?' she said quietly. 'So why did you turn him down?'

'Because... because we've both changed and because it's fifty years too late as I've finally realised marriage to Mario isn't the be all and end all of things. D'you think I should have said yes and agreed to marry him?'

'Not if you don't want to,' Carla said. 'Do you think he's changed that much?'

'He's still as impetuous as ever,' Josette said. 'Like today, when he asked me to marry him. It's far too soon to be talking about marriage. We need time to readjust to each other. To get used to being back in each other's lives, and for his family to accept the news.'

'He does seem very keen to introduce everyone,' Carla said. 'To surround himself with a big happy family. Maybe that's the Italian in him?'

Josette laughed. 'Peut être. Now he knows about you he's on a high and seems to think that the two of us getting back together is a foregone conclusion.' She glanced anxiously at

Carla. 'I realise it would bring our lives a full circle. But getting married won't cancel out all the years we've lost. It certainly won't turn us into a proper family overnight. The world will just see an old couple who got their act together too late, call it romantic, and forget us.' She sighed. 'What I do know is I can't just jump straight back into a relationship I'm not sure I want any more.' There, she had voiced her fears.

'Then don't,' Carla said, catching hold of her hand. 'You get to make all the decisions this time – no one is forcing you to do anything. If you want to settle for friendship, then that's your choice.'

Josette smiled a watery smile. 'I always dreamt about us having these mother-daughter chats and now we are – except it's you being the sensible one. Come on, let's get to the station and go home.' Arm in arm, they turned and walked back along the esplanade.

During the train ride back to Antibes, the two of them sat companionably looking out at the scenery, both deep in their own thoughts. As they left the train at Antibes, Carla said, 'Come back to the villa with me for tea?'

Josette shook her head. 'Lovely thought, but I promised Gordon I'd go to the apartment as soon as I returned and tell him how lunch and everything went.'

'Okay. Maybe both of you come for supper tomorrow night?'

'Looking forward to it already,' Josette said. 'Ciao'.

* * *

Five minutes later, she pressed Gordon's buzzer on the

entrance door to his building and slipped inside when the door opened. Climbing the stairs to Gordon's apartment, Josette felt an inner strength she'd forgotten she'd ever possessed. She had a second chance of happiness and she was determined to grasp it unreservedly. No way would she make the mistake of fifty years ago and simply accept things. Carla was right. She was in command now and in turning Mario down had made one of the most important decisions of her life. It also meant that everything that had happened between them was now firmly where it belonged – in that foreign country known as the past.

Gordon was standing at the open door of his apartment holding his arms out wide, ready to enclose her in a bear-tight hug as she reached the top floor. 'Come through to the terrace, there's a slight breeze out there. Would you like a drink?'

'A glass of iced water would be great,' Josette said.

Twenty seconds later, Gordon handed her the water and regarded her anxiously. 'How did Mario react?'

Quickly Josette described the meeting to Gordon. 'He accused me of lying to him initially but calmed down when I explained. He's more than happy to accept Carla and the twins' presence in his life. He has plans for a big family get-together.' She took a sip of water. 'There was an interesting moment after lunch finished. Mario proposed to me. Said the three of us could finally be a proper family.'

Josette felt Gordon tense and stiffen beside her as he stared intently at her face and waited for her to finish.

'Sadly for Mario his proposal has come fifty years too late. I turned him down as I no longer want to marry him.' Josette looked at Gordon and held his gaze.

For several seconds the two of them simply stared at each

other before a broad smile crossed Gordon's face and Josette smiled back.

'Carla and I went for a walk when we left the restaurant. One of the things she pointed out was that this time nobody would force me to do anything I didn't want to.'

Josette caught her breath and watched as Gordon put his hand in the pocket of his shorts and pulled a small box out. Surely he wasn't about to say, to do, what she suddenly suspected?

'I saw this on that antique stall down in the market the other day and thought – hoped – you'd like it.' Gently, he took hold of her left hand and carefully slid an old-fashioned, wide gold ring set with three garnet stones on to her third finger. 'It's vintage like us, and it's not a traditional engagement ring, but I thought it's more you than diamonds. We don't have to get married if you don't want to, but I hope you do.'

'It's beautiful,' Josette said, looking at the ring. 'And if that little speech means you've just proposed to me – the answer is yes.'

Gordon pulled her into his arms, looking at her as he held her tight. 'I was so afraid you would choose Mario over me.'

'I've already told you that I can't imagine my life now without you in it,' Josette said. 'But...' she added.

'Oh, there's always a but,' Gordon said. 'Not sure I want to hear it.'

'But,' Josette continued. 'Because of Carla and the twins, I will be staying in touch with him – as a friend of the family. I couldn't explain things to him over lunch very well, so I said I'd ring him tonight. I'm also going to write that letter I tried to start the other week.' She looked at Gordon questioningly.

'D'accord? He's going to be back in my life as a friend. Please say you're okay with that? There will be times socially when we will all meet up and I can't bear the thought of there being an atmosphere between us.'

'Just friends? Not friends with benefits?'

'I promise you – no benefits,' Josette said.

'Good. Having got that out of the way, I need a drink. I'll fetch the bubbly and we can celebrate,' Gordon said, making for the kitchen.

Josette stayed where she was, deep in thought. Two proposals in one day. Who'd ever have thought it? And who'd have thought it would be the unconventional Scotsman who'd literally snowballed his way to her side that would be the man she'd fall in love with at this time of her life?

'To the future and us,' Gordon said, handing her a glass of champagne.

'To the future and us,' Josette said, echoing his words.

45

When Josette and Gordon arrived hand in hand for supper the following evening carrying a bottle of champagne, Carla and Joel were waiting for them out on the terrace.

'Are we celebrating something?' Carla said.

'Definitely,' Josette said, smiling, and held out her left hand.

Carla looked at the ring and then at the two of them. 'Wow. Congratulations. I'm so happy for you both. I'll fetch some glasses and the nibbles.'

Josette followed her into the kitchen, leaving Gordon and Joel to talk.

Carla looked at her. 'After yesterday's proposal from Mario, I wasn't expecting this news.'

'Quelle surprise for me too,' Josette said. 'But it feels right. I'm so happy.'

'Aren't you worried about how Mario might react? Have you told him yet?'

'I rang him last night as I promised, but I didn't tell him

about Gordon and me,' Josette said. 'I concentrated on explaining why I couldn't slip back into a relationship with him after all this time. I didn't feel it was fair to then blithely announce I just got engaged to Gordon.' She'd caused him enough hurt for one lifetime. She would try and break the news of her engagement to Gordon gently.

'Probably a wise move,' Carla said. 'You'll have to tell him, though, before the twins arrive for this family get-together he wants.'

'I've got some time then,' Josette said. 'No?' as Carla shook her head and handed her the plate of nibbles to carry outside.

'Mario rang me earlier insisting I arranged a meeting asap. They're coming over this weekend. I told them I needed them here for an urgent family conference. Had to assure them I wasn't ill, which was their first thought, but it was something serious I needed to talk to them about. Probably made it sound a bit too mysterious, but I wanted to make sure they came.'

'When and where's the family get-together happening?' Josette said.

'Saturday afternoon. Not sure where yet. I'm hoping here, but Mario said he'd like to show everyone his place in San Remo. Right, that's everything, let's go and celebrate your news. Oh, and there's something I need to show you in the garden.'

After Gordon had poured the champagne and a toast had been drunk to everyone's future happiness, Carla took Josette down to the wild garden at the side of the pool house. The white roses had died back, but the bees and butterflies were still humming around the buddleia and a blue aster had taken the place of the daisies. Carla waited for Josette to register the urn placed in the middle of the area.

'Amelia?' Josette said softly.

Carla nodded. 'What d'you think? I know you weren't happy initially with the thought of her being here, but I didn't know what else to do with her.'

'Like you said before, she turned into a tortured soul, didn't she?' Josette said. 'I'd give anything to be able to talk to the loving sister I knew long ago for five minutes and put everything right between us. But she's gone, leaving a vindictive letter telling me how much she hated me. I'm not sure I'll ever be able to forgive her for that, but I can't find it in me to throw her in the rubbish bin like I wanted to earlier. I also can't tell her how sorry I am for the consequences of the mistake I made all those years ago.' Josette turned to look at Carla. 'If you're happy with the urn here then I think it's the perfect spot. Even tortured souls deserve to find peace.' Josette turned back to look directly at the urn. 'R.I.P. Amelia.' She leant in closer and whispered, 'Start haunting us though and I promise I'll scatter you far and wide in the Mediterranean.'

Carla laughed. 'I'd loved to have spent time with you both when you still liked each other. I bet you were fun to be around and used each other as sparring partners.'

'I have to admit we had our moments,' Josette said. 'We fell out frequently, mind, but I never expected the final fallout to last forever,' and she turned away, hoping that Carla wouldn't notice her eyes glistening with tears.

* * *

An hour or so later after Gordon and Josette had said their

goodbyes, Carla and Joel remained sitting out on the terrace chatting. Leroy was stretched out on a patch of warm earth asleep in front of them.

'I love how eating al fresco is such a way of life down here,' Carla said. 'It's a real treat in the UK, but here it's possible to do it nearly every day all year round.'

'The heat and lack of rain makes my job difficult though,' Joel said. 'Especially lawns. They're always the first to go brown in the heat. I've just taken on a client with a new house and a garden full of rubble. He wants a lawn fit to play croquet on by next summer. I've told him the problems, but he seems to think I can work a miracle for him.'

'How's being totally freelance working out for you?' Carla asked. 'Are you finding enough new clients?'

Joel nodded. 'I signed three this week – two of whom need their gardens landscaping rather than just weeding, which is great for me.' He glanced at Carla before looking away and saying, 'One of the gardens has a small cottage in it being renovated. The owners have offered to rent it to me when it's ready.'

Carla tried to hide her dismay. Of course the room in the villa had always been a stopgap for Joel until he found another place. She'd known that but had pushed the knowledge it was a temporary solution for him to the back of her mind. She'd got so used to him being around that she'd begun to think he'd be living with her forever.

'When will it be ready for you?'

'They reckon another six weeks. Time for me to save some rent money.'

Time for me to try and change your mind about leaving, Carla thought.

'I shall miss you when you go. As for Leroy, he'll think

you're deserting him. Oh – you're not planning on taking him with you, are you?'

Joel shook his head. 'No. I'm hoping you'll grant me visiting rights. To see both of you,' he added quietly.

Carla felt her heart soar at his words. 'You're welcome any time. I know having just the one room and,' she made quotation marks in the air with her fingers, 'sharing "the facilities" with me isn't ideal, but you don't have to move out at all if you don't want to. I've really liked having you around – you're a great housemate.' The words, *I thought you liked me as much as I'm beginning to realise I like you*, stayed unspoken.

'Once you've opened your chambre d'hôte you'll need the spare room for when Maddy and Ed visit.'

'Doubt that that's going to happen this year now,' Carla said. 'With everything else happening... anyway, right now I don't think I could cope with other people in the house. I'd...' she hesitated, 'I'd quite like it if you stayed, Joel.'

Joel was silent for several seconds. 'It's better if I do move out – give you space to enjoy life as a single woman for a while, but that doesn't mean I don't care about you.' Joel said quietly. 'But your life has been turned upside down this past year, I think you need to take some time for you.'

Carla, remembering Joel's door closing the evening she'd arrived home late after having dinner with Bruno, hoped she was reading the right message into his words. He did like her but wanted to give her time to recover from the divorce.

'You've got my number on speed dial,' Joel said. 'So you know I can be here within minutes if you need me. I'm also looking forward to you spending time with me in my new place.' He glanced at her. 'Whenever you need me, I'll be there, okay?'

Carla nodded. 'Okay.' She smiled at him. 'How d'you feel about this weekend? I definitely need you here then for moral support, that's for sure. I'm praying that introducing Mario to the twins doesn't turn out be too nerve wracking.'

'I'll be here,' Joel promised.

46

Carla found it impossible to settle to anything as the weekend approached. Mario rang again, trying to persuade her to bring everyone to San Remo, but Carla held firm about this first meeting being at the Villa Mimosa. It was her home and she wanted the twins to at least be in a familiar place rather than in a strange house in yet another country when they met Mario for the first time.

'It's going to be a huge shock for them, discovering they have a new grandfather,' she said. 'I promise we'll all come to San Remo another time for a family get-together.' She crossed her fingers as she made the promise. What would happen if the twins flatly refused to embrace Mario as their grandfather? They'd both adored Grampa Robert and Carla suspected they'd have the same reaction she'd had to the news of Mario's relationship to them all. Robert was irreplaceable either as a father or grandfather.

Early Saturday afternoon found Carla in the kitchen baking scones and a sponge cake for the tea she was planning on offering Mario and whomever of his family he brought with him. Maybe he'd bring his brother Alexandro, who had known Josette in the past? Would Bruno accompany him?

Joel had gone into town but had promised to be back before everyone arrived. Carla found herself getting more and more stressed as it got closer to the time for Maddy and Ed to arrive. She wished Sam was coming with Maddy. He seemed to know how to calm her down when she became agitated or unhappy over something, although Ed too, was also good at that. Ed himself seemed to take everything life threw at him in his stride and Carla prayed the latest revelation wouldn't prove to be the exception.

Josette arrived alone just as Carla was taking the sponge out of the oven.

'Where's Gordon? I thought he was coming to give you some moral support,' Carla said, glancing at Josette's left hand. 'You've taken your ring off.'

Josette held up her right hand. 'Changed hands just for the afternoon. Gordon's coming later. I said I'd text him when... when I've spoken to Mario about us.'

Carla stared at her. 'You mean he doesn't know yet you turned him down and then accepted Gordon on the same day?'

Josette nodded miserably. 'I have written him a letter like I promised, repeating everything I told him on the phone about why getting back together is not possible for so many reasons. But somehow telling him in a letter I am now engaged to Gordon seemed too brutal. Be kinder to tell him face to face.'

'And there was me thinking introducing the twins to Mario was going to be stressful enough,' Carla said, shaking her head.

'Who's Mario?' Maddy asked, walking into the kitchen.

'Darling, I didn't hear you arrive,' Carla said, turning round and hugging her. 'Where's Ed?'

'Being a good brother and getting our overnight bags out of the car,' Maddy said. 'So, come on, answer the question.' And she looked at her mother and grandmother expectantly.

'I'll just put the kettle on for tea and wait for Ed,' Carla said. 'It's all part of the reason for getting you to come down this weekend.'

'Okay, I'll go and have a quick dip in the pool while we wait,' Maddy said.

'It would be better if you waited until after we've talked, please,' Carla said.

Maddy stared at her and was just about to open her mouth to say something when Ed walked in.

'Hi Ma, Grandma Josette, so what's this urgent meeting all about then?'

It was Josette who answered him. 'Let's all go and sit on the terrace and I'll start to explain while your mother makes the tea. Although after you hear what I've got to say, you might prefer something stronger.'

Carla deliberately took her time in the kitchen, feeling that it was Josette's story to explain to the twins how they now had a new Italian grandfather and various other relations in their lives. One or more of whom were coming to meet them this afternoon.

When Carla carried the tray out, both the twins were sat there listening to their grandmother with stunned expressions on their faces.

'I can only keep repeating how sorry I am that my action so long ago has caused such distress to the people I love. The truth is out in the open now and we all have adjustments to make,' Josette said. 'It's an unhappy story, but hopefully we're at the beginning of a happier time for our family.' She took a deep breath. 'My sister spent the majority of her life hating, wanting and instigating revenge against me, which sadly hurt other innocent people as well as me. I was brought up to never speak ill of the dead, but Amelia's action in keeping the DNA result secret was a deliberate and unforgivable act of cruelty. I can only guess at the disturbed state of her mind. If she'd told me those results when she first got them, then we wouldn't be here today. You would have all known the truth far earlier. Lives could have been very different.'

'I think you and Mum are the ones who have suffered the most in all this,' Ed said quietly. 'I'm glad the two of you have the chance now to get to know one another.' He turned to look at Carla. 'I think it's been easier for you to accept the shock news of Josette being your mother because of the way Amelia treated you, but you and Granddad were so close. Learning about Mario must have been an even bigger shock.'

Carla nodded. 'True.'

'Have you met this Mario?' Maddy said.

'Yes, I went with Josette to Ventimiglia and met him. He's... very Italian,' Carla said. 'As shocked by the news as we all are, of course.'

'Do we get to meet this new grandfather? Or doesn't he want to know?' Maddy asked, an edge to her voice.

'He's longing to meet you both. He'll be here in about an hour,' Carla said.

47

An hour later, an overwhelmed Carla sat on the terrace next to Joel.

'Are you all right?' Joel asked. 'The awkward introductions have passed, now everyone needs to spend time getting to know each other. Seems to be going well so far,' he added, looking across to where the twins were talking to Stéphanie and Bruno, while Josette was talking to Mario and his son, Antoine.

Carla nodded absently. 'It's just that I hadn't given a single thought to my own reaction to Mario's family. I was too busy worrying about the twins and their feelings. And Josette's too, of course.' She looked at Joel. 'I'd forgotten that Mario's son is my brother – well, half-brother.'

'He seems a nice man,' Joel said. 'You're both too old for any sort of attention-seeking sibling rivalry, so I expect you'll get on,' he said, a teasing note in his voice.

'I'd forgotten I've become an instant auntie too,' Carla said, hearing Stéphanie, Antoine's daughter, laugh at something Ed said. 'That the twins have a cousin. Suddenly, I've got more family than I know what to do with. Family that are strangers, with a history I know nothing about – any more than they know about mine. It could all end in a big disaster.'

Joel took her hand. 'Stop worrying. Comme une famille – as a family – they look good. In a year or two, after a few lunches and dinners with them, celebrating birthdays, Christmas and various other things, you'll wonder why you were so anxious over everything. So stop stressing about things. Relationships will sort themselves out.' He stood up. 'I'm going to go and potter in the garden. I think you need to talk to your relatives. I'll be back in time for a cup of tea and a slice of the cake I saw in the kitchen earlier. If you need me, come and find me.'

Watching him walk away, Carla realised he was right. She did need to talk to her new family. Before she could make her way across to anyone, she saw Bruno say something quickly to the others and begin to walk towards her. She smiled up at him as he reached her side.

'I was going to ring you, but when Mario invited me to accompany him today I decided I'd rather see you. I can't believe I'm related to the beautiful lady I rescued earlier this year. My uncle is delighted with me and I'm glad I was there, but right now I wish we weren't related.'

Carla laughed. 'Just as well you didn't know at the time or you'd have been in a bit of a quandary – to save me or to leave me.'

'No quandary at all. I'd always opt to save you,' Bruno said seriously. 'Any chance of us being kissing cousins?' He added, laughing.

Carla smiled. 'As much as I like you, I'm afraid not. Friends though, I hope?'

'Of course. At least I'll get to see you on family occasions,' and Bruno smiled at her.

Carla glanced over to where Mario, Antoine and Josette had now joined the twins and Stéphanie. 'How's Mario taken all the unexpected family news?'

'On the one hand he's delighted about you and the twins, but on the other hand, he's upset over the unhappiness that Amelia caused for others as well as suffered herself.'

'I think we can all agree with that,' Carla said.

Bruno looked at her. 'Josette was the love of his life, you know. I know he loved his wife, Concheta, but he never forgot Josette. The one thing he longed for when he knew Josette was back in Antibes was to see her, for her to be free and for them to get back together.'

Carla let out a regretful sigh and shook her head. 'I know that's not going to happen and I'm sorry about it too, in a way. It would make for a lovely and very satisfying end to their young love.'

Bruno nodded. 'He showed me the letter she wrote explaining why their getting back together was not possible. He has an argument for every single reason she put up, he told me, but felt he had to accept her decision.'

'He's being extremely intuitive,' Carla said. 'And I hope he'll be equally understanding when...' she stopped. 'Sorry, I'm getting ahead of things here.'

Bruno looked at her questioningly, but she shook her head and, after waiting for a few seconds, he spoke again. 'One thing he is determined on, though, is embracing you and the twins as his family. Now he knows about you, he will try and make up for all the missing years. I hope you're ready for the full onslaught of an Italian man intent on gathering his family to his side.'

'I'll warn the twins,' Carla said, smiling at the thought.

'Right, I think it's time to get everyone round the table for cake and tea. I'll go put the kettle on.'

'I'll give you a hand with things,' Bruno said.

Josette, seeing Carla go indoors followed by Bruno, guessed that tea was on its way and she wanted to be able to text Gordon to join them. But it was imperative she talked to Mario before that could happen. She looked around. The twins and Stéphanie were getting along well, Antoine was wandering off in Joel's direction and Mario... was walking towards her. The tight feeling in her tummy increased and she felt nauseous. It was time for her to face things and tell Mario the last painful reason she couldn't marry him.

'Josie amore mio,' Mario said. 'Isn't this wonderful? Two halves of our family meeting for the first time. If only you would change your mind about marrying me, life would be perfect. Maybe one day I'll be able to persuade you?' The sentence hung in the air. 'I'll play the long game if I have to,' he added softly, looking at her intently.

Josette bit her lip. 'I've already told you over the telephone and in my letter the main reasons why I can't marry you, but there is also another reason,' she said. 'And that reason is a man.'

Mario stilled. 'Gordon?'

'Yes. He also has asked me to marry him and... and I've said yes.'

Mario turned slightly away from her but not before she saw the emotion etched across his face.

'I'm sorry if this is painful for you. I've never met anyone I wanted to marry other than you, until now. Sadly the right time for us to marry passed long ago. And whereas you had a good family life with Concheta and Antoine, I wasn't that lucky. My time to marry, though, has finally come now I've met Gordon.' Josette took a breath. 'I've explained to him, that you and I will be forever linked via Carla and the twins. He knows when I marry him he has to accept me and all my baggage and be happy to be part of my newly discovered family unit. A family unit which will always include you.' She looked anxiously at Mario and reached for his hand. His fingers gripped hers. 'Gordon doesn't see any of this being a problem. For my sake, I hope you don't see any problems either?'

Mario shook his head as he looked at her. 'To think we finally came back into each other's lives, only for it to be too late and to learn that there is no hope for us in the future. I can't say I'm not hurt that you're marrying someone else, because I am. But I do wish you every happiness with Gordon. If anyone deserves to be happy it's my Josie.' He squeezed her hand tightly.

Josette blinked hard. 'Thank you. That means everything to me.'

Mario caught hold of her other hand and, pulling her towards him, pressed his lips against her forehead gently for several seconds before moving back and saying. 'I want you to promise me a couple of things though.'

Josette looked at him and waited.

'If you ever need help of any kind, you let me know. Promise? Good. The other thing is – you tell me if this Gordon doesn't treat you right. I have friends who'd be only too willing to show him how to treat a lady.'

Josette laughed. 'Mario Grimaud – only a true Italian man would dare to offer something like that!'

48

While Carla organised everyone with cake and tea, Josette quickly walked round to the front garden to text Gordon.

All explained. Tea is being served. See you soon.

She pressed send.

'I'm hoping that is my cue to arrive,' Gordon said, walking up the drive towards her. 'Sorry. I've been loitering outside for ages waiting for your message.' He looked at her questioningly. 'How's it going?'

Josette shrugged. 'D'accord I think. You'll be able to judge for yourself when you meet everyone. Although I do need to warn you that Mario has threatened to send in "certain" Italian friends if you don't treat me right.'

'Dinee worry, lass,' Gordon said, putting on a dreadful fake Scottish accent and placing his arm around her shoulders. 'I'll tell him I'll gae him a Glaswegian kiss if he makes a move on my girl. Now,' he said in his normal voice. 'Please can I put your ring back on the right finger?'

* * *

Out on the terrace, Carla had decided to forgo the tea and opened the large bottle of Prosecco Mario had brought instead. As everyone picked up their glasses, Mario got to his feet and proposed a toast.

'Here's to extended families and lots of happy meet-ups in the future. Saluti!'

With Joel on one side, her new half-brother Antoine on the other and surrounded by the rest of her family, old and new, Carla felt a frisson of happiness. The past year had been traumatic to say the least, but things now appeared to have levelled out in ways she could never have anticipated. When Mario proposed the next meet-up should be in San Remo at his place, she readily agreed. She'd already overheard Maddy and Stéphanie planning a London shopping trip.

As Gordon moved across to speak to Mario, Carla briefly wondered how Josette felt seeing the two men together. It couldn't be easy knowing that they both loved her and she'd chosen one over the other. Carla tensed as she saw the two men do a sort of high five – only with their fists rather than their hands. But it was clearly a man thing as afterwards they stayed chatting and laughing together.

Not long afterwards, Mario said it was time for them to leave and there was a flurry of goodbyes and promises to see each other soon.

After Mario and his family had left, Josette insisted she, Gordon and the twins would clear up and Carla was to relax. When she went to protest, Joel said, 'Good idea. I need you to come with me for five minutes. I want to show you something.' He held out his hand. 'You remember I did some pottering in the garden earlier? It wasn't just about giving you space to talk to your relatives.'

Carla took his hand and he led her towards the wild bit of the garden behind the pool house where she'd placed Amelia's urn. Right at the front in a freshly cleared patch, a garden plaque had been pushed into the ground.

As Carla read the words engraved on the stone plaque, Joel put his arm around her shoulders and squeezed her tightly. 'I found it in the market and thought this would be a good place for these sentiments. And,' he hesitated. ''C'est a perfect saying for us to remember in our future lives.'

> Starting Today,
> I need to forget what's gone, appreciate what still
> remains,
> and look forward to what's coming next. (anon.)

Carla turned into him and as he put both his arms around her she raised her face to his, for the kiss that she knew would seal the beginning of her future.

ACKNOWLEDGMENTS

Thank you 'Team Boldwood' for helping me to make this book the best it could be. A thank you to my online writing group who keep me sane and boost me up when I'm in need – you all know who you are. Thanks also to Linda Mitchelmore and Jan Wright – one a friend for many years in real life, one I've never met, but both are so supportive of me. Last but by no means least, my heartfelt thanks must go to my readers – without you I wouldn't be doing a job I love, so a big THANK YOU to everyone.

MORE FROM JENNIFER BOHNET

We hope you enjoyed reading *Villa of Sun and Secrets*. If you did, please leave a review.

If you'd like to gift a copy, this book is also available as a ebook, digital audio download and audiobook CD.

Sign up to Jennifer Bohnet's mailing list for news, competitions and updates on future books.

ABOUT THE AUTHOR

Jennifer Bohnet is the bestselling author of over 10 women's fiction novels, including *Rosie's Little Cafe on the Riviera* and *The Little Kiosk By The Sea*. She is originally from the West Country but now lives in the wilds of rural Brittany, France.

Visit Jennifer's website: http://www.jenniferbohnet.com/

Follow Jennifer on social media:

- facebook.com/Jennifer-Bohnet-170217789709356
- twitter.com/jenniewriter
- instagram.com/jenniebohnet

ABOUT BOLDWOOD BOOKS

Boldwood Books is a fiction publishing company seeking out the best stories from around the world.

Find out more at www.boldwoodbooks.com

Sign up to the Book and Tonic newsletter for news, offers and competitions from Boldwood Books!

http://www.bit.ly/bookandtonic

We'd love to hear from you, follow us on social media:

 facebook.com/BookandTonic

 twitter.com/BoldwoodBooks

 instagram.com/BookandTonic

Made in the USA
Middletown, DE
12 May 2020